A RE

M O

C L A

A PARTY FOR THE GIRLS

Also by H. E. Bates

A Month by the Lake & Other Stories

With an introduction by Anthony Burgess

H.E. BATES

A PARTY FOR THE GIRLS

SIX STORIES

A NEW DIRECTIONS BOOK

Manufactured in the United States of America
First published clothbound and as New Directions Paperbook 653 in 1988

Library of Congress Cataloging-in-Publication Data

Bates, H. E. (Herbert Ernest), 1905–1974.
    A party for the girls : six stories / by H.E. Bates.
(A New Directions Book)

        p.   cm.—(Revived modern classic)
    ISBN 0-8112-1050-2.   ISBN 0-8112-1051-0 (pbk.)
    I. Title.   II. Series.
PR6003.A965P3 1988   87-26874
823'.912—dc19   CIP

New Directions Books are published for James Laughlin
by New Directions Publishing Corporation
80 Eighth Avenue, New York 10011

CONTENTS

A PARTY FOR THE GIRLS

A PARTY FOR THE GIRLS

Miss Tompkins, who was seventy-six, bright pink-looking in a bath-salts sort of way and full of an alert but dithering energy, looked out of the drawing-room window for the twentieth time since breakfast and found herself growing increasingly excited. The weather, she thought, really was improving all the time it got better. It was going to be marvellous for the party after all.

The morning had improved so much and so fast, in fact, that all the azaleas, mere stubby fists of rose and apricot and yellow the day before, were now fully expanded in the sun, raising the most delicate open hands to a cloudless summer sky. They were very late this year and perhaps that was why, she thought, they seemed to be so much more beautiful. After all, she told herself, you couldn't hurry nature; everything had its appointed time; everything that was really good was worth waiting for. During all the wet cold weeks of May she had watched the barely colouring buds apparently clenching themselves tighter and tighter and once or twice she had actually prayed for them, in true earnest, against the dreaded threat of frost.

Now they were all in blossom. Great banks of them rose splendidly from the far side of the lawn. As if by a miracle they were all at their best on the appointed day: the day of the party for the girls.

"If that's the telephone I'll answer it," Miss Tompkins called to the invisible presence of Maude Chalmers, who was very busy filling the last vol-au-vent cases with cold fresh salmon and mayonnaise in the kitchen, "if it isn't you go."

No answering word came from Maude Chalmers, her companion-housekeeper, who was working in a silent and practical vacuum at the vols-au-vents, with the kitchen door closed, unable to hear the ringing of the bell that flew with tremulous persistence through the house. Sometimes Miss Tompkins vowed that Maude, who was seventy-eight, actually feigned deafness: either that, she thought, or her hearing deliberately deteriorated the moment she wanted it to get worse.

"I think it's the telephone after all!" she called and rushed into the hall, picking up the receiver and pouring excited 'Hullos' into it, only to discover after some seconds that the line was dead. "No, it isn't. I'll go. It's the front door."

"Oh! it's the smoked sprats! You splendid man!" She took from the fishmonger's man a small parcel, hands clutching it with new excitement. "How clever of you to have got them in time. They're such lovely things for someone who's never had them before."

She had read about the sprats in a magazine. They were one of the things by which she hoped to give the party a touch of the unusual, a bit of exciting tone. For the same reason she had decided it should be a morning party. Morning parties were, she thought, different. For one thing they were kinder to the girls, most of whom were no longer quite so young. Some were early-to-bedders; many of them played bridge in the afternoon or had sleeps and later went out to tea. At noon they would, she thought, be fresher, in the mood to peck at something and ready for a well-iced drink or two. They could wander in the garden, gaze at the azaleas, take their plates and glasses with them and chat happily in the sun.

A bell rang stridently in the house again and automatically she picked up the telephone receiver, at the same time calling:

"Maude, the smoked sprats have come. Isn't that heaven?"

"Is that you, Tommy?" a voice said over the phone. Most of her friends called her Tommy; she never paused to wonder if it suited her. "It's Phoebe here. What was that about sprats? You sound like a warbling thrush."

"Oh! I am—I did. I feel like that. Did I say sprats? I suppose I did—I didn't want you to know. What is it, Phoebe? Could something be the matter? Don't say you can't come."

"Not a thing, dear. It was simply—I wondered if you'd mind—"

"Mind? Mind what?"

"I just wondered if I might bring Horace, that's all."

"Horace? Who's Horace?"

"My brother." Phoebe Hooper's voice was deep, throaty, oiled and persuasive in tone; over the telephone it greatly belied her years. "He's eighteen months younger than me." Phoebe Hooper was a mere seventy. "Would you mind? He's here staying with me for a week or two."

"Well, it was really a party for the girls—"

"Yes, I know. But you know how it is. Either I've got to leave the poor man cold lunch on a tray or something or he goes to the pub for a lonely Guinness and a sandwich. He's harmless, really. He just needs pushing around, that's all."

A sense of uneasiness, touched with disappointment, crept over Miss Tompkins. The fond bright illusion of her female party seemed suddenly to fade. She had created in her mind for so long a picture of the girls wandering through the house, all permed and gay in summer dresses, and about the garden, against the background of azaleas in all their freshest colours, that the thought of a solitary male stranger among them seemed now to obtrude unpleasantly.

"But it's just for the girls, Phoebe. It's all hen, I mean. I'm sure he'll be frightfully, frightfully bored—"

"Oh! not Horace. He'll make himself useful. He'll buttle for you. He'll mix the drinks. He mixes beautiful Moselle cup. I'm sorry I left it so late, Tommy—"

"Late?" Miss Tompkins felt suddenly helpless and at the mercy of time. It always went so much faster when you thought it was earlier than it was. "Is it late? What time is it now?"

"I make it five to twelve. Is it really all right about Horace?"

"I must fly. Twelve? It was half-past ten five minutes ago. Yes, it's all right about—yes, please—perfectly—"

"You're a lamb, dear." Phoebe Hooper's voice, smooth as oil, sent yet another tremor through Miss Tompkins, once more despoiling her confidence. "We'll be over in a few minutes. Heavenly day."

Breathlessly Miss Tompkins flew to the kitchen, actually unwrapping smoked sprats as she went and finally saying to Maude Chalmers: "It's twelve already. That was Phoebe Hooper on the phone. She wants to bring her brother to the party. His name's Horace. I thought we'd put the sprats on the green dish—you know, the Spode. The green would match so well with the gold."

"Green dish? Spode? People are going to eat them," Maude Chalmers said, "aren't they? Not use them for interior decorating."

Maude Chalmers, who spoke tartly, was surprisingly solid, almost beefy, for a woman in her late seventies. Her hair was dark and strong, if rather stringy, and untidy bits of smoky whisker grew out of her upper lip and under-chin in irregular tufts, rather as if left there after a hasty shave.

"What about the drinks?" Miss Tompkins said. She was going to serve sherry and gin with tomato juice for those who preferred it, though most of the girls, as she knew, adored gin in some form or another. But looking distractedly round the kitchen she saw neither drinks nor glasses and was unpacified by Maude Chalmers' level, practical voice saying:

"The drinks are where they should be. On the sideboard in the drawing-room. What are people going to eat the sprats with by the way? Their fingers?"

"Oh! forks, forks."

Ignoring this desperate remark except for a sideways hitch of her hairy chin, Maude Chalmers picked up a large Sheffield plate tray filled with canapés, delicate little sandwiches sprinkled with emerald threads of mustard and cress, cold chipolata sausages, rounds of stuffed hard boiled eggs and slices of toast spread with liver pâté and topped with olives. While Miss Tompkins had been fussing with idle fears over the weather, the sprats and whether the azaleas would open in time or not she had prepared every crumb of food herself. Everything, as far as she was concerned, was done. Everything was ready.

"I feel there's such heaps still to do," Miss Tompkins said. "Shouldn't we have a table or two put out on the lawn? Don't you think?—"

In fresh, fussy alarm, she followed Maude Chalmers to the drawing-room, taking out her powder compact as she went. Drinks, glasses, plates, dishes, napkins, olives, radishes, cigarettes and even forks were, to her trembling astonishment, placed about the room in perfect order everywhere. The silvery tray of food brought in by Maude Chalmers merely crowned the waiting pattern.

"Everything looks so cool," she said. "Where are you going?"

"To fetch your precious sprats, dear."

"Oh! I see. Yes, yes, I see." Miss Tompkins held the mirror of her compact so close to her face that she actually recoiled sharply from the reflection of the one jellied uneasy eye that stared back at her. "Oh! I look a mess. I'm an absolute sight." She hastily salted herself with ill-timed generous dabs of her powder puff, making her face look more sharply pink than ever. Powder flew everywhere, prompting her to give three or four spurting little sneezes, cat-fashion, the last of which seemed to be echoed in a gentle buzz at the front door-bell, so polite as to be almost a whisper.

"Was that the bell?" she called. "Maude, was that you? Did you hear?" Maude, she thought, was feigning deafness again, but a moment later Maude was answering with customary tartness from the kitchen:

"It's the Miss Furnivals, you bet your life. They're always on the dot. Can you go? I've still got to do the sprats—"

Two ladies of undernourished appearance, greyish and wrinkled as a pair of barely wakening chrysalids, almost fell into the house, as if from sheer surprise or weakness, or even both, as Miss Tompkins opened the front door. Wheezes of timid breath escaped from them in matching rhythm, offering greetings that were not really audible as words. Their shrunken little bodies seemed to float across the hall-way, their sharp triangular noses thrusting piercingly ahead, as if already scenting food.

Before Miss Tompkins could dispose of the two drifting bodies with politeness, Maude Chalmers was back from the kitchen carrying in her hands a golden star of sprats, shining on a green dish, phosphorescently. A moment later a car hooted with a challenge of greeting from the driveway outside, but before Miss Tompkins could recover from the start of surprise it gave her the front door was actually opened to admit a throaty solo chorus of laughter, followed by words which came with liquid undulation:

"It's only me, it's only me. My god-fathers, Tommy, you chose a thirsty day."

"Connie, my angel," Miss Tompkins said.

She ran forward to press powdery caressive cheeks on the face of a tallish woman in her late seventies who recoiled slightly as if thinking of tossing back the low-cut fringe of her curled coppery hair. As she did so she raised her hand to her hat as if feeling that it might suddenly fall off. Instead the hat, a very small one, sat with surprising firmness on her flaming hair, looking like a white cake decorated with spring-like airiness in a design of narcissi, pink rosebuds and lily-of-the-valley.

"I saw Phoebe Hooper driving up." Connie Stevens bore widow-hood with a sort of metallic serenity, perhaps because a third excursion into it had given her both confidence and practice. "And with a man. I thought this was just for the old hens today?"

"Her brother. His name's Horace. He had to be left alone—"

"Horace? I've heard of Horace somewhere. Isn't he in tea or something?"

Suddenly the door-bell rang again, to be answered this time with calm and beefy promptitude by Maude. At the sound of voices Miss Tompkins turned with the expectation of seeing Phoebe Hooper and her brother Horace, but to her surprise—it was her day of surprises, she suddenly thought, first the azaleas, then the weather, then—it was Dodie Sanders and her mother.

Dodie Sanders, tall, thin and sallow, with depressed fair hair, had a mouth that was not only unrouged but almost perpetually open in a low droop that gave her a look not at all unlike that of a lean, long fish that had been landed and left on a river bank in a state of gentle expiration. Her eyes were reddish and globular; the lashes were like little gingery red ants nervously dancing up and down.

"Please do go in. Maude will look after you." Miss Tompkins felt suddenly, as she always did in the presence of Dodie Sanders and her mother, slightly ill-at-ease. Dodie, although sixty, was like a girl who had never grown up. With fish-like coldness she swam away under the big fin of her mother, who in a shining dress of steel-blue silk glided away to the drawing-room like a watchful shark.

"Ah! it's us at last!" Phoebe Hooper, with habitual domination, was already in the hall-way, not having bothered with the formality of the bell. "You must blame Horace for it. He's such a slow coach. He was simply ages getting ready."

Horace had very much the appearance of a shy and inattentive prawn: the cushiony splendour of Phoebe Hooper, immense in bust and hips, overwhelmed him. Modest grey curls encircled his crimson ears like tufts of sheep wool and two small sepia bull's eyes stared with wandering apprehension from under mild whiskery grey brows. In one hand he was clutching two long green bottles of wine and in the other a siphon of soda and a third bottle of wine. The strain of this overloading had driven his cream collar and rose-brown bow tie slightly askew and somehow at the same time the trousers of his crumpled fawn suit had become unevenly hitched up, revealing glimpses of white socks that had fallen down.

"This is Horace," Phoebe Hooper said. "I made him bring the wine because I knew he'd adore making that cup for you. It's his great specialty—"

"Oh! I don't know about—" Horace smiled shyly. Unable to shake hands or finish his mildly protesting sentence, he stood between the two girls with an air of indecisive, wistful meditation. He seemed to be thinking of something far outside the walls of Miss Tompkins' house: perhaps a quiet glass of Guinness, a walk with a dog, a game of golf somewhere.

"Oh! it's my day of surprises," Miss Tompkins said. "First the azaleas, then the sprats and now—this, wine! And of course, the weather—all the time improving as it gets better."

Horace reacted to these inconsequential statements with a solemnity far greater than mere surprise. The sheer weight of the wine bottles seemed to drag him down.

"You'd better lead him to the kitchen," Phoebe said. "Get him to work. Don't let him get lazy."

"Oh! yes, of course. This way, this way, Mr. Hooper," Miss Tompkins said. "Maude will find you all you need."

In the kitchen Maude was topping shining dishes of early strawberries with large blobs of cream. At the sudden appearance of Horace and Miss Tompkins she drew herself straight up, as if about to be tartly affronted, but something about Horace's modest and crumpled appearance made her pause, spoon in air, while blobs of cream slowly dropped to the tablecloth.

"This is Phoebe's brother, Horace. He's going to make us the most delicious cup or something with wine. Is it Hock, did you say, Mr. Hooper, or Moselle? I think you need lemons for that, don't you? Do you need lemons?"

Horace, unloading wine bottles and siphon on the kitchen table with evident relief, said yes, he needed lemons and also ice and a little mint, please, if they had it.

"Plenty of mint in the garden," Maude said, her voice brusque as sandpaper. "Under the first apple-tree."

"I must fly back," Miss Tompkins said. "I hear the bell again."

In her light thrush-warbling fashion she flew away, half-singing, "I'm coming! I'm coming! I'll be there!"

"I suppose you'll need jugs and glasses," Maude said. "Anything else?"

"A little sugar."

"Lump or gran?"

"About a dozen lumps, I'd say. And a cup of brandy."

"Brandy? All we've got is cooking."

"That will do nicely."

Maude, returning from a kitchen cupboard with a meagre quarter bottle of brandy, paused to eye the three bottles of Moselle and their companion siphon with flinty disapproval. What were people coming to suddenly, bringing their own bottles to a party? They'd be bringing their own nuts or something next.

She supposed Mr. Hooper needed a corkscrew too, she said. He'd brought plenty of bottles, she must say. Did he want to get them all squiffy or something?

Horace, who had no intention whatever of getting anybody squiffy and who hadn't in the least wanted to make the Moselle cup in the first place but was merely doing so because his sister was a bully and insisted he do a good turn of some kind as a reward for being invited, merely smiled with excruciating shyness again and said:

"It was really my sister's idea. She gets rather carried away."

Something about the smile and the retreating tone of Horace's apologetic voice made Maude suddenly think of a dog about to cower into a corner after some dire misdeed. She suddenly felt unaccountably sorry for Horace. She knew it was all that Phoebe Hooper's fault, puffing herself up like a majordomo. The woman was always bossing. She woke up every morning, Maude was sure, with great ambitious ideas bouncing about her head like electrons or whatever they were—let's all have a picnic, let's do *Twelfth Night* out of doors or something—and then made somebody else do all the donkey work. The woman was infuriatingly domineering; she made you wild.

Horace, now armed with a corkscrew, pulled the first cork with such clean, snapping precision that Maude was actually startled and gave a giggle and said Mr. Hopper sounded very expert. She supposed he was doing things like making Moselle cup all the time?

Horace, who hadn't made Moselle or any other cup since his sister's sixtieth birthday, to celebrate which she had inveigled the two Miss Furnivals into lending their large bushy garden for an Edwardian street pageant accompanied by three cornet and barrel-organ players and a fish-and-chip van, said:

"Well, as a matter of fact, not really. Might I have the ice now? And two jugs please?"

Obediently she rushed to find ice and jugs. Two tall Venetian glasses of rose-purple colour seemed to her the very things for the cup and after putting down the ice-tray on the kitchen table she started polishing them vigorously with a cloth, saying at the same time:

"You said mint. What about mint now? Shall I go and get it? We've got lemon mint too, I think."

Horace, who was trying hard to remember the exact proportions of the cup's ingredients, put a dozen cubes of ice in a jug and coloured them with a golden film of brandy. Hesitant about something, he stood biting his lip. Oughtn't there to be a dash or two of *curaçao*? Something seemed to tell him so.

"You haven't a spot of *curaçao*, I suppose?"

No, but they had *maraschino*, Maude said, and she thought also a little *cointreau*.

By now Horace was mildly confused. He couldn't remember for the life of him whether it was *curaçao, cointreau* or *maraschino* that the cup demanded and again he stood biting his lip with that shy perplexity that affected Maude far more sharply than any look of open appeal.

Was something the matter? she said and Horace assured her that no, it was nothing, merely that he wondered if *maraschino* or—

Before she could allow herself a second of rational thought Maude made the astonishingly impetuous suggestion that they should be devils—they should put them both in!

Maude's unexpected suggestion of devilry was accompanied by another giggle or two, and had the instant effect of making Horace

stir ice with an over-vigorous rattling spoon, as if uneasily anxious
to drown the odd sounds that Maude was making. Any moment
now his sister would be storming the kitchen, imperiously calling
for the cup, scolding him again for being a slow-coach.

"Oh! all right, let's put them both in—"

"Do!" Maude said. "Use them up. It'll be a way of clearing them
out. I'll get the mint now."

By the time Maude came back with a handful of fresh mint from
the garden the tall Venetian jugs were looking frosty. A translucent
glow of green, fresh and light as that of a half-bleached leaf,
streamed softly through the rosy-purple patterns of the glass.
Finally crowned by mint and ice and lemon the cup looked, as
Maude had suggested it would, very expert.

Shyly Horace resisted flattery. It wasn't after all, the looks—it
was, he reminded her, the taste of the thing.

"May I taste?" Maude said. "Just the weeniest—"

Maude was quick to find glasses and Horace poured out two cold
and inviting measures of the cup, at one of which Maude drank
deeply enough to leave a bead or two of green on the lower and
longer sprouts of her moustaches.

"I've never tasted anything quite like it before," she said. "I think
it's most unique."

Under this generous tribute Horace looked shyer than ever. At
the same time, he had to admit, the fragrant coldness of the cup
seemed good. It had something to it. It wasn't bad at all.

Maude, under the stimulus of a strong second gulp, was about to
say again that it was far better than that. The word 'genius' hung on
her lips. She giggled again and was on the point of asking Horace to
top her up when an intruding voice arrested her:

"What's all this we hear about punch? Or cup or something? Or
aren't we allowed into the wine sanctum?"

Connie Stevens' coppery head, arresting as a shining helmet,
appeared suddenly in the kitchen doorway. Maude, unable to
explain why, felt the moisture all over her body run cold and with a
sudden return to customary tartness she said:

"Mr. Hooper will bring the wine-cup when it's ready. Things
take time."

Without quite knowing what she was doing she snatched up a

pair of kitchen scissors and disappeared into the garden, half-running, beefy hindquarters bumping up and down.

"Everybody's dilating," Connie Stevens said. "That's why I came to peep. They all say you're mixing a beaut."

"Oh! I don't know—"

"The girls are lapping up gin like stink already," she said. "Are you trying to get them all spellbound? By the way, my name's Connie Stevens. Phoebe told me about you once. Aren't you in tea?"

Horace, spurting a final squeeze of soda into the wine-cup said no, he wasn't in tea. He had been in plastics. Now he was retired.

"Nonsense. You look far too young to retire."

He was afraid it was a fact, Horace said.

"I used to have shares in plastics once. Plastic Research Foundation or something like that it was called. They did marvellously."

"My company."

"No wonder. I'm sure you were the wizard."

Connie Stevens peered with a sort of spry innocence, eyelashes dancing, into the wine-cup. "It looks so artistic," she said. "I love drinks that look artistic. May one taste? I mean the merest *soupçon*?"

"I rather think it still needs another stir—"

"The artist's touch. I know. Will it knock us all flying?"

Connie Stevens gave Horace a look of slow, exploratory charm. In contrast to Maude, who found herself under the spell of the brown shy eyes, she found herself suddenly engrossed by his ears. They were firm but delicate; they were like a pair of clean rosy fossils. Something about their recurring lines spiralling perfectly inward sent the strangest voluptuous spasm through her, so that she felt sharply annoyed when Maude Chalmers burst in through the garden door like a clumsy bear and said acidly:

"Here's the lemon mint. I suppose it goes in whole? Or do you chop it?"

Bear-like still, she threw the stalks of mint on the table and retreated with sweeping haste in the direction of the sitting-room. Connie Stevens merely stared and shrugged her shoulders.

"Strange woman. Embittered. I can't think why Tommy keeps on with her."

Without answering, Horace dropped a sprig or two of lemon mint into the wine-cup, giving it a final stir with a spoon.

"May one taste? You said I might."

Horace, uneasy at Maude's acid departure, poured out half a glass of wine-cup. Connie Stevens took it, held her little delicate hat with her free hand and sipped at the glass with lips that, heavy with lipstick of a deep shade of coppery rose, were designed to match her hair.

After drinking, she paused, held up her eyes in a half-voluptuous glance to heaven and said that some of them would certainly know when they'd had this. This was it: the real McCoy.

"It's pretty mild really," Horace said. "It's just refreshing. I think we'd better take it in."

The sitting-room was electric with female voices and springing laughter. Miss Tompkins greeted the arrival of the wine-cup with rising warbles of delight. Her hands played scales in the air. A whole regiment of hats swivelled sharply to concentrate on Horace, modestly bearing the two jugs, but had scarcely a glance for Connie Stevens, carrying a tray of glasses, until Maude rushed up with something like outrage and took it away.

"On the table here, on the table here," she commanded. "Set it down here."

Horace, dutifully setting down the two jugs on a corner table, looked like a one-man patrol ambushed and far outnumbered. Elderly ladies, gay as dolls, seemed to spring from everywhere. Miss Tompkins warbled, for perhaps the tenth time, that when they each had their cup they must take it outside: it was so sunny, so absolutely perfect, they mustn't miss the azaleas. There mightn't be another day.

"Well, young man," a clear soprano voice said and Horace, in infinite astonishment, suddenly realised that this could only mean himself. He turned from pouring the first of the wine-cup into glasses to find himself confronted by a neat vision in a white silk suit threaded with narrow charcoal stripes and a little hat, not unlike a silvery pineapple, with an inch or two of light grey veil, that sat slightly tilted on a head of impeccably curled dark grey hair. Lithe and straight as a cane, with eyes as blue as larkspur, she didn't look a day over sixty, Horace thought. "What's all this about your Moselle-cup I hear?"

"This is Miss La Rue," Miss Tompkins told him. She longed to tell him too that, as all the girls knew, Miss La Rue was within a month or so of ninety, but Miss La Rue was so engrossed in sprightly appreciation of both Horace and the glass of wine-cup he had by now put into her hands that Miss Tompkins realised sadly that she was very much *de trop* and said only, before moving away: "You must talk to her. She has the most wonderful memory. Astonishing. She remembers everything."

"I certainly remember this," Miss La Rue said. No tremor of age was detectable in voice, air or eye as she lifted her glass and stared at Horace through it, as if with the intention of examining him microscopically. "I first had this at Ascot in '89. That was a glorious day too. Rather like today."

She drank, afterwards sucking delicately at her firm moist lips.

"No *curaçao*?"

No, Horace had to confess, no *curaçao*.

"Great pity," she said. "It gives that touch."

She nevertheless gave him a glance of matchless gratitude, eyes glowing with the iridescence of young petals. Receiving it, Horace felt for some reason extraordinarily young, almost boyish; he was suddenly a character in some distant, long-lost school party.

"You're spilling it, you're spilling it!" It was Maude Chalmers now, in rigid reprimand. "All over the place. Give it to me, do give it to me." She snatched the jug from his hands. "You can't trust them, Miss La Rue, can you? You can't trust them."

In contrast to this dark insinuation Miss La Rue looked, as her eyes smiled under the grey fringe of veil, all trust and light.

"What of these azaleas I hear so much about?" she said. "Aren't you going to take me to see them?"

"Of course. Whenever you wish."

Horace, less shy now and suddenly feeling more youthful than ever, prepared to move away.

"Not without your cup, surely?" she said. "I'll take a little more too before we go."

Armed with full glasses, they walked slowly into a garden so drenched with sunlight that it gave a fantastic acidity to the brightness of the lawn's new-mown grass. The amazing transparence of blue sky seemed to lift the whole world up. The voices of several ladies chirping about the thick orange and pink and yellow forest of azaleas might have been the cries of birds.

Presently Horace was uneasily astonished to find Miss La Rue taking his arm: not lightly, but in an earnest lock, almost a cuddle. A breath of perfume, so delicate that the mere movement of her arm might have released it, rose in the air. It might have been mignonette, he thought.

"I'm walking slowly," she said, "only because I don't want to get anywhere," and looked down for some moments in silence at her feet.

Horace looked at them too. The ankles were surprisingly small, delicate and well-shaped. Each of her grey shoes had a black frontal bow with a single white spot on the wings, giving the effect of a resting butterfly.

"Women chatter so," she said. "The nice thing about you is you don't talk too much."

She sipped wine-cup as she walked along, a feat of such accurate balance and ease, with no hint of haste or awkwardness, that she might have been doing it every day.

"Why was Maude Chalmers so vinegary?" she said.

"I didn't notice it."

"Of course you noticed it."

"I suppose the party makes a lot of work," he said. He recalled the incident of the mint; though so small it now seemed embarrassing. "I suppose the wine-cup put her out of her stride."

"She was angry with you."

"With me? Oh! dear no."

"Flaming." She turned and looked him squarely in the eye. It was a look of both intimacy and penetration. "You'd been flirting with her."

"Oh! never!"

"Of course you had. She was red all over."

Ahead, the azaleas flamed. No single petal had yet fallen from the thickly fringed branches. Below them, and to one side, a platoon of delphiniums, palest blue to near black, stood in arrested grandeur, unshaken by wind.

"I see there's a seat over there," she said. "It's easier to drink wine sitting down—"

"No, you don't. No, you don't. I'm stealing him. Tommy's desperate." It was the strident voice of Connie Stevens metallically beating across the lawn. "The wine-cup's giving out fast. And Phoebe says you have another bottle left."

Horace, jerked to his feet as by an invisible string, uttered very small disturbed noises.

"Come, come, come," Connie Stevens said, as if bringing a poodle to heel. "Oh! he shall come back. I'll send him back."

"Take my glass, young man," Miss La Rue drained her glass, lifted it towards Horace and fixed him with a sort of accusative charm. "Don't let them keep you. I want to talk to you."

As if actually ordered to do so, Horace drained his glass too and then, half-dragged by the imperative hand of Connie Stevens, took both empty glasses away.

"Oh! you dear man, we work you to death." In the drawing-room Miss Tompkins, flushed with gin and after-doses of wine-cup, was full of giddy solicitude. "Empty glasses too! Empty glasses! No one should empty a glass when they can have it filled up." She laughed on dithering notes, at the same time grabbing from a table a consolatory glass of something that Horace presently discovered was gin and tonic. He drank at it timidly. "Oh! drink up, you dear man. You need it. We've got work for you to do. That comes of being so popular."

Popular? The word, sped on its way by gin and wine-cup, rushed through the chattering wings of female voices like an arrow. A bare feminine arm, belonging to someone he didn't recognize, held him momentarily suspended, just long enough for him to hear:

"Absolutely marvellous, your cup. Making the party."

Another voice, cooing gently, primed him to beware. "I'm after you for the recipe. Don't forget, will you? Just scribble it down. I'm after you."

"I go for this cup," he heard another one of the girls saying. "I really do."

"You can feel it going down," another girl said. "You know—creeping."

Horace presently found himself back in the kitchen. Maude who had the two Venetian jugs, the remaining bottle of wine and a fresh nosegay of mint in readiness on the table, greeted him with the long rattle of an ice-tray and the voice of a skeleton:

"Oh! you're back, are you?"

A certain chill in the air was softened by the unexpected discovery by Horace that he was still holding the glass of gin and tonic in his hands. He drained it gratefully.

"No more brandy," Maude said, in a tersely detached voice, rather as if it were his fault, "and the *maraschino*'s nearly all gone. But I found some *Kirsch*. Cherry, isn't it? Tommy brought it from Germany once. Will it do?"

Horace didn't know and suddenly, impelled by gin mixing itself with wine-cup, didn't care. He started shovelling cubes of ice into a jug. Popular, was he? He poured generous measures of *Kirsch* over the ice and stirred madly with a spoon. Popular? Peals of laughter coming from across the lawn made him pause abruptly and gaze through the window. The garden was bright with chattering, wine-flushed girls.

"Seem to be enjoying themselves," Horace said. "Gay sight."

Maude, otherwise speechless, gave a snort that clearly dismissed all other womenfolk as worse than pitiful. Horace, hardly noticing, pulled the remaining Moselle cork and tipped the bottle upside down, vertically, in a gesture meant to be expert. The neck of the bottle struck his gin glass, sending it crashing to the floor.

Unserene and lightly silent, Maude swept up the broken glass with brush and dust-pan and then left the kitchen abruptly, in even higher silence, carrying with her a tray of strawberries and cream.

Left alone, Horace discovered that he was actually laughing to himself. Popular, eh? It was getting to be rather fun. Popular? He stirred with joyful energy at the nearly completed cup, raising a veritable sonata from the ice as it went swirling round and round. An over-generous squirt of soda sent the level of liquid too high in the jug and suddenly it was all brimming over. Horace, laughing to himself again, remedied the situation by pouring himself a generous glass of wine-cup and then tasting it deeply. Not bad at all, he thought. Not bad. Small wonder it was popular. The *Kirsch*, allied to *maraschino*, had undoubtedly given it a remarkably bizarre and haunting flavour.

After giving the jug its final garnish of mint he bore it back to the drawing-room, now three parts empty. One of the girls, elderly by any standards, was holding trembling court in a corner by the fireplace, listened to by Mrs. Sanders and three others, who now and then responded by laughing sweetly and bobbing up and down, like puppies.

Another, crowned by a precious piece of millinery in black velvet, dancing bits of jet and what seemed to be the hind part of a vermilion cockatoo, suddenly bore down on him as from some secret hiding place, saying:

"Ah! Ha, ha. I've caught you."

A smoked sprat, speared on the end of a silver fork, waved merrily in front of his face.

"The pageant, wasn't it? I've been drilling my brain all morning trying to remember. You haven't forgotten, have you?"

Horace had hardly begun to protest that he had indeed forgotten when the waving golden sprat cautioned him, with the accompaniment of laughter as thin as a tin-whistle, not to be silly. Of course he hadn't forgotten.

"Gorgeous day, that. I ran a fish-for-the-bottle stall. You won nearly every time. You knew the knack. I knew you did. I knew all the time you knew the knack, but I wouldn't split. You did know, didn't you?"

A moment later the sprat described a smart elliptical dive in the air and fell on the floor. Horace, hastily setting down the jug of wine-cup on a side-table, rushed to pick it up, holding it by its tail.

"Well, that's the end of that." The precious piece of millinery suddenly disdained all connexion with the sprat. "I hardly knew what it was for, anyway."

"You mean you don't want it?"

Horace, left suddenly alone, turned to dispose of the sprat by dropping it into a vase of irises but then thought better of it. At the same time he recalled the excellence of the fresh-made cup and told himself that now was as good a time as any to sample it again. But before he could pick up the jug the peremptory hands of his sister had snatched it away and the bullying voice was at him again:

"Where on earth have you been? They're all panting with thirst outside. And what's that in your hand?"

Phoebe Hooper actually pushed him through the open french windows and into the garden. It was blissfully warm outside and her voice was jagged as glass as it nagged him about his duty and the way he had neglected it. He wondered how and where he had failed and, still holding the sprat by its tail, wondered equally what on earth he should do with it. He made as if to throw it casually into a bed of pansies but at once she positively flew at him:

"Not in there. That's disgusting. Put it in your pocket or something."

He dutifully put the sprat in his pocket. He then remembered Miss La Rue and how much she wanted to talk to him and that it was his urgent duty to take her another glass of the cup.

He hurried back into the house for glasses, only to be met on the threshold by Maude, bearing another tray of strawberries and cream. She made way for him in silence; their paths might never have crossed; she was a cold stranger a thousand miles away.

In the corner of the drawing-room the elderly girl and her court were all eating strawberries and cream, bending closely over their plates like lapping puppies at their dinners.

Horace picked up a pair of empty glasses and started to pursue his sister across the lawn. The girls were scattered everywhere in the sun and now in his haste he half ran into one of them. Solitary and confined as if by an invisible wall of glass Dodie Sanders held him for the swiftest moment in too exquisite embarrassment, eyes dropping into excruciating shyness a moment later.

Something made him say: "You haven't got a glass," but a moment later she timidly lifted one containing a thimbleful of sherry, as if from somewhere up her sleeve. The smile on her face was wan; the three words she dropped were a ghostly trinity of whispers:

"Quite all right—"

Disturbed, and with some of his own shyness unaccountably returning, Horace was about to tell her that he would be back in a minute with more sherry when Phoebe Hooper, accusing him yet again of slacking about and doing nothing when everybody was dying of thirst, thrust the Venetian jug into his hands and flew away.

He paused to look at Dodie Sanders. The lids of her eyes quivered and fell again. She looked for a moment like a fish embalmed in the centre of a dazzling aquarium of aimless light.

"Have you tried my cup?"

No, the droopy lids confessed, she hadn't—she—

"Try it."

Horace waited for her to drain her glass of sherry. He thought he actually saw her start to smile, and then think better of it, as he poured a little of the cup for her.

"Did you try the first lot?" he said. "This is different. Would you hold my glass? I'd like a drop myself. No harm in the barman having—"

Eyes downwardly fixed on the two glasses, she was utterly silent as Horace poured wine-cup from the jug. The interlude, Horace thought, was almost like a dreamy doze after all his hectic travellings between kitchen and garden, with Maude and his sister and the various girls at his heels, but he woke suddenly to hear:

"Popular man, popular man. Can't have you being cornered." Miss Tompkins, laughing frivolously, caught his arm and started to pilot him away. He had just time to grab his glass from Dodie Sanders and take a hurried drink at it before she set him fully on his course. "Miss La Rue was one of those who was asking—"

He moved about the lawn, topping up glasses. A group of five girls, standing by a magnolia that had only recently shed the last of its blossom in big ivory curls, were clearly telling stories of doubtful character, he thought, and a hush like a straight jacket encircled them tightly as he arrived.

One by one they all refused the cup. They were all ginny girls, they said. Eyes much reddened, they laughed with unseemly pleasure into his face as he prepared to retreat with jug and glasses, but just before he turned his back one called to him with arresting winsomeness:

"I'll have a spot. I'll try it. They all tell me it's been 'normously popular."

A well-built girl of seventy, with hair as light as the head of a seeded dandelion, came forward to capture him with a pair of violet eyes brimming over with alcohol. A pair of heavy garnet earrings dangled against her neck. The front of her carmine dress was low. Her bosom, unusually white, exposed itself like the upper portions of a pair of wrinkled turnips. She gazed down on it with the most possessive and flirtatious of glances, all the creases of her neck quivering like crumpled lace, and said, laughing:

"One man and his jug, eh? Well, let's try it." Horace, now laughing too, the word popular again dancing mystically in his ears, poured wine-cup into his own glass—it was important to keep the other one, he thought, for Miss La Rue—and the well-built girl drank with heartiness, telling him:

" 'Licious. Absolutely 'licious. Can't think why you didn't come before. Nice to share your glass—"

She gave it back to him, empty. The possessive and inviting glance that she had previously reserved for her own bosom was now suddenly turned on Horace. She muttered a few low, amorous words about his big, brown eyes, at the same time gazing into them, and Horace glowed.

"Got to do the rounds!" he suddenly told her in an amazing burst of abandon. "Customers everywhere." An abrupt turn of the heel caused him to stagger slightly. "Too damn popular, this stuff. That's the trouble."

" 'Licious. 'Bye," she said. She waved a hand infantile in its spidery fluttering, her seedy violet eyes overflowing. "Quite 'licious—"

He went in search of Miss La Rue. He found her beyond the azaleas, alone, sitting on a white iron seat against the trunk of a vast acacia. Although she sat with grace, legs crossed, she had allowed the skirt of her costume to ride up, exposing a shapely silken knee. A delicate and bewitching smile accompanied her invitation to Horace to come and sit close to her. She actually patted the seat an inch or two from her thigh, affectionately scolding him at the same time:

"You've been naughty. Where have you been? You neglected me."

Horace protested that he had been rushed off his feet. The cup had taken some time to make and there were customers everywhere.

"Nonsense. You've been flirting again."

"My goodness, no."

"I saw you. I watched you from here. First Miss Sanders and then the creature in the red dress."

From somewhere behind the acacia a fountain tinkled. Its bright and spirited notes might have been Horace's own responses to Miss La Rue's flattering, warming words.

"Well, now that you're here you might at least give me some cup. Of course if you're too engrossed in looking at my knee—"

"Oh! I'm sorry. I'm so sorry."

"Oh! I don't mind." She turned the knee delicately from side to side, appraising it. "I'm rather proud of it. Not at all bad, I think, do you?"

"Well, certainly it—"

"Don't be afraid. You were going to say for a woman of my age, weren't you?"

Horace, embarrassed, started to pour out the remainder of the wine-cup, at the same time making apologetic noises intended to indicate that he couldn't agree with her at all.

"Oh! yes you were," she said. "The trouble is you've no idea how old I am, have you?" Not waiting for an answer, she raised her eyes to the sky, wonderfully remote and ethereal in its clear blue spaciousness beyond the little white flowers of the gigantic acacia. "I am a little older than the tree—the acacia, I mean. It's eighty-five. I know to the day. I remember it being planted."

It was on the tip of Horace's tongue to pay her an immediate compliment but shyness overcame him again and he stopped in the middle of his opening syllable.

"Well?" she said.

"Oh! nothing, nothing."

"I thought for a moment you were going to flatter me."

"Oh! no, no."

"How disappointing," she said. "I hoped you were."

Glass in hand now, she moved more closely to him, squeezing his elbow gently with her free hand. She drank, raising miraculously bright eyes to the summer sky.

"You've been experimenting with the cup."

Horace, once again engrossed in the shining silken knee, confessed that as a matter of fact he had. It had been forced upon him.

"*Kirsch*," she said. She drank again and smacked her lips appreciatively, with the utmost delicacy. "And a touch of *maraschino*. Strange combination but clever of you. Fill me up."

She gave him a flattering and vivacious glance and he filled her up, at the same time topping his own glass too. Freed of his sister and the chattering demands of the girls, Horace was beginning to feel absolutely splendid again. Clever, was he? Popular? Popular and clever! Ah! well, the party was terrific too. He was very glad, after all, that he'd come. He was just the chap to have around at a party. All the girls appreciated him.

He drank again and Miss La Rue moved closer. All the warm intoxication of the summer day seemed suddenly to descend like a pillar of light fire from heaven and Horace gave the exposed shining knee a long look, covetous and almost idolatrous at the same time.

Miss La Rue was quick to notice it and beguiled him further by saying:

"Go on. You may squeeze my knee if you want to."

Horace, freshly flushed with wine-cup, started to protest that nothing was further from his mind but she merely laughed, mocking him slightly.

"Don't be silly. You've been wanting to for some time."

The beginnings of an outrageous fire started to dart about Horace's veins. He felt himself drawn with irresistible force to the knee and suddenly, with an impulse of considerable abandon, started caressing it.

"It's perfectly all right," she said with a light coolness that was also slightly mocking. "Don't be afraid. No one's watching."

Horace, encouraged, squeezed the knee with relish, at the same time laughing a little tipsily. Miss La Rue laughed too and pressed the side of her face close to his ear, the little veil of her hat touching and slightly tickling him. The whisper she gave him a moment later might have been a thunderclap of emotional surprise:

"It isn't the first time it's been squeezed. Nor, I hope, the last."

"No?" Horace said exultantly. "No?"

The noise of the fountain ran thrillingly in his ears, to be echoed suddenly by the notes of a blackbird almost bursting its breast in song somewhere at the very pinnacle of the acacia tree.

"You do it rather well, too," she said.

"My God," Horace said all of a sudden, "you must have been absolutely great when you were young!"

Instantly she regarded him with sly petulance, eyes bright with overtones of mocking reproval.

"After that remark," she said, "I think I should take my leave."

"Oh! no, no. Please," Horace said. He felt suddenly reduced to the proportions of a small boy again. "I didn't mean—no, please—"

"Up to that moment you'd been very tactful."

"Oh! no please—"

"It was heaven sitting here under the acacia and you went and spoilt it all."

"Now, really, listen—"

"You wouldn't say a thing like that to the tree, would you? My tree, I mean."

"Yes, but that's different—"

"How?" she said. She gave him a glance of flirtatious severity, at the same time lifting his hand from her knee rather as if she were lifting up the arm of a gramophone. "The acacia is far more beautiful now than the day it was planted."

"So are you," Horace said. "So are you. I mean—"

"It's all very well to say that now."

"Yes, but I mean it." In an effort to exert physical as well as moral pressure Horace again put his hand on her knee. She moved it away at once, with a gesture aloof and almost prudish.

"Oh! look, we were getting on so well—"

"We were indeed. In fact I was thinking of letting you—"

"Letting me what? Letting me what?"

"It's too late now."

"Oh! what was it?" Horace said. "Please."

"I was thinking of letting you kiss me." She smiled teasingly. "My hand, of course." To Horace's dismay and astonishment she drained the last of her wine-cup, gave him the glass and actually stood up. "But it's too late now. You can kiss Miss Sanders instead."

"Miss Sanders?" Either he or she was going mad, Horace thought. "Miss Sanders? Why on earth Miss Sanders?"

"Because she's coming this way. She's looking terribly soulful. She's obviously looking for someone like you to talk to."

Horace turned his head to see, coming from the direction of the flaming azaleas, the wandering Dodie Sanders. Alone and shy, she seemed about to turn away when Miss la Rue waved her hand and called:

"Dodie. Come over and sit down. Mr. Hooper's dying to talk to you."

"Don't," Horace said. "Don't. Please. Don't."

"Don't be silly. She's charming when you get to know her."

"I don't want to get to know her."

"Don't be unkind. She's a girl who needs company."

"But not mine, for God's sake."

"Don't talk like that. It's tactless." She gave him a maddening smile of mocking intimacy, with the added pain of a slight touch on his arm. "Of course you're very young. You'll learn better as you grow up."

Speechlessly, crushed and in positive pain, Horace watched the arrival of Dodie Sanders as if she were chief mourner at the sudden and cruel demise of the summer morning. He was no longer aware of the thrilling voices of the fountain and the blackbird.

"Come along, Dodie dear. Sit down," Miss La Rue said. Once again the polished curve of her chin caught for a moment a reflection of sunlight as on a shell. Her neat light figure, belying all its years, turned away with grace and poise. "There's a little of Mr. Hooper's wine-cup left. You can have my glass. Mr. Hooper will wash it out in the fountain, won't you, Mr. Hooper?"

She walked away, airily, a moment later. When she had gone Dodie Sanders sat down on the seat, Miss La Rue's empty glass in her hands.

"Give it to me and I'll wash it," Horace said.

"Oh! please don't bother."

"It's no trouble."

"Oh! please don't bother."

After that Dodie Sanders stared, in complete silence, at the distances.

Across the lawn some of the girls were drifting away in groups or in ones and twos. The casual uplift of semi-distant voices only seemed to deepen the pall of silence that hung between Horace and the shy Miss Sanders, who sat twisting the empty glass in her hands.

"My Heavens it's hot," Horace said. A long and intolerable interval of utter silence had left him constrained and sweating. "I really think I shall have to go in."

A moment later he took out his handkerchief to mop his forehead and as he did so the smoked sprat fell to the ground.

For almost half a minute Dodie Sanders gazed down at it with uninspired gravity. Once she lifted her head and stared up into the acacia tree, as if thinking perhaps that the sprat might mysteriously have dropped from there.

"Where did that come from?"

"It fell out of my pocket."

"It's one of those sprats, isn't it?"

Horace said it was. After another silence of considerable length, during which Horace suffered himself to be tortured by a vision of Miss La Rue's brilliant ageless eyes seemingly doting on him to a mocking chorus of fountain and blackbird, she made a remark so astonishing that it reduced him to a profound and impotent silence too.

"In a way sprats are rather beautiful," she said, "aren't they?"

Horace squirmed; he uttered, mentally, a protesting 'Blast!' And suddenly, as if the imposition of yet another awful silence were not enough, he heard a familiar goading voice driving across the lawn:

"Horace! Time to go! We're departing!"

"My sister," he explained. "I'm afraid I'll have to say good-bye—"

He fled across the lawn. Hastily he bore the Venetian jug and the last dregs of its wine-cup out of the deep acacia shade, past the flaring azaleas, across the lawn and through the drifting procession of departing girls. A late glimpse of Miss La Rue getting nimbly into a black limousine aroused an echo so searing that he uttered, aloud this time and almost involuntarily, another monumental "Blast! and blast again!"

"What's the matter with you?" Phoebe Hooper said. "Didn't you enjoy the party? I thought it was you who was the great success?"

"Of course he was, of course he was." Miss Tompkins, in almost passionate assertion, waved delighted and almost tipsy hands to the sky.

"He was like the weather. He was wonderful. He improved all the time he got better."

Half an hour later the lawn was empty. The heat of early afternoon had already woven a hush so deep that each water-note from the fountain beyond the acacia tree could be distinctly heard in a separate crystal fall. The only figures to be seen now were those of Maude and Miss Tompkins, occasionally darting into the garden to pick up a glass, and the solitary figure of Dodie Sanders, silent under the old acacia, staring down at the fallen sprat, golden at her feet.

She alone did not seem to realize that the party for the girls was over.

THE MILL

[I]

A Ford motor-van, old and repainted green with *Jos. Hartop, greengrocer, rabbits,* scratched in streaky white lettering on a flattened-out biscuit tin nailed to the side, was slowly travelling across a high treeless stretch of country in squally November half-darkness. Rain hailed on the windscreen and periodically swished like a sea-wave on the sheaves of pink chrysanthemums strung on the van roof. Jos. Hartop was driving: a thin angular man, starved-faced. He seemed to occupy almost all the seat, sprawling awk-wardly; so that his wife and their daughter Alice sat squeezed up, the girl with her arms flat as though ironed against her side, her thin legs pressed tight together into the size of one. The Hartops' faces seemed moulded in clay and in the light from the van-lamps were a flat swede-colour. Like the man, the two women were thin, with a screwed-up thinness that made them look both hard and frightened. Hartop drove with great caution, grasping the wheel tightly, braking hard at the bends, his big yellowish eyes fixed ahead, protuberantly, with vigilance and fear. His hands, visible in the faint dashboard light, were marked on the backs with dark smears of dried rabbits' blood. The van fussed and rattled, the chrysanthemums always swishing, rain-soaked, in the sudden high wind-squalls. And the two women sat in a state of silent apprehen-sion, their bodies not moving except to lurch with the van their clayish faces continuously intent, almost scared, in the lamp-gloom. And after some time Hartop gave a slight start, and then drew the van to the roadside and stopped it.

"Hear anything drop?" he said. "I thought I heard something."

"It's the wind," the woman said. "I can hear it all the time."

"No, something dropped."

They sat listening. But the engine still ticked, and they could hear nothing beyond it but the wind and rain squalling in the dead grass along the roadside.

"Alice, you git out," Hartop said.

The girl began to move herself almost before he had spoken.

"Git out and see if you can see anything."

Alice stepped across her mother's legs, groped with blind instinct for the step, and then got out. It was raining furiously. The darkness seemed solid with rain.

"See anything?" Hartop said.

"No."

"Eh? What? Can't hear."

"No!"

Hartop leaned across his wife and shouted: "Go back a bit and see what it was." The woman moved to protest, but Hartop was already speaking again: "Go back a bit and see what it was. Something dropped. We'll stop at Drake's Turn. You'll catch up. I know something dropped."

"It's the back-board," the woman said. "I can hear it all the time. Jolting."

"No, it ain't. Something dropped."

He let in the clutch as he was speaking and the van began to move away.

Soon, to Alice, it seemed to be moving very rapidly. In the rain and the darkness all she could see was the tail-light, smoothly receding. She watched it for a moment and then began to walk back along the road. The wind was behind her; but repeatedly it seemed to veer and smash her, with the rain, full in the face. She walked without hurrying. She seemed to accept the journey as she accepted the rain and her father's words, quite stoically. She walked in the middle of the road, looking directly ahead, as though she had a long journey before her. She could see nothing.

And then, after a time, she stumbled against something in the road. She stooped and picked up a bunch of pink chrysanthemums. She gave them a single shake. The flower-odour and the rain seemed to be released together, and then she began to walk back with them along the road. It was as though the chrysanthemums were what she had expected to find above all things. She showed no surprise.

Before very long she could see the red tail-light of the van again. It was stationary. She could see also the lights of houses, little squares of yellow which the recurrent rain on her lashes transformed into sudden stars.

When she reached the van the back-board had been unhooked. Her mother was weighing out potatoes. An oil lamp hung from the van roof, and again the faces of the girl and her mother had the appearance of swede-coloured clay, only the girl's bleaker than before.

"What was it?" Mrs. Hartop said.

The girl laid the flowers on the back-board. "Only a bunch of chrysanthemums."

Hartop himself appeared at the very moment she was speaking.

"Only?" he said, "Only? What d'ye mean by only? Eh? Might have been a sack of potatoes. Just as well. Only! What next?"

Alice stood mute. Her pose and her face meant nothing, had no quality except a complete lack of all surprise; as though she had expected her father to speak like that. Then Hartop raised his voice:

"Well, don't stand there! Do something. Go on. Go on! Go and see who wants a bunch o' chrysanthemums. Move yourself!"

Alice obeyed at once. She picked up the flowers, walked away and vanished, all without a word or a change of that expression of unsurprised serenity.

But she was back in a moment. She began to say that there were chrysanthemums in the gardens of all the houses. Her voice was flat. It was like a pressed flower, a flat faint impression of a voice. And it seemed suddenly to madden her father:

"All right, all right. Christ, all right. Leave it."

He seized the scale-pan of potatoes and then walked away himself. Without a word the girl and her mother chained and hooked up the back-board, climbed up into the driving seat, and sat there with the old intent apprehension, staring through the rain-beaded windscreen, until the woman spoke in a voice of religious negation, with a kind of empty gentleness:

"You must do what your father tells you."

"Yes," Alice said.

Before they could speak again Hartop returned, and in a moment
the van was travelling on.

When it stopped again the same solitary row of house-lights as
before seemed to appear on the roadside and the Hartops seemed to
go through the same ritual of action: the woman unhooking the
back-board, the man relighting the oil lamp, and then the girl and
the woman going off in the rain to the backways of the houses. And
always, as they returned to the van, Hartop grousing, nagging:

"Why the 'ell don't you speak up? Nothing? Well, say it then, say
it!"

Finally the girl took a vegetable marrow from the skips of
potatoes and oranges and onions, carried it to the houses and then
returned with it, and Hartop flew into a fresh rage:

"I'd let 'em eat it if I was you, let 'em eat it. Take the whole
bloody show and let 'em sample. Go on. I'm finished. I jack up. I've
had a packet. I jack up."

He slammed down the scale-pan, extinguished the oil lamp,
began to chain up the back-board. On the two women his rage had
not even the slightest effect. Moving about in the rain, slowly, they
were like two shabby ducks, his rage rolling off the silent backs of
their minds like water.

And then the engine, chilled by the driving rain, refused to start.
Furious, Hartop gave mad jerks at the starting handle. Nothing
happened. The two women, silently staring through the windscreen, never moved. They might even have been in another world,
asleep or dead.

Swinging viciously at the starting handle Hartop shouted:
"When I swing, shove that little switch forward. *Forward!* Christ.
Forward! I never seen anything to touch it. Never. *Forward!* Now
try. Can't you bloody well hear?"

"Yes."

"Then act like it. God, they say there's no peace for the wicked.
Forward!"

Then when the engine spluttered, fired, and at last was revolving
and the van travelling on and the women were able to hear again,
Hartop kept repeating the words in a kind of comforting refrain.
No peace for the wicked. No bloody peace at all. He'd had enough.
Just about bellyful. What with one thing—Christ, what was the use

of talking to folks who were deaf and dumb? Jack up. Better by half to jack up. Bung in. No darn peace for the wicked.

And suddenly, listening gloomily to him, the woman realized that the road was strange to her. She saw trees, then turns and gates and hedges that she did not know.

"Jos, where are we going?" she said.

Hartop was silent. The mystery comforted him. And when at last he stopped the van and switched off the engine it gave him great satisfaction to prolong the mystery, to get down from the van and disappear without a word.

Free of his presence, the two women came to life. Alice half rose from the seat and shook her mackintosh and skirt and said, "Where have we stopped?" Mrs. Hartop was looking out of the side window, peering with eyes screwed-up. She could see nothing. The world outside, cut off by blackness and rain, was strange and unknown. Then when Mrs. Hartop sat down again the old state of negation and silence returned for a moment until Alice spoke. It seemed to Alice that she could hear something, a new sound, quite apart from the squalling of wind and rain; a deeper sound, quieter, and more distant.

The two women listened. Then they could hear the sound distinctly, continuously, a roar of water.

Suddenly Mrs. Hartop remembered. "It's the mill," she said. She got up to look through the window again. "We've stopped at Holland's Mill." She sat down slowly. "What's he stopped here for? What've we—?"

Then she seemed to remember something else. Whatever it was seemed to subdue her again, sealing over her little break of loquacity, making her silent once more. But now her silence had a new quality. It was very near anxiety. She would look quickly at Alice and then quickly away again.

"Is there any tea left?" Alice said.

Mrs. Hartop bent down at once and looked under the seat. She took out a thermos flask, two tea-cups, and an orange. Then Alice held the cups while her mother filled them with milky tea. Then Mrs. Hartop peeled and quartered the orange and they ate and drank, warming their fingers on the tea-cups.

They were wiping their juice-covered fingers and putting away the tea-cups when Hartop returned. He climbed into the cab, slammed the door, and sat down.

"What you been to Hollands' for?" the woman said.

Hartop pressed the self-starter. It buzzed, but the engine was silent. The two women waited. Then Hartop spoke.

"Alice," he said, "you start in service at Hollands' Monday morning. His wife's bad. He told me last Wednesday he wanted a gal about to help. Five shillin' a week and all found."

"Jos!"

But the noise of the self-starter and then the engine firing drowned what the women had to say. And as the van moved on she and Alice sat in silence, without a sound of protest or aquiescence, staring at the rain.

[II]

At night, though so near, Alice had seen nothing of the mill, not even a light. On Monday morning, from across the flat and almost treeless meadows, she could see it clearly. It was a very white three-storeyed building, the whitewash dazzling, almost incandescent, against the wintry fields in the morning sunshine.

Going along the little by-roads across the valley she felt extraordinarily alone, yet not lonely. She felt saved from loneliness by her little leather bag; there was comfort in the mere changing of it from hand to hand. The bag contained her work-apron and her nightgown, and she carried it close to her side as she walked slowly along, not thinking. "You start in good time," Hartop had said to her, "and go steady on. The walk'll do you good." It was about five miles to the mill, and she walked as though in obedience to the echo of her father's command. She had a constant feeling of sharp expectancy, not quite apprehension, every time she looked up and saw the mill. But the feeling never resolved itself into thought. She felt also a slight relief. She had never been, by herself, so far from home. And every now and then she found herself looking back, seeing the house she had left behind, the blank side-wall gas-tarred, the wooden shack in the back-yard where Hartop kept the motor-van, the kitchen where she and her mother bunched the chrysanthemums or sorted the oranges. It seemed strange not to be doing those things: she had sorted oranges and had bunched whatever flowers were in season for as long as she could remember. She had done it all without question, with instinctive obedience. Now, suddenly, she was to do something else. And whatever it was she knew without thinking that she must do it with the same unprotesting obedience. That was right. She had been brought up to it. It was going to be a relief to her father, a help. Things were bad and her going might better them. And then—five shillings a week. She thought of that with recurrent spasms of wonder and incredulity. Could it be true? The question crossed her mind more often than her bag crossed from hand to hand, until it was mechanical and unconscious also.

She was still thinking of it when she rapped at the back door of the mill. The yard was deserted. She could hear no sound of life at all except the mill-race. She knocked again. And then, this time, as she stood waiting, she looked at the yard more closely. It was a chaos of derelict things. Everything was derelict: derelict machinery, old iron, derelict motor cars, bedsteads, wire, harrows, binders, perambulators, tractors, bicycles, corrugated iron. The junk was piled up in a wild heap in the space between the mill-race and the backwater. Iron had fallen into the water. Rusty, indefinable skeletons of it had washed up against the bank-reeds. She saw rust and iron everywhere, and when something made her look up to the mill-windows she saw there the rusted fly-wheels and crane-arms of the mill machinery, the whitewashed wall stained as though with rusty reflections of it.

When she rapped on the door again, harder, flakes of rust, little reddish wafers, were shaken off the knocker. She stared at the door as she waited. Her eyes were large, colourless, fixed in vague penetration. She seemed to be listening with them. They were responsive to sound. And they remained still, as though of glass, when she heard nothing.

And hearing nothing she walked across the yard. Beyond the piles of rusted iron a sluice tore down past the mill-wall on a glacier of green slime. She stooped and peered down over the stone parapet at the water. Beyond the sluice a line of willows were shedding their last leaves, and the leaves came floating down the current like little yellow fish. She watched them come and surge through the grating, and then vanish under the water-arch. Then, watching the fish-like leaves, she saw a real fish, dead, caught in the rusted grating, thrown there by the force of descending water. Then she saw another, and another. Her eyes registered no surprise. She walked round the parapet, and then, leaning over and stretching, she picked up one of the fish. It was cold, and very stiff, like a fish of celluloid, and its eyes were like her own, round and glassy. Then she walked along the path, still holding the fish and occasionally looking at it. The path circled the mill pond and vanished, farther on, into a bed of osiers. The mill-pond was covered in duck-weed, the green crust split into blackness here and there by chance currents of wind or water. The osiers were leafless, but quite still in the windless air. And standing still, she looked at the tall osiers for a moment, her eyes reflecting their stillness and the strange persistent absence of all sound.

And then suddenly she heard a sound. It came from the osiers. A shout:

"You lookin' for Mus' Holland?"

She saw a man's face in the osiers. She called back to it: "Yes."

"He ain't there."

She could think of nothing to say.

"If you want anythink, go in. She's there. A-bed." A shirt-sleeve waved and vanished. "Not that door. It's locked. Round the other side."

She walked back along the path, by the sluice and the machinery and so past the door and the mill-race to the far side of the house. A stretch of grass, once a lawn and now no more than a waste of dead grass and sedge, went down to the backwater from what she saw now was the front door.

At the door she paused for a moment. Why was the front door open and not the back? Then she saw why. Pushing upon the door she saw that it had no lock; only the rusty skeleton pattern of it remained imprinted on the brown sun-scorched paint.

Inside, she stood still in the brick-flagged passage. It seemed extraordinarily cold; the damp coldness of the river air seemed to have saturated the place.

Finally she walked along the passage. Her lace-up boots were heavy on the bricks, setting up a clatter of echoes. When she stopped her eyes were a little wider and almost white in the lightless passage. And again, as outside, they registered the quietness of the place, until it was broken by a voice:

"Somebody there? Who is it?" The voice came from upstairs. "Who is it?"

"Me."

A silence. Alice stood still, listening with wide eyes. Then the voice again:

"Who is it?"

"Me. Alice."

Another silence, and then:

"Come up." It was a light voice, unaggressive, almost friendly. "Come upstairs."

The girl obeyed at once. The wooden stairs were steep and carpetless. She tramped up them. The banister, against which she rubbed her sleeve, was misted over with winter wetness. She could smell the dampness everywhere. It seemed to rise and follow her.

On the top stairs she halted. "In the end bedroom," the voice called. She went at once along the wide half-light landing in the direction of the voice. The panelled doors had at one time been painted white and blue, but now the white was blue and the blue the colour of greenish water. The doors had old-fashioned latches of iron and when she lifted the end latch she could feel the first thin leaf of rust on it ready to crumble and fall. She hesitated a moment before touching the latch, but as she stood there the voice called again and she opened the door.

Then, when she walked into the bedroom, she was almost surprised. She had expected to see Mrs. Holland in bed. But the woman was kneeling on the floor, by the fireplace. She was in her nightgown. The gown had come unbuttoned and Alice could see Mrs. Holland's drooping breasts. They were curiously swollen, as though by pregnancy or some dropsical complaint. The girl saw that Mrs. Holland was trying to light a fire. Faint acrid paper-smoke hung about the room and stung her eyes. She could hear the tin-crackle of burnt paper. There was no flame. The smoke rose up the chimney and then, in a moment, puthered down again, the paper burning with little running sparks that extinguished themselves and then ran on again.

"I'm Alice," the girl said. "Alice Hartop."

She stared fixedly at the big woman sitting there with her nightgown unbuttoned and a burnt match in her hands and her long pigtail of brown hair falling forward over her shoulders almost to the depths of her breasts. Her very largeness, her soft dropsical largeness, and the colour of that thick pigtail were somehow comforting. They were in keeping with the voice she had heard, the voice which spoke to her quite tenderly again now:

"I'm so glad you've come, Alice, I am so glad."

"Am I late?" Alice said. "I walked."

Then she stopped. Mrs. Holland had burst out laughing. The girl stood vacant, at a loss, her mouth fallen open. The woman gathered her nightgown in her hands and held it tight against her breasts, as though she feared that the laughter might suddenly flow out of them like milk. And the girl stared until the woman could speak:

"In your hand! Look, look. In your hand. Look!"

Then Alice saw. She still had the fish in her hand. She was clutching it like a little siver-scaled purse.

"Ohdear! ohdear!" she said. She spoke the words as one word: a single word of unsurprised comment on the unconscious folly of her own act. Even as she said it Mrs. Holland burst out laughing again. And as before the laughter seemed as if it must burst liquidly or fall and run over her breasts and hands and her nightgown. The girl had never heard such laughter. It was far stranger than the fish in her own hand. It was almost too strange. It had a strangeness that was only a shade removed from hysteria, and only a little further from inanity. "She's a bit funny," the girl thought. And almost simultaneously Mrs. Holland echoed her thought:

"Oh! Alice, you're funny." The flow of laughter lessened and then dried up. "Oh, you are funny."

To Alice that seemed incomprehensible. If anybody was funny it was Mrs. Holland, laughing in that rich, almost mad voice. So she continued to stare. She still had the fish in her hand. It added to her manner of uncomprehending vacancy.

Then suddenly a change came over her. She saw Mrs. Holland shiver and this brought back at once her sense of almost subservient duty.

"Hadn't you better get dressed and let me light the fire?" she said.

"I can't get dressed. I've got to get back into bed."

"Well, you get back. You're shivering."

"Help me."

Alice put down her bag on the bedroom floor and laid the fish on top of it. Mrs. Holland tried at the same moment to get up. She straightened herself until she was kneeling upright. Then she tried to raise herself. She clutched the bedrail. Her fat, almost transparent-fleshed fingers would not close. They were like thick sausages, fat jointless lengths of flesh which could not bend. And there she remained in her helplessness, until Alice put her arms about her and took the weight of her body.

"Yes, Alice, you'll have to help me. I can't do it myself any longer. You'll have to help me."

Gradually Alice got her back to bed. And Alice, as she helped her, could feel the curious swollen texture of Mrs. Holland's flesh. The distended breasts fell out of her unbuttoned nightgown, her heavy thighs lumbered their weight against her own, by contrast so weak and thin and straight. And then when Mrs. Holland was in bed, at last, propped up by pillows, Alice had time to look at her face. It had that same heavy water-blown brightness of flesh under the eyes and in the cheeks and in the soft parts of the neck. The gentle dark brown eyes were sick. They looked out with a kind of gentle sick envy on Alice's young movements as she straightened the bedclothes and then cleaned the fireplace and finally as she laid and lighted the fire itself.

And then when her eyes had satisfied themselves Mrs. Holland began to talk again, to ask questions.

"How old are you, Alice?"

"Seventeen."

"Would you rather be here with me than at home?"

"I don't mind."

"Don't you like it at home?"

"I don't mind."

"Is the fire all right?"

"Yes."

"When you've done the grate will you go down and git the taters ready?"

"Yes."

"It's cold mutton. Like cold mutton, Alice?"

"I don't mind."

Then, in turn, the girl had a question herself.

"Why ain't the mill going?" she asked.

"The mill? The mill ain't been going for ten years."

"What's all that iron?"

"That's the scrap. What Fred buys and sells. That's his trade. The mill ain't been worked since his father died. That's been ten year. Fred's out all day buying up iron like that, and selling it. Most of it he never touches, but what he don't sell straight off comes back here. He's gone off this morning. He won't be back till night-time. You'll have to get his tea when he comes back."

"I see."

"You must do all you can for him. I ain't much good to him now."

"I see."

"You can come up again when you've done the taters."

Downstairs Alice found the potatoes in a wet mould-green sack and stood at the sink and pared them. The kitchen window looked out on the mill-stream. The water foamed and eddied and kept up a gentle bubbling roar against the wet stone walls outside. The water-smell was everywhere. From the window she could see across the flat valley: bare willow branches against bare sky, and between them the bare water.

Then as she finished the potatoes she saw the time by the blue tin alarm clock standing on the high smoke-stained mantelpiece. It was past eleven. Time seemed to have flown by her faster than the water was flowing under the window.

[III]

It seemed to flow faster than ever as the day went on. Darkness began to settle over the river and the valley in the middle afternoon: damp, still November darkness preceded by an hour of watery half-light. From Mrs. Holland's bedroom Alice watched the willow trees, dark and skeleton-like, the only objects raised up above the flat fields, hanging half-dissolved by the winter mist, then utterly dissolved by the winter darkness. The afternoon was very still; the mist moved and thickened without wind. She could hear nothing but the mill-race, the everlasting almost mournful machine-like roar of perpetual water, and then, high above it, shrieking, the solitary cries of sea-gulls, more mournful even than the monotone of water.

They were sounds she had heard all day, but had heard unconsciously. She had had no time for listening, except to Mrs. Holland's voice calling downstairs its friendly advice and desires through the open bedroom door: "Alice, have you put the salt in the taters? You'll find the onions in the shed, Alice. The oil-man calls today, ask him to leave the usual. When you've washed up you can bring the paper up, Alice, and read bits out to me for five minutes. Has the oil-man been? Alice, I want you a minute, I want you." So it had gone on all day. And the girl, gradually, began to like Mrs. Holland; and the woman, in turn, seemed to be transported into a state of new and stranger volatility by Alice's presence. She was garrulous with joy. "I've been lonely. Since I've been bad I ain't seen nobody, only Fred, one week's end to another. And the doctor. It's been about as much as I could stan'." And the static, large-eyed, quiet presence of the girl seemed to comfort her extraordinarily. She had someone to confide in at last. "I ain't had nobody I could say a word to. Nobody. And nobody to do nothing for me. I had to wet the bed one day. I was so weak I couldn't get out. That's what made Fred speak to your dad. I couldn't go on no longer."

So the girl had no time to listen except to the voice or to think or talk except in answer to it. And the afternoon was gone and the damp moving darkness was shutting out the river and the bare fields and barer trees before she could realise it.

"Fred'll be home at six," Mrs. Holland said. "He shaves at night. So you git some hot water ready about a quarter to."

"All right."

"Oh! and I forgot. He allus has fish for his tea. Cod or something. Whatever he fancies. He'll bring it. You can fry it while he's shaving."

"All right."

"Don't you go and fry that roach by mistake!"

Mrs. Holland, thinking again of the fish in Alice's hand, lay back on the pillows and laughed, the heavy ripe laughter that sounded as before a trifle strange, as though she were a little mad or hysterical in the joy of fresh companionship.

Mrs. Holland and Alice had already had a cup of tea in the bedroom. That seemed unbelievably luxurious to Alice, who for nearly five years had drunk her tea from a thermos flask in her father's van. It brought home to her that she was very well off: five shillings a week, tea by the fire in the bedroom, Mrs. Holland so cheerful and nice, and an end at last to her father's ironic grousing and the feeling that she was a dead weight on his hands. It gave her great satisfaction. Yet she never registered the emotion by looks or words or a change in her demeanour. She went about quietly and a trifle vaguely, almost in a trance of detachment. The light in her large flat pellucid eyes never varied. Her mouth would break into a smile, but the smile never telegraphed itself to her eyes. And so with words. She spoke, but the words never changed that expression of dumb content, that wide and in some way touching and attractive stare straight before her into space.

And when she heard the rattling of a motor-van in the mill-yard just before six o'clock she looked suddenly up, but her expression did not change. She showed no flicker of apprehension or surprise.

About five minutes later Holland walked into the kitchen.

" 'Ullo," he said.

Alice was standing at the sink, wiping the frying pan with a dishcloth. When Holland spoke and she looked round at him her eyes blinked with a momentary flash of something like surprise. Holland's voice was very deep and it seemed to indicate that Holland himself would be physically very large and powerful.

Then she saw that he was a little man, no taller than herself, and rather stocky, without being stiff or muscular. His trousers hung loose and wide, like sacks. His overcoat, undone, was also like a sack. The only unloose thing about him was his collar. It was a narrow stiff celluloid collar fixed with a patent ready-made tie. The collar was oilstained and the tie, once blue, was soaked by oil and dirt to the appearance of old *crêpe*. The rest of Holland was loose and careless and drooping. A bit of an old shack, Alice thought. Even his little tobacco-yellowed moustache drooped raggedly. Like his felt hat, stuck carelessly on the back of his head, it looked as though it did not belong to him.

" 'Ullo," he said. "You *are* 'ere then. I see your dad. D'ye think you're going to like it?"

"Yes."

"That's right. You make yourself at 'ome." He had the parcel of

fish under his arm and as he spoke he took it out and laid it on the
kitchen table. The brown paper flapped open and Alice saw the tail-
cut of a cod. She went at once to the plate-rack, took a plate and
laid the fish on it.

"Missus say anythink about the fish?" Holland said.

"Yes."

"All right. You fry it while I git shaved."

"I put the water on," she said.

Holland took off his overcoat, then his jacket, and finally his collar
and tie. Then he turned back the greasy neck-band of his shirt and
began to make his shaving lather in a wooden bowl at the sink,
working the brush and bowl like a pestle and mortar. Alice put the
cod into the frying-pan and then the pan on the oil-stove. Then as
Holland began to lather his face, Mrs. Holland called downstairs:
"Fred. You there, Fred? Fred!" and Holland walked across the
kitchen, still lathering himself and dropping spatters of white lather
on the stone flags as he went, to listen at the stairs door.

"Yes, I'm 'ere, Em'ly. I'm—Eh? Oh! all right."

Holland turned to Alice. "The missus wants you a minute
upstairs."

Alice ran upstairs, thinking of the fish. After the warm kitchen
she could feel the air damper than ever. Mrs. Holland was lying
down in bed and a candle in a tin holder was burning on the chest
of drawers.

"Oh! Alice," Mrs. Holland said, "you do all you can for Mr.
Holland, won't you? He's had a long day."

"Yes."

"And sponge his collar. I want him to go about decent. It won't
get done if you don't do it."

"All right."

Alice went downstairs again. Sounds of Holland's razor scraping
his day-old beard and of the cod hissing in the pan filled the
kitchen. She turned the cod with a fork and then took up Holland's
collar and sponged it with the wetted fringe of her pinafore. The
collar came up bright and fresh as ivory, and when finally Holland
had finished shaving at the sink and had put on the collar again it
was as though a small miracle had been performed. Holland was
middle-aged, about fifty, and looked older in the shabby overcoat

and oily collar. Now, shaved and with the collar cleaned again, he looked younger than he was. He looked no longer shabby, a shack, and a bit nondescript, but rather homely and essentially decent. He had a tired, rather stunted and subservient look. His flesh was coarse, with deep pores, and his greyish hair came down stiff over his forehead. His eyes were dull and a little bulging. When Alice put the fried fish before him he sat low over the plate, scooped up the white flakes of fish with his knife and then sucked them into his mouth. He spat out the bones. Every time he spat out a bone he drank his tea, and when his cup was empty, Alice, standing by, filled it up again.

None of these things surprised the girl. She had never seen anyone eat except like that, with the knife, low over the plate, greedily. Her father and mother ate like it and she ate like it herself. So as she stood by the sink, waiting to fill up Holland's cup, her eyes stared with the same abstract preoccupation as ever. They did not even change when Holland spoke, praising her:

"You done this fish all right, Alice."

"Shall I git something else for you?"

"Git me a bit o' cheese. Yes, you done that fish very nice, Alice. Very nice indeed."

Yet, though her eyes expressed nothing, she felt a sense of reassurance, very near to comfort, at Holland's words. It was not deep: but it was enough to counteract the strangeness of her surroundings, to help deaden the perpetual sense of the mill-race, to drive away some of the eternal dampness about the place.

But it was not enough to drive away her tiredness. She went to bed very early, as soon as she had washed Holland's supper things and had eaten her own supper of bread and cheese. Her room was at the back of the mill. It had not been used for a long time; its dampness rose up in a musty cloud. Then when she lit her candle and set it on the washstand she saw that the wallpaper, rotten with dampness, was peeling off and hanging in ragged petals, showing the damp-green plaster beneath. Then she took her nightgown out of her case, undressed and stood for a moment naked, her body as thin as a boy's and her little lemon-shaped breasts barely formed, before dropping the nightgown over her shoulders. A moment later she had put out the candle and was lying in the little iron bed.

Then, as she lay there, curling up her legs for warmth in the damp sheets, she remembered something. She had said no prayers. She got out of bed at once and knelt down by the bed and words of mechanical supplication and thankfulness began to run at once through her mind: "Dear Lord, bless us and keep us. Dear Lord, help me to keep my heart pure," little impromptu gentle prayers of which she only half-understood the meaning. And all the time she was kneeling she could hear a background of other sounds: the mill-race roaring in the night, the wild occasional cries of birds from up the river, and the rumblings of Holland and his wife talking in their bedroom.

And in their room Holland was saying to his wife: "She seems like a good gal."

"She is. I like her," Mrs. Holland said. "I think she's all right."

"She done that fish lovely."

"Fish." Mrs. Holland remembered. And she told Holland of how Alice had brought up the roach in her hand, and as she told him her rather strange rich laughter broke out again and Holland laughed with her.

"Oh dear," Mrs. Holland laughed. "She's a funny little thing when you come to think of it."

"As long as she's all right," Holland said, "that's all that matters. As long as she's all right."

[IV]

Alice was all right. It took less than a week for Holland to see that, although he distrusted a little Alice's first showing with his fish. It seemed too good. He knew what servant girls could be like: all docile, punctual and anxious to please until they got the feeling of things, and then haughty and slovenly and sulky before you could turn round. He wasn't having that sort of thing. The minute Alice was surly or had too much lip she could go. Easy get somebody else. Plenty more kids be glad of the job. So for the first few nights after Alice's arrival he would watch her reflection in the soap-flecked shaving-mirror hanging over the sink while he scraped his beard. He watched her critically, tried to detect some flaw, some change, in her meek servitude. The mirror was a big round iron-framed concave

mirror, so that Alice, as she moved slowly about with the fish-pan
over the oil-stove, looked physically a little larger, and also vaguer
and softer, than she really was. The mirror put flesh on her bony
arms and filled out her pinafore. And looking for faults, Holland saw
only this softening and magnifying of her instead. Then when he had
dried the soap out of his ears and had put on the collar Alice had
sponged for him he would sit down to the fish, ready to pounce on
some fault in it. But the fish, like Alice, never seemed to vary.
Nothing wrong with the fish. He tried bringing home different sorts
of fish, untried sorts, tricky for Alice to cook; witch, whiting, sole
and halibut, instead of his usual cod and hake. But it made no
difference. The fish was always good. And he judged Alice by the
fish: if the fish was all right Alice was all right. Upstairs, after supper,
he would ask Mrs. Holland: "Alice all right to-day?" and Mrs.
Holland would say how quiet Alice was, or how good she was, and
how kind she was, and that she couldn't be without her for the
world. "Well, that fish was lovely again," Holland would say.

And gradually he saw that he had no need for suspicion. No need
to be hard on the kid. She was all right. Leave the kid alone. Let her
go on her own sweet way. Not interfere with her. And so he swung
round from the suspicious attitude to one almost of solicitude.
Didn't cost no more to be nice to the kid than it did to be
miserable. "Well, Alice, how's Alice?" The tone of his evening
greeting became warmer, a little facetious, more friendly. "That's
right, Alice. Nice to be back home in the dry, Alice." In the
mornings, coming downstairs, he had to pass her bedroom door.
He would knock on it to wake her. He got up in darkness, running
downstairs in his stockinged feet, with his jacket and collar and tie
slung over his arm. And pausing at Alice's door he would say
"Quart' t' seven, Alice. You gittin' up, Alice?" Chinks of candlelight round and under the door-frame, or her sleepy voice, would
tell him if she were getting up. If the room were in darkness and she
did not answer he would knock and call again. "Time to git up,
Alice. Alice!" One morning the room was dark and she did not
answer at all. He knocked harder again, hard enough to drown any
sleepy answer she might have given. Then, hearing nothing and
seeing nothing, he opened the door.

At the very moment he opened the door Alice was bending over the washstand, with a match in her hands, lighting her candle. "Oh! Sorry, Alice, I din't hear you." In the moment taken to speak the words Holland saw the girl's open nightgown, and then her breasts, more than ever like two lemons in the yellow candlelight. The light shone straight down on them, the deep shadow of her lower body heightening their shape and colour, and they looked for a moment like the breasts of a larger and more mature girl than Holland fancied Alice to be.

As he went downstairs in the winter darkness he kept seeing the mirage of Alice's breasts in the candlelight. He was excited. A memory of Mrs. Holland's large dropsical body threw the young girl's breasts into tender relief. And time seemed to sharpen the comparison. He saw Alice bending over the candle, her nightgown undone, at recurrent intervals throughout the day. Then in the evening, looking at her reflection in the shaving-mirror, the magnifying effect of the mirror magnified his excitement. And upstairs he forgot to ask if Alice was all right.

In the morning he was awake a little earlier than usual. The morning was still like night. Black mist shut out the river. He went along the dark landing and tapped at Alice's door. When there was no answer he tapped again and called, but nothing happened. Then he put his hand on the latch and pressed it. The door opened. He was so surprised that he did not know for a moment what to do. He was in his shirt and trousers, with the celluloid collar and patent tie and jacket in his hand, and no shoes on his feet.

He stood for a moment by the bed and then he stretched out his hand and shook Alice. She did not wake. Then he put his hand on her chest and let it rest there. He could feel the breasts unexpectedly soft and alive, through the nightgown. He touched one and then the other.

Suddenly Alice woke.

"All right, Alice. Time to git up, that's all," Holland said. "I was trying to wake you."

[V]

"I 'spect you want to git home weekends, don't you, Alice?" Mrs. Holland said.

Alice had been at the mill almost a week. "I don't mind," she said.

"Well, we reckoned you'd like to go home a' Sundays, anyway. Don't you?"

"I don't mind."

"Well, you go home this week, and then see. Only it means cold dinner for Fred a' Sundays if you go."

So after breakfast on Sunday morning Alice walked across the flat valley and went home. The gas-tarred house, the end one of a row on the edge of the town, seemed cramped and a little strange after the big rooms at the mill and the bare empty fields and the river.

"Well, how d'ye like it?" Hartop said.

"It's all right."

"Don't feel homesick?"

"No, I don't mind."

Alice laid her five shillings on the table. "That's my five shillings," she said. "Next Sunday I ain't coming. What shall I do about the money?"

"You better send it," Hartop said. "It ain't no good to you there if you keep it, is it? No shops, is they?"

"I don't know. I ain't been out."

"Well, you send it." Then suddenly Hartop changed his mind. "No, I'll tell you what. You keep it and we'll call for it a' Friday. We can come round that way."

"All right," Alice said.

"If you ain't coming home," Mrs. Hartop said, "you'd better take a clean nightgown. And I'll bring another Friday."

And so she walked back across the valley in the November dusk with the nightgown wrapped in brown paper under her arm, and on Friday Hartop stopped the motor-van outside the mill and she went out to him with the five shillings Holland had left on the table that morning. "I see your dad about the money, Alice. That's all right." And as she stood by the van answering in her flat voice the questions her father and mother put to her, Hartop put his hand in his pocket and said:

"Like orange, Alice?"

"Yes," she said. "Yes, please."

Hartop put the orange into her hand. "Only mind," he said. "It's tacked. It's just a bit rotten on the side there." He leaned out of the driver's seat and pointed out the soft bluish rotten patch on the orange skin. "It's all right. It ain't gone much."

"You gittin' on all right, Alice?" Mrs. Hartop said. She spoke from the gloom of the van seat. Alice could just see her vague clay-coloured face.

"Yes. I'm all right."

"See you a' Friday again then."

Hartop let off the brake and the van moved away simultaneously as Alice moved away across the millyard between the piles of derelict iron. Raw half-mist from the river was coming across the yard in sodden swirls and Alice, frozen, half-ran into the house. Then, in the kitchen, she sat by the fire with her skirt drawn up above her knees, to warm herself.

She was still sitting like that, with her skirt drawn up to her thighs and her hands outstretched to the fire and the orange in her lap, when Holland came in.

"Hullo, Alice," he said genially. "I should git on top o' the fire if I was you."

Alice, wretched with the cold, which seemed to have settled inside her, scarcely answered. She sat there for almost a full minute longer, trying to warm her legs, before getting up to cook Holland's fish. All the time she sat there Holland was looking at her legs, with the skirt pulled up away from them. The knees and the slim thighs were rounded and soft, and the knees and the legs themselves a rosy flame-colour in the firelight. Holland felt a sudden agitation as he gazed at them.

Then abruptly Alice got up to cook the fish, and the vision of her rose-coloured legs vanished. But Holland, shaving before the mirror, could still see in his mind the soft firelight on Alice's knees. And the mirror, as before, seemed to magnify Alice's vague form as it moved about the kitchen, putting some flesh on her body. Then when Holland sat down to his fish Alice again sat down before the fire and he saw her pull her skirt above her knees again as though he did not exist. And all through the meal he sat looking at her. Then suddenly he got tired of merely looking at her. He wanted to be closer to her. "Alice, come and 'ave a drop o' tea," he said. "Pour yourself a cup out. Come on. You look starved." The orange

Hartop had given Alice lay on the table, and the girl pointed to it.
"I'm going to have that orange," she said. Holland picked up the
orange. "All right, only you want summat. Here, I'm going to
throw it." He threw the orange. It fell into Alice's lap. And it
seemed to Holland that its fall drew her dress a little higher above
her knees. He got up. "Never hurt you, did I, Alice?" he said. He
ran his hands over her shoulders and arms, and then over her thighs
and knees. Her knees were beautifully warm, like hard warm
apples. "You're starved though. Your knees are like ice." He began
to rub her hands a little with his own, and the girl, her flat
expression never changing, let him do it. She felt his fingers harsh
on her bloodless hands and then on her shoulders. "Your chest ain't
cold, is it?" Holland said. "You don't want to git cold in your
chest." He was feeling her chest, above the breasts. The girl shook
her head. "Sure?" Holland said. He kept his hands on her chest.
"You put something on when you go out to that van again. If you
git cold on your chest . . ." And as he was speaking his hands moved
down until they covered her breasts. They were so small that he
could hold them easily in his hands. "Don't want to git cold in
them, do you?" he said. "In your nellies?" She stared at him
abstractedly, not knowing the word, wondering what he meant.
Then suddenly he was squeezing her breasts, in a bungling effort of
tenderness. The motion hurt her. "Come on, Alice, come on. I
shan't do nothing. Let's have a look at you, Alice. I don't want to
do nothing. Alice. All right. I don't want to hurt you. Undo your
dress, Alice." And the girl, mechanically, to his astonishment, put
her hands to the buttons. As they came undone he put his hands on
her chest and then on her bare breasts in clumsy and agitated efforts
to caress her. She sat rigid, staring, not fully understanding. Every
time Holland squeezed her he hurt her. But the mute and fixed look
on her face and the grey flat as though motionless stare in her eyes
never changed. She listened only vaguely to what Holland said.

"Come on, Alice. You lay down. You lay down on the couch. I
ain't going to hurt you, Alice. I don't want to hurt you."

For a moment she did not move. Then she remembered, flatly,
Mrs. Holland's injunction. "You do all you can for Mr. Holland,"
and she got up and went over to the American leather couch.

"I'll blow the lamp out," Holland said. "It's all right. It's all right."

[VI]

"Don't you say nothing, Alice. Don't you go and tell nobody."

Corn for Mrs. Holland's chickens, a wooden potato-tub of maize and another of wheat, was kept in a loft above the mill itself, and Alice would climb the outside loft-ladder to fill the chipped enamel corn-bowl in the early winter afternoons. And standing there, with the bowl empty in her hands, or with a scattering of grain in it or the full mixture of wheat and maize, she stared and thought of the words Holland said to her almost every night. The loft windows were hung with skeins of spiderwebs, and the webs in turn were powdered with pale and dark grey dust, pale flour-dust never swept away since the mill had ceased to work, and a dark mouse-coloured dust that showered constantly down from the rafters. The loft was always cold. The walls were clammy with river damp and the windows misty with wet. But Alice always stood there in the early afternoons and stared through the dirty windows across the wet flat valley. Seagulls flew wildly above the floods that filled the meadows after rain. Strings of wild swans flew over and sometimes came down to rest with the gulls on the waters or the islands of grass. They were the only moving things in the valley. But Alice stared at them blankly, hardly seeing them. She saw Holland instead; Holland turning out the lamp, fumbling with his trousers, getting up and relighting the lamp with a tight scared look on his face. And she returned his words over and over in her mind. "Don't you say nothing. Don't you say nothing. Don't you go and tell nobody." They were words not of anger, not threatening, but of fear. But she did not see it. She turned his words slowly over and over in her mind as she might have turned a ball or an orange over and over in her hands, over and over, round and round, the surface always the same, the shape the same, for ever recurring, a circle with no end to it. She reviewed them without surprise and without malice. She never refused Holland. Once only she said, suddenly scared: "I don't want to, not tonight. I don't want to." But Holland cajoled, "Come on, Alice come on. I'll give you something. Come on. I'll give y' extra sixpence with your money, Friday, Alice. Come on."

And after standing a little while in the loft she would go down the ladder with the corn-bowl to feed the hens that were cooped up behind a rusty broken-down wire-netting pen across the yard, beyond the dumps of iron. "Tchka! Tchka! Tchka!" She never varied the call. "Tchka! Tchka!" The sound was thin and sharp in the winter air. The weedy fowls, wet-feathered, scrambled after the yellow corn as she scattered it down. She watched them for a moment, staying just so long and never any longer, and then went back into the mill, shaking the corn-dust from the bowl as she went. It was as though she were religiously pledged to a ritual. The circumstances and the day never varied. She played a minor part in a play which never changed and seemed as if it never could change. Holland got up, she got up, she cooked breakfast. Holland left. She cleaned the rooms and washed Mrs. Holland. She cooked the dinner, took half up to Mrs. Holland and ate half herself. She stood in the loft, thought of Holland's words, fed the fowls, then ceased to think of Holland. In the afternoon she read to Mrs. Holland. In the evening Holland returned. And none of it seemed to affect her. She looked exactly as she had looked when she had first walked across the valley with her bag. Her eyes were utterly unresponsive, flat, never lighting up. They only seemed if anything greyer and softer, a little fuller if possible of docility.

And there was only one thing which in any way broke the ritual; and even that was regular, a piece of ritual itself. Every Wednesday, and again on Sunday, Mrs. Holland wrote to her son.

Or rather Alice wrote. "You can write better 'n me. You write it. I'll tell you what to put and you put it." So Alice sat by the bed with a penny bottle of ink, a steel pen and a tissue writing tablet, and Mrs. Holland dictated. "Dear Albert." There she stopped, lying back on the pillows to think. Alice waited. The pen dried. And then Mrs. Holland would say: "I can't think what to put. You git th' envelope done while I'm thinking." So Alice wrote the envelope:

'Pte Albert Holland, 94167, B Company, Fifth Battalion 1st Rifles, British Army of Occupation, Cologne, Germany.'

And then Mrs. Holland would begin, talking according to her mood: "I must say, Albert, I feel a good lot better. I have not had a touch for a long while." Or: "I don't seem to get on at all somehow. The doctor comes every week and says I got to stop here. Glad to say though things are well with your Dad and trade is good and he is only waiting for you to come home and go in with him. There is a good trade now in old motors. Your Dad is very good to me I must say and so is Alice. I wonder when you will be home. Alice is writing this."

All through the winter Alice wrote the letters. They seemed always to be the same letters, slightly changed, endlessly repeated. Writing the letters seemed to bring her closer to Mrs. Holland. "I'm sure I don't know what I should do without you, Alice." Mrs. Holland trusted her implicitly, could see no wrong in her. And it seemed to Alice as if she came to know the soldier too, since she not only wrote the letters which went to him but read those which came in return.

"Dear Mum, it is very cold here and I can't say I shall be very sorry when I get back to see you. Last Sunday we . . ."

It seemed almost as if the letters were written to her. And though she read them without imagination, flatly, they gave her a kind of pleasure. She looked forward to their arrival. She shared Mrs. Holland's anxiety when they did not come. "It seems funny about Albert, he ain't writ this week." And they would sit together in the bedroom, in the short winter afternoons, and talk of him and wonder.

Or rather Mrs. Holland talked. Alice simply listened, her large grey eyes very still with their expression of lost attentiveness.

[VII]

She began to be sick in the early mornings without knowing what was happening to her. It was almost spring. The floods were lessening and vanishing and there was a new light on the river and the grass. The half-cut osier-bed shone in the sun like red corn, the bark varnished with light copper. She could dimly feel the change in the life about her: the new light, the longer days, thrushes singing in the willows above the mill-water in the evenings, the sun warm on her face in the afternoons.

But there was no change in her own life. Or if there was a change she did not feel it. There was no change in Mrs. Holland's attitude

to her and in her own to Mrs. Holland. And only once was there a
change in her attitude to Holland himself. After the first touch of
sickness she could not face him. The life had gone out of her. "I
ain't well," she kept saying to Holland. "I ain't well." For the first
time he went into a rage with her. "It ain't been a week since you
said that afore! Come on. Christ! You ain't goin' to start that
game." He tried to put his arms round her. She struggled a little,
tried to push him away. And suddenly he hit her. The blow struck
her on the shoulder, just above the heart. It knocked her silly for a
moment and she staggered about the room, then sat on the sofa,
dazed. Then as she sat there the room was suddenly plunged into
darkness. It was as though she had fainted. Then she saw that it was
only Holland. He had put out the lamp.

   After that she never once protested. She became more than ever
static, a neutral part of the act in which Holland was always the
aggressor. There was nothing in it for her. It was over quickly, a
savage interlude in the tranquil day-after-day unaltered life of Mrs.
Holland and herself. It was as regular almost as the sponging of
Holland's collar and the cooking of his fish, or as the Friday visit of
her mother and father with the van.

   "How gittin' on? You don't look amiss. You look as if you're
fillin' out a bit." Or "This is five and six! Is he rised you? Mother,
he give her a rise. Well, well, that's all right, that is. That's good, a
rise so soon. You be a good gal and you won't hurt." And finally:
"Well, we s'll ha' to git on. Be dark else," and the van would move
away.

   She was certainly plumper: a slight gentle filling of her breasts
and her face were the only signs of physical change in her. She
herself scarcely noticed them; until standing one day in the loft,
gazing across the valley, holding the corn-bowl pressed against her,
she could feel the bowl's roundness hard against the hardening
roundness of her belly. Then she could feel something wrong with
herself for the first time. And she stood arrested, scared. She felt
large and heavy. What was the matter with her? She stood in a
perplexity of fear. And finally she put the corn-bowl on the loft
floor and then undid her clothes and looked at herself. She was
round and hard and shiny. Then she opened the neck of her dress.
Her breasts were no longer like little hard pointed lemons, but like

half-blown roses. She put her hand under them, and under each breast, half in fear and half in amazement, and lifted them gently. They seemed suddenly as if they would fall if she did not hold them. What was it? Why hadn't she noticed it? Then she had suddenly something like an inspiration. It was Mrs. Holland's complaint. She had caught it. Her body had the same swollen shiny look about it. She could see it clearly enough. She had caught the dropsy from Mrs. Holland.

For a time she was a little frightened. She lay in bed at night and touched herself, and wondered. Then it passed off. She went back into the old state of unemotional neutrality. Then the sickness began to get less severe; she went for whole days without it; and finally it ceased altogether. Then there were days when the heaviness of her breasts and belly seemed a mythical thing, when she did not think of it. And she would think that the sickness and the heaviness were passing off together, things dependent on each other.

By the late spring she felt that it was all right, that she had nothing to fear. Summer was coming. She would be better in summer. Everybody was better in the summer.

Even Mrs. Holland seemed better. But it was not the spring weather or the coming of summer that made her so, but the letters from Germany. "I won't say too much, Mum, in case. But very like we shall be home afore the end of this year."

"I believe I could git up, Alice, if he come home. I believe I could. I should like to be up," Mrs. Holland would say. "I believe I could."

And often, in the middle of peeling potatoes or scrubbing the kitchen bricks, Alice would hear Mrs. Holland calling her. And when she went up it would be, "Alice, you git the middle bedroom ready. In case Albert comes," or "See if you can find Albert's fishing-tackle. It'll be in the shed or else the loft. He'll want it," or "Tell Fred when he comes home I want him to git a ham. A whole 'un. In case." And always the last flickering desire: "If I knowed when he was coming I'd git up. I believe I *could* git up."

But weeks passed and nothing happened. Mid-summer came, and all along the river the willow-leaves drooped or turned, green and silver, in the summer sun and the summer wind. And the hot still days were almost as uneventful and empty as the brief damp days of winter.

Then one afternoon in July Alice, standing in the loft and gazing through the dusted windows, saw a solider coming up the road. He was carrying a white kitbag and he walked on rather splayed flat feet.

She ran down the loft steps and across the dump-yard and up into Mrs. Holland's bedroom.

"Albert's come!"

Mrs. Holland sat straight up in bed, as though by a miracle, trembling.

"Get me out, quick, let me get something on. Get me out. I want to be out for when he comes. Get me out."

The girl took the weight of the big woman as she half slid out of bed, Mrs. Holland's great breasts falling out of her nightgown, Alice thinking all the time, "I ain't got it as bad as her, not half as bad. Mine are little side of hers. Mine are little." She had never realised how big Mrs. Holland was. And she had never seen her so distressed—distressed by joy and anticipation and her own sickness. Tears were flowing from her eyes. Alice struggled with her desperately. But she had scarcely put on her old red woollen dressing-jacket and helped her to a chair before there was a shout:

"Mum!"

Alice was at the head of the stairs before the second shout came. She could see the solider in the passage below looking up. His tunic collar was unbuttoned and thrown back from his sun-red neck.

"Where's mum?"

"Up here."

Albert came upstairs. Alice had expected a young man, very young. Albert seemed about thirty-five, perhaps older. His flat feet, splayed out, and his dark loose moustache gave him a slightly old-fashioned countrified look, a little stupid. He was very like Holland himself. His eyes bulged, the whites glassy.

"Where is she?" he said.

"In the bedroom," Alice said. "In there."

Albert went past her and along the landing without another word, scarcely looking at her. Alice could smell his sweat, the pungent sweat-soaked smell of khaki, as he went by. In another moment she heard Mrs. Holland's cries of delight and his voice in answer.

From that moment she began to live in a changed world. Albert's coming cut her off at once from Mrs. Holland; she was pushed aside like an old love by a new. But she was prepared for that. Not consciously, but by intuition, she had seen that it must come, that Albert would usurp her place. So she had no surprise when Mrs. Holland scarcely called for her all day, had no time to talk to her except of Albert, and never asked her to sit and read to her in the bedroom as she had always done in the past. She was prepared for all that. What she was not prepared for at all was to be cut off from Holland himself too. It had not occurred to her that in the evenings Albert might sit in the kitchen, that there might be no lying on the sofa, no putting out of the light, no doing as Holland wanted.

She was so unprepared for it that for a week she could not believe it. Her incredulity made her quieter than ever. All the time she was waiting for Holland to do something: to come to her secretly, into her bedroom, anywhere, and go on as he had always done. But nothing happened. For a week Holland was quiet too. He did not speak to her. Every evening Alice fried a double quantity of fish for Holland and Albert, and after tea the two men sat in the kitchen and talked, or walked through the osier-bed to the meadows and talked there. Holland scarcely spoke to her. They were scarcely ever alone together. Albert was an everlasting presence, walking about aimlessly, putteeless, his splayed feet shuffling on the bricks, stolid, comfortable, not speaking much.

And finally when Holland did speak to her it was with the old words: "Don't you say nothing! See?" But now there was not only fear in the words, but anger. "You say half a damn word and I'll break your neck. See? I'll smash you. That's over. Done with. Don't you say a damn word! See?"

The words, contrary to their effect of old, no longer perturbed or perplexed her. She was relieved, glad. It was all over. No more putting out the lamp, lying there waiting for Holland. No more pain.

[VIII]

Outwardly she seemed incapable of pain, even of emotion at all. She moved about with the same constant large-eyed quietness as ever, as though she were not thinking or were incapable of thought. Her eyes were remarkable in their everlasting expression of mute steadfastness, the same wintry grey light in them as always, an unreflective, almost lifeless kind of light.

And Albert noticed it. It struck him as funny. She would stare at him across the kitchen, dishcloth in hand, in a state of dumb absorption, as though he were some entrancing boy of her own age. But there was no joy in her eyes, no emotion at all, nothing. It was the same when, after a week's rest, Albert began to repair the chicken-coop beyond the dumps of old iron. Alice would come out twice a day, once with a cup of tea in the morning, once when she fed the hens in the early afternoon, and stand and watch him. She hardly ever spoke. She only moved to set down the tea-cup on a box or scatter the corn on the ground. And standing there, hatless, in the hot sunlight, staring, her lips gently parted, she looked as though she were entranced by Albert. All the time Albert, in khaki trousers, grey army shirt, a cloth civilian cap, and a fag-end always half burning his straggling moustache, moved about with stolid countrified deliberation. He was about as entrancing as an old shoe. He never dressed up, never went anywhere. When he drank, his moustache acted as a sponge, soaking up a little tea, and Albert took second little drinks from it, sucking it in. Sometimes he announced, "I don't know as I shan't go down Nenweald for half hour and look round," but further than that it never went. He would fish in the mill-stream instead, dig in the ruined garden, search among the rusty iron dumps for a hinge or a bolt, something he needed for the hen-house. In the low valley the July heat was damp and stifling, the willows still above the still water, the sunlight like brass. The windless heat and the stillness seemed to stretch away infinitely. And finally Albert carried the wood for the new hen-house into the shade of a big cherry-tree that grew between the river and the house, and sawed and hammered in the cherry-tree shade all day. And from the kitchen Alice could see him. She stood at the sink, scraping potatoes or washing dishes, and watched him. She did it unconsciously. Albert was the only new thing in the square of landscape seen from the window. She had nothing else to watch. The view was even smaller than in winter time, since summer had filled the cherry-boughs, and the tall river reeds had shut out half the world.

It went on like this for almost a month, Albert tidying up the garden and remaking the hen-house, Alice watching him. Until finally Albert said to her one day:

"Don't you ever git out nowhere?"

"No."

"Don't you want to git out?"

"I don't mind."

The old answer: and it was the same answer she gave him, when, two days later, on a Saturday, he said to her: "I'm a-going down Nenweald for hour. You git ready and come as well. Go on. You git ready."

She stood still for a moment, staring, not quite grasping it all.

"Don't you wanna come?"

"I don't mind."

"Well, you git ready."

She went upstairs at once, taking off her apron as she went, in mute obedience.

Earlier, Albert had said to Mrs. Holland: "Don't seem right that kid never goes nowhere. How'd it be if I took her down Nenweald for hour?"

"It's a long way. How're you going?"

"Walk. That ain't far."

"What d'ye want to go down Nenweald for?" A little sick petulant jealousy crept into Mrs. Holland's voice. "Why don't you stop here?"

"I want some nails. I thought I'd take the kid down for hour. She can drop in and see her folks while I git the nails."

"Her folks don't live at Nenweald. They live at Drake's End."

"Well, don't matter. Hour out'll do her good."

And in the early evening Albert and Alice walked across the meadow paths into Nenweald. The sun was still hot and Albert, dressed up in a hard hat and a blue serge suit and a stand-up collar, walked slowly, with grave flat-footed deliberation. The pace suited Alice. She felt strangely heavy; her body seemed burdened down. She could feel her breasts, damp with heat, hanging heavily down under her cotton dress. In the bedroom, changing her clothes, she could not help looking at herself. The dropsy seemed to be getting worse. It was beyond her. And she could feel the tightly swollen nipples of her breasts rubbing against the rather coarse cotton of her dress.

But she did not think of it much. Apart from the heaviness of her

body she felt strong and well. And the country was new to her, the
fields strange and the river wider than she had ever dreamed.

It was the river, for some reason, which struck her most. "Don't
it git big?" she said. "Ain't it wide?"

"Wide," Albert said. "You want to see the Rhine. This is only a
brook." And he went on to tell her of the Rhine. "Take you quarter
of hour to walk across. And all up the banks you see Jerry's grapes.
Growing like twitch. And big boats on the river, steamers. I tell
you. That's the sort o' river. You ought to see it. Like to see a river
like that, wouldn't you?"

"Yes."

"Ah, it's a long way off. A thousand miles near enough."

Alice did not speak.

"You ain't been a sight away from here, I bet, 'ave you?" Albert
said.

"No."

"How far?"

"I don't know."

"What place? What's the farthest place you bin?"

"I don't know. I went Bedford once."

"How far's that? About ten miles, ain't it?"

"I don't know. It seemed a long way."

And gradually· they grew much nearer to each other, almost
intimate. The barriers of restraint between them were broken down
by Albert's talk about the Rhine, the Germans, the war, his funny
or terrible experiences. Listening, Alice forgot herself. Her eyes
listened with the old absorbed unemotional look, but in reality
with new feelings of wonder behind them. In Nenweald she
followed Albert through the streets, waited for him while he bought
the nails or dived down into underground places or looked at comic
picture post-cards outside cheap stationers. They walked through
the Saturday market, Albert staring at the sweet stalls and the caged
birds, Alice at the drapery and the fruit stalls, remembering her old
life at home again as she caught the rich half-rotten fruit smells,
seeing herself in the kitchen at home, with her mother, hearing the
rustle of Spanish paper softly torn from endless oranges in the
kitchen candlelight.

Neither of them talked much. They talked even less as they

walked home. Albert had bought a bag of peardrops and they sucked them in silence as they walked along by the darkening river. And in silence Alice remembered herself again: could feel the burden of her body, the heavy swing of her breasts against her dress. She walked in a state of wonder at herself, at Albert, at the unbelievable Rhine, at the evening in the town.

It was a happiness that even Mrs. Holland's sudden jealousy could not destroy or even touch.

Suddenly Mrs. Holland had changed. "Where's that Alice! Alice! Alice! Why don't you come when I call you? Now just liven yourself, Alice, and git that bedroom ready. You're gettin' fat and lazy, Alice. You ain't the girl you used to be. Git on, git on, do. Don't stand staring." Alice, sackcloth apron bundled loosely round her, her hair rat-tailed about her face, could only stare in reply and then quietly leave the bedroom. "And here!" Mrs. Holland would call her back. "Come here. You ain't bin talking to Albert, 'ave you? He's got summat else to do 'sides talk to you. You leave Albert to 'isself. And now git on. Bustle about and git some o' that fat off."

The jealousy, beginning with mere petulancy, then rising to reprimand, rose to abuse at last.

"Just because I'm in bed you think you can do so you like. Great slommacking thing. Lazy ain't in it. Git on, do!"

And in the evenings:

"Fred, that Alice'll drive me crazy."

"What's up?" Holland's fear would leap up, taking the form of anger too. "What's she bin doing? Been saying anything?"

"Fat, slommacking thing. I reckon she hangs round our Albert. She don't seem right, staring and slommacking about. She looks half silly."

"I'll say summat to her. That fish ain't very grand o' nights sometimes."

"You can say what you like. But she won't hear you. If she does she'll make out she don't. That's her all over. Makes out she don't hear. But she hears all right."

And so Holland attacked her:

"You better liven yourself up. See? Act as if you was sharp. And Christ, you ain't bin saying nothing, 'ave you? Not to her?"

"No."

"Not to nobody?"

"No."

"Don't you say a damn word. That's over. We had a bit o' fun and now it's finished with. See that?"

"Yes." Vaguely she wondered what he meant by fun.

"Well then, git on. Go on, gal, git on. Git on! God save the King, you make my blood boil. Git on!"

The change in their attitude was beyond her: so far beyond her that it created no change in her attitude to them. She went about as she had always done, very quietly, with large-eyed complacency, doing the dirty work, watching Albert, staring at the meadows, her eyes eternally expressionless. It was as though nothing could change her.

Then Albert said, "How about if we go down Nenweald again Saturday? I got to go down."

She remembered Mrs. Holland, stared at Albert and said nothing.

"You git ready about five," Albert said. "Do you good to git out once in a while. You don't git out half enough." He paused, looking at her mute face. "Don't you want a come?"

"I don't mind."

"All right. You be ready."

Then, hearing of it, Mrs. Holland flew into a temper of jealousy:

"You'd take a blessed gal out but you wouldn't stay with me, would you? Not you. Away all this time, and now when you're home again you don't come near me."

"All right, all right. I thought'd do the kid good, that's all."

"That's all you think about. Folks'll think you're kidnappin'!"

"Ain't nothing to do with it. Only taking the kid out for an hour."

"Hour! Last Saturday you'd gone about four!"

"All right," Albert said, "we won't go. It don't matter."

Mrs. Holland broke down and began to weep on the pillow.

"I don't want a stop you," she said. "You can go. It don't matter to me. I can stop here be meself. You can go."

And in the end they went. As before they walked through the meadows, Albert dressed up and hot, Alice feeling her body under her thin clothes as moist and warm as a sweating apple with the heat. In Nenweald they did the same things as before, took the same time, talked scarcely at all, and then walked back again in the summer twilight, sucking the peardrops Albert had bought.

The warm air lingered along by the river. The water and the air and the sky were all breathless. The sky was a soft green-lemon colour, clear, sunless and starless. "It's goin' to be a scorcher again tomorrow," Albert said.

Alice said nothing. They walked slowly, a little apart decorously. Albert opened the towpath gates, let Alice through, and then splay-footed after her. They were like some countrified old fashioned couple half-afraid of each other.

Then Albert, after holding open a towpath gate and letting Alice pass, could not fasten the catch. He fumbled with the gate, lifted it, and did not shut it for about a minute. When he walked on again Alice was some distance ahead. Albert could see her plainly. Her pale washed-out dress was clear in the half light. Albert walked on after her. Then he was struck all of a sudden by the way she walked. She was walking thickly, clumsily, not exactly as though she were tired, but heavily, as though she had iron weights in her shoes.

Albert caught up with her. "You all right, Alice?" he said.

"I'm all right."

"Ain't bin too much for you? I see you walking a bit lame like."

Alice did not speak.

"Ain't nothing up, Alice, is there?"

Alice tried to say something, but Albert asked again: "Ain't bin too hot, is it?"

"No. It's all right. It's only the dropsy."

"The what?"

"What your mother's got. I reckon I catched it off her."

"It ain't catchin', is it?"

"I don' know. I reckon that's what it is."

"You're a bit tired, that's all 'tis," Albert said. "Dropsy. You're a funny kid, no mistake."

They walked almost in silence to the mill. It was dark in the kitchen, Holland was upstairs with Mrs. Holland, and Albert struck a match and lit the oil-lamp.

The burnt match fell from Albert's fingers. And stooping to pick it up he saw Alice, standing sideways and full in the lamplight. The curve of her pregnancy stood out clearly. Her whole body was thick

and heavy with it. Albert crumbled the match in his fingers, staring
at her. Then he spoke.

"Here kid," he said. "Here."

She looked at him.

"What'd you say it was you got? Dropsy?"

"Yes. I reckon that's what it is I caught."

"How long you bin like it?"

"I don't know. It's bin coming on a good while. All summer."

He stared at her, not knowing what to say. All the time she stared
too with the old habitual muteness.

"Don't you know what's up wi' you?" he said.

She shook her head.

When he began to tell her she never moved a fraction. Her face
was like a lump of unplastic clay in the lamplight.

"Don't you know who it is? Who you bin with? Who done it?"

She could not answer. It was hard for her to grapple not only
with Albert's words but with the memory of Holland's: "You tell
anybody and I'll smash you. See?"

"You better git back home," Albert said. "That's your best
place."

"When?"

"Soon as you can. Git off tomorrow. You no business slaving
here."

And then again:

"Who done it? Eh? Don't y' know who done it? If you know who
done it he could marry you."

"He couldn't marry me."

Albert saw that the situation had significance for him.

"You better git off to bed quick," he said. "Go on. And then be
off in the morning."

In the morning Alice was up and downstairs soon after sunlight,
and the sun was well above the trees as she began to walk across the
valley. She walked slowly, carrying her black case, changing it now
and then from one hand to another. Binders stood in the early
wheatfields covered with their tarpaulins, that were in turn covered
with summer dew. It was Sunday. The world seemed empty except
for herself, rooks making their way to the cornfields, and cattle in
the flat valley. She walked for long periods without thinking. Then

when she did think, it was not of herself or the mill or what she was doing or what was going to happen to her, but of Albert. An odd sense of tenderness rose up in her simultaneously with the picture of Albert rising up in her mind. She could not explain it. There was something singularly compassionate in Albert's countrified solidity, his slow voice, his flat feet, his concern for her. Yet for some reason she could not explain, she could not think of him with anything like happiness. The mere remembrance of him sawing and hammering under the cherry-tree filled her with pain. It shot up in her breast like panic. "You better git back home." She could hear him saying it again and again.

And all the time she walked as though nothing had happened. Her eyes had the same dull mute complacency as ever. It was as though she were only half-awake.

When she saw the black gas-tarred side of the Hartop's house it was about eight o'clock. She could hear the early service bell. The sight of the house did not affect her. She went in by the yard gate, shut it carefully, and then walked across the yard to the back door.

She opened the door and stood on the threshold. Her mother and her father, in his shirt-sleeves, sat in the kitchen having breakfast. She could smell tea and bacon. Her father was sopping up his plate with bread, and seeing her he paused with the bread half to his lips. She saw the fat dripping down to the plate again. Watching it, she stood still.

"I've come back," she said.

Suddenly the pain shot up in her again. And this time it seemed to shoot up through her heart and breast and throat and through her brain.

She did not move. Her face was flat and blank and her body static. It was only her eyes which registered the suddenness and depths of her emotions. They began to fill with tears.

It was as though they had come to life at last.

SUMMER IN SALANDAR

Manson lifted one corner of the green gauze window blind of the shipping office and watched, for an indifferent moment or two, the swift cortege of a late funeral racing up the hill. It flashed along the water-front like a train of cellulose beetles, black and glittering, each of the thirty cars a reflection of the glare of sun on sea. He wondered, as the cars leapt away up the avenue of jade and carmine villas, eyeless in the bright evening under closed white shades, why funerals in Salandar were always such races, unpompous and frenzied, as if they were really chasing the dead. He wondered too why he never saw them coming back again. They dashed in black undignified weeping haste to somewhere along the sea-coast, where blue and yellow fishing boats beat with high moon-like prows under rocks ashen with burnt seaweed, and then vanished for ever.

He let the blind fall into place again, leaning spare brown elbows on the mahogany lid of his desk. He was thinking that that evening a ship would be in. It could not matter which ship—he was pretty sure it was the *Alacantara*—since nobody in their senses ever came to Salandar in the summer. There would in any case be no English passengers and he would meet it out of pure routine. After that he would go home to his small hotel and eat flabby oil-soaked *esparda* that had as much taste in it as a bath sponge and drink export beer and read the English papers of a week last Wednesday. In the street outside men would sit on dark door-steps and spit golden melon seeds into gutters, coughing with tubercular mournfulness. The flash of an open-air cinema down the street would drench the plumb-black air above the surrounding courtyards with continuous gentle fountains of light, above little explosions of applause and laughter. In one of the old houses behind the hotel a woman would lull her baby to sleep with a prolonged soft song that was probably as old as the moon-curve of the fishing boats that lined the shore. Under the infinite stars the red beacons on the radio masts would flame like big impossible planets above the mass of the fortress that obscured, with its vast and receding walls, nearly half the sky. And that would be his evening: a lonely and not surprising conclusion to a tiring day when nothing had happened, simply because nothing ever happened in summer in Salandar.

From across the quayside, out on the landing pier, he suddenly heard the sound of more voices than he thought was customary. He got up and parted the slats of the window shade. The pier was massed with emigrants, emigrant baggage, emigrant noises, the messy struggle of emigrant farewells. He remembered then that the *Alacantara* was not coming in. It was the *Santa Maria,* coming from precisely the opposite way.

That sort of trick of memory always overtook him at the height of summer, two months after the tourist season had died. It was the delayed shock of seasonal weariness. He was as unprepared for it as he was unprepared for the sight of the *Santa Maria* herself, a ship of pale green hulls with funnels of darker green, suddenly coming round the westerly red-black cliffs of the bay. It made him less annoyed to think that he had to meet her. He did not like to hurry. There was no need to hurry. There was nothing to hurry for. He was not going anywhere. He was not meeting anyone. The point of his meeting a ship on which he had no passenger was purely one of duty. Like most of the rest of his life on Salandar it was a bore.

Was there a passenger? With the precision of habit he turned up a black ledger of passengers' names that gave him nothing in answer. It was nice to be assured, anyway, that he was not mistaken.

A moment later he called to the only clerk to tell the porter that he wanted the launch in five minutes. His voice was dry from the summer catarrh that came from living low down, at sea-level, in the rainless months, in the sandy dust of the port. He cleared his throat several times as he went out into the street and the sun struck him below the eyebrows with pain. On the corner of the pavement he stood and closed his eyes briefly before he crossed to the waterfront and as he opened them again the last black beetle of the funeral cortege flashed past him, expensively glittering, lurching dangerously, chasing the dead: a car filled with weeping men.

[2]

On the ship the air seemed absorbent. It sucked up the life of the fanless purser's cabin on the middle deck.

"She got on at Lisbon, Mr. Manson," the purser said. "She said she cabled you from there."

A small quantity of pearl-grey luggage, splashed with varnished scarlet labels, among them the letter V, stood by the purser's door. Staring down at it, Manson tried to remember back through a long drowsy day to some point where a cable might have blown in, rushed past him and, like the cortege of racing mourners, have disappeared. He could not recall any cable and the purser said:

"I had better take her luggage up. I promised to look after her." He began to pick up suitcases, tucking the smallest under his arms. "She seems to like being looked after. Perhaps you will bring the last one, Mr. Manson?—thank you."

No one else had come aboard except a harbour policeman in flabby grey ducks, so thin that he seemed impossibly weighed down by black bayonet and revolver, and a customs officer in crumpled washed-out sienna gabardine. These two stood sweating at the head of the companionway, the policeman with thumbs in his drooping belt. There was not even the usual collection of hotel porters' caps on the ship simply because every hotel was closed.

"Where is she staying?" Manson called. "There isn't a single hotel open."

"I told her that. She said she did not mind. I told her you would see all about it."

"She's nothing to do with me."

"She's English. I told her you would do it—"

"Do what? I'm not a sight-seeing guide for anybody who comes and dumps themselves down here in the middle of summer."

He felt his hands grow sweaty on the high-polished fabric of the suitcase handle. He knew, he thought, all that English women could be. Ill-clad in worsted, horribly surpliced in porridge-coloured shantung, they arrived sometimes as if expecting the island to yield the horse-drawn charm of 1890, where everything could be had or done by the clapping of hands.

"Anyway I had no warning," he said. "What warning had I?"

He thought he saw the customs officer grin at this, and it annoyed him still further.

"She said she cabled you herself, Mr. Manson," the purser said.

"I've seen no sign of a cable," he said. "And anyway cable or no cable—"

"It was awfully good of you to meet me," a voice said.

When he turned, abruptly, at the same time as the sweat-bright faces of the policeman, the customs officer, and the purser, he saw her standing behind him: a tall black-haired girl, with an amazing combination of large pure blue eyes and black lashes, her hair striped across the front with a leonine streak of tawny blonde.

He found himself at once resenting and resisting this paler streak of hair.

"It was really very good of you," she said. "My name is Vane."

He checked an impulse to say "Spelt in which way?" and she held out a hand covered with a long cream glove. This glove, reaching to her elbow, matched a sleeveless dress of light cool linen.

"I know you think I've come at the wrong time of year," she said.

"Not at all."

"No?" she said. "I thought I heard you say so."

He was so irritated that he was not really conscious of helping her down the gangway. He felt instead that the gangway had begun to float on air. It was nothing but a shaky ladder of cotton-reels swaying above the calm sea. It seemed almost perpendicular, pitching him forward as he went down first and waited to help her into the launch below.

The red triangular pennant of the company drooped above the burnished deck house and she said, staring beyond it:

"Everyone told me it was so brilliant. So much flashing colour. But the rocks are black. It looks burnt out, somehow."

"That's just the summer," he said.

Out of politeness he stared with her at the shore. He thought there was a great deal of colour. It was simply that it was split into a fractional mosaic of blacks and browns, of bleached pinks and the dull ruby reds of house-tops, half-smothered by green. A tower of pale yellow, the new school, was raised like a fresh sugar stick above the black sand of the shore, at the end of which an astonishing summer residence of blue tiles, polished as a kitchen stove, was wedged into the cliff. Two or three rowing-boats, piled with white baskets, with curtains of island embroideries in scarlet and green, were motionless on the oily bay, where in the high season a hundred of them clamoured about liners like fighting junks, manned by brown shivering men diving for coins. Lines of high-prowed fishing boats, up-curved like horns, striped in green and blue and ochre, were pulled up along the water-front, and far away and high above them he could see the water splash of a spouting *levada*, poised like gathered spittle in a fissure of rock and eucalyptus forest, pure white in the blinding sun.

He suddenly felt himself defending all he saw. He wanted to say that there was plenty of colour. Only the sun, burning ferociously, created an illusion of something cindery, melting dully away.

"It's just a question of—"

"Oh! my bag," she said.

She stood on the lowest rung of the gangway, lifting helpless arms, imploring with a smile.

"In my cabin—so sorry—twenty-three—you'll see it. Probably on the bed."

As he mounted the ladder quickly, more insecure than when he had come down, he remembered that cabin twenty-three was one of four on the boat deck and he walked straight for it, before the purser could speak or stop him.

He found her handbag on the bed. Unstripped, the bed was disorderly and the bag, which was why she had forgotten it, was partly covered by her pillow. Its clasp sprang open as he picked it up. Its white jaws spilled lipstick and handkerchief, a few letters, a mirror, a little diary in black morocco.

He felt intensely curious and wanted to open the diary. The bag gave out a perfume that floated about him for a moment, arousing in him a startling sensation of intimacy.

Then he felt nervous and shut the bag quickly and rushed out of the cabin, only to find the purser coming to meet him on the deck, saying:

"What was it, Mr. Manson? Was it something you could not find?"

He went on without answering, slipping hastily once again on the insecure mahogany cotton-reels of the gangway, down to a sea on which the launch's scarlet pennant and the yellow dress were the only things that did not melt and sway.

"You were very quick," she said. "It was very kind of you."

The sea was so calm that it was possible for himself and the girl to stand motionless on the launch all the way from ship to shore. She stood erectly looking about her, searching the bay, the shore, and the abrupt hills above the town for colour.

"It surprises me," she said. "I'd expected something more exotic."

"It's exotic in winter," he said. "It's all colour then. You should have come in the winter. That's when everybody comes."

It suddenly struck him that, after all, she was really not looking at the approaching shore. Something about her eyes made them seem glazed with preoccupation.

"I'm afraid it was my fault about the cable," she said. "It should have been sent. But I was in a dreadful hurry. I made up my mind all of a sudden and then somehow—"

"I don't know what you had in mind about hotels."

"I suppose they're all shut," she said.

"All the recognized ones."

"Where do you live? In one not recognized?"

"I wouldn't recommend it," he said.

Forgetfulness about the cable, forgetfulness about the bag—he stood pondering uncertainly, staring at the approaching harbour pier, wondering where to take her.

"I do apologize about the cable," she said. "I'm afraid you're peeved."

"I was trying to think of a possible solution to the hotel problem."

"It's no problem," she said. "I'm not particular. I shall find something. I always do."

"Had you any idea of how long you were staying?"

"As long as I like it."

"It isn't always possible to leave when you think you will," he said. "Ships are very irregular here. They don't just happen when you think they're going to."

"Does anything?" she said.

The launch began to make its curve to the landing pier, the

change of course uplifting the scarlet pennant very slightly. Above steps of baked white concrete a line of idle taxis stretched out, with a few ox-carts, in the shade of flowerless jacarandas. A smell of oil and hot bullock dung and rotting sea-weed seethed in the air and he said:

"I'm afraid you'll find anything down here in the port very hot."

As the launch came into the jetty he leapt out. On the steps he held out his hand to her and she lifted the long cream glove.

"The man will bring the bags up to the top," he said.

At the top of the jetty he realized with concern that she was hatless. Heat struck down on concrete and then back again as if pitilessly forced down through a tube, dangerously compressed under the high enclosure of hills.

"I hope you're all right?" he said. "I mean the heat?—the air is terribly clear and you don't always realize—"

"I don't feel it," she said. "I never feel it." She touched her hair, running her fingers through it. The paler streak of it, uplifted, exposed the mass of pure black hair below, and he realized how thick and strong and wiry it was. Its heavy sweep, shot with the curious blonde streak, aroused in him the same odd sensation of uneasy intimacy he had experienced in the cabin, smelling the perfume of the handbag, by the disordered bed.

For a moment longer she stood engrossed by the sight of him staring at her hair, and he did not realize how absorbed and uncomfortable it had made him feel until she said:

"Where do we go from here? Where can I get a taxi?"

"I was thinking you could come to the office and leave your things—"

"I'd rather get a hotel," she said. "What's the name of yours?"

"Mafalda," he said. "It's terribly small and they don't really cater—"

"It doesn't matter if it's reasonable and the beds are clean. Are the beds clean?"

"Quite clean."

She looked at him without any kind of disturbance, the clear, rather too large blue eyes fixing him with exacting softness and said:

"I think any beds that are clean enough for you ought to be clean enough for me."

"You can always try it temporarily."

From the hot taxi she leaned her long body forward and looked at the mounting hillside. Above it successive folds of rock, exposed in crags that seemed sun-blackened, submerged under encrustations of blue-green forests of pine and eucalyptus, fascinated her large blue eyes into a larger stare.

"What's up there?" she said. "I mean the other side of the mountain?"

"Not much," he said. "More rock and forests and so on. Not many people. Over the other side there's a power station. It's lonely. There are places you can't get to."

She smiled and sat back beside him on the seat, wrapping the surprisingly cool cream gloves deftly one over the other.

"That's where I'd like to go," she said.

Then, without attaching importance to what she said, without really giving it another thought, he was inspired to remark with sudden cheerfulness that there would probably be, at the hotel, a cup of tea.

[3]

There were mice in the upper ceilings of the old hotel and he lay listening to them half the night, turning over in his mind what seemed to him the vexing problem of her being there, in that highly unsuitable, dark, cheap hotel where no English visitor ever came except for a temporary night, in sheer high season desperation. He had carefully warned her a number of times that the food would not be English. "It will be oily and all that," he said. "It's something it takes a long time to get used to." When she reminded him that he at any rate appeared to survive it he did not dare tell her that it was simply because he could not afford anything else. He had just had to get used to it; and now he did not ask for anything better and in his limited way he was perfectly happy. At least he supposed he was.

But something troubled him much more than this. He was perplexed and worried by a phrase she had used.

"What are you going to to do with yourself?" he asked her. "It can be terribly exhausting at this time of the year—"

"I'm going to poke about," she said. "I want things to do. I want to see things."

He grew increasingly uneasy about this as the evening went on. It was not a good thing to poke your nose into things in Salandar. It was a place, in the right season, in the delicious winter flower days, of infinite surface charm. Bougainvilleas covered with steep massive curtains of purple and sienna-rose all the dry ravines coming down from the hills; starry scarlet poinsettias lined the potato patches; a honey odour of incense trees hung over the old streets at night-time. If underneath all this there were people who had not enough to eat, who were afraid of something or somebody, who were tubercular or illiterate or superfluous or resentful, that was no concern of visitors.

"Don't you ever poke about and find out how things really are?" she said.

"No."

"Have you been here long?" she said. "How many years have you been here?"

"I came here about three and a half years ago. Nearly four."

It was getting so long ago he could hardly remember exactly. His time there had gradually become, in the Salandar fashion, a succession of dull tomorrows.

"How long is it since you went over to the other side of the island?" she said.

"I'm afraid I've never been over to the other side."

"By the way you spoke I thought you'd been there often," she said.

"No," he said, "I've never been there."

"Haven't you any inclination at all to see what it's like?"

"Not particularly."

It seemed to him that she did not speak her questions so much as impose them on him with the too large, too brilliant, uneasy eyes.

"What about Santo Carlo?" she said. "They say that's very interesting. Have you been there?"

No: he had not been to Santo Carlo either.

He found, presently, what seemed to him a happy solution to her restlessness, to the problem of what she should do with herself. It was also a tremendous relief to be able at last to change an uncomfortable subject.

"You could join the club," he said. "I don't know why I didn't think of it before."

"Do you belong?"

"Not now," he said. "I gave it up."

In winter the club was crowded with visitors he did not know; in summer there was no one there. After six months of it he had not considered it worth while to renew the subscription. He decided he would save the money. He had to think of the future.

"What happens there?"

"People play bridge and tennis and that sort of thing and there's a small golf course," he said. "It's rather beautiful," and then added, as if it was an extra thought to impress her: "You can get tea."

She did not say anything and he went on:

"You can get a temporary subscription—I think for even a week. I can find out for you—but then if you don't know how long you're going to stay—"

"That was something I was going to talk to you about," she said.

In speaking of the times of ships he felt more certain of himself. That at least was his job.

"It depends where you want to go from here," he said. "If you'll give me some idea of times and places I'll have—"

"When is the next ship in?"

"There'll be nothing in this week. Not until after the weekend," he said. "Then the *Alacantara* is due. She's pleasant."

"It would be nice just to have the sailing times of what's likely to be coming in," she said. "Could you? It would be very sweet of you."

She had asked him so many questions that this final acutely personal one, delivered more softly, in a lowered voice, made him more uneasy than he had been before. He did not grasp even that the conversation had been largely about himself. He felt only another rush of feeling about her: a repetition of the sensation he had had in the cabin, over the handbag and the disorderly bed, and from the way she had run her fingers through her thick black hair.

"You look tired," she said to him at last. "It's time you got into that good clean bed."

In the morning he woke to an air that had in it the breath of ashes. It sprang at his already catarrhal throat with windy choking heat. He grasped then the reason for his lethargy of the previous day, his soporific irritations as he met the boat that he had not expected. The *leste* was blowing: the wind from the northeast that burned with pure incineration off the mainland sand.

This had not prevented Miss Vane from getting up at five o'clock and watching the night-boats, like slowly extinguishing fireflies, bringing in their fish across the bay.

"They looked wonderful," she said. "Haven't you ever seen them come in?"

"No."

"I talked to some of them—the men, I mean. There were two brothers from Santo Carlo—"

"You should be very careful how you talk to these people," he said.

At breakfast which they had together in the already shuttered little dining-room, in a queer kind of morning twilight through which even her large and exceptionally blue eyes looked almost white in their diffusion, he warned her about the intolerable burning wind.

"It will probably last for two days," he said. "Perhaps three. I'm afraid you'll find it very exhausting."

In a white dress of low cut, with a transparent organdie insertion across the breast, she looked remarkably cool and she said:

"Isn't it a good chance to get up into the hills? Couldn't you take a day off and come with me?"

He rested easily on the firm ground of his local knowledge.

"That's the curious thing about the *leste*," he said. "It's even hotter in the hills. You'd hardly believe it, but the coast is going to be the cooler place."

"I might go myself."

"Oh! no," he said. "Don't think of doing that."

"Why not?"

"Oh! in the first place—Well, it's hardly the thing. You see you can only drive so far. After that it's a question of mule-track. You need several days—"

"I have plenty of days."

"Yes, but not while the *leste* is on," he said. "Really not. It can be ghastly up there when the *leste* is on."

"How would you know?" she said. "You've never been."

His coffee, which should have been cool after so much conversation, sprang down his already anguished throat like hot acid. He felt unable to speak for some moments and at last she said:

"I think you look awfully tired. Don't you ever want to get away from here?"

"Not particularly. I suppose eventually—"

"Not when the ships come in? Don't you ever suddenly feel hell, for God's sake let me get away—don't you ever feel like that?"

"I can't say I do."

"I think it might do you good to get away."

For a second he was touched, and then bewildered, by her concern. He was disturbed too because she had, as he now noticed for the first time, no coffee to drink.

"Didn't you have any coffee?"

"I had orange instead," she said. "It's cooler."

"I suppose I ought to have done that," he said. "But I always have coffee. I can't get out of the habit of it somehow—"

"Would you come on this trip to the hills?" she said.

"I honestly don't know."

"I shall go," she said. "I'll fix it up. I like fixing things. Would you come if I fixed it?"

"It's awfully difficult for me to say," he said. "You see, everybody's on leave. Charlton, my chief, is on leave. The only really good local clerk has gone to Lisbon for a week. It's very doubtful if I could leave the office in any case—"

"You've got the weekend."

"I know, but—" He found himself being hopelessly absorbed, as his breath had been absorbed in the stifling purser's cabin on the ship, by her enlarged diffused eyes, almost pure white, their true colour extinguished until they gave out a curious impression of nakedness in the dark morning shadow. "And apart from anything else there's the *leste*—"

"If we wait till the *leste* is over?" she said. "If it blows for two or three days it ought to be over by the weekend, oughtn't it?"

"Well, you can't tell—"

"Shall we chance it?" she said. "Shall I fix it up?"

"Will it do if I decide this evening?"

"I'm going to fix it during the day," she said. "If the *Alacantara* comes next week I haven't much time."

"All right," he said. "I suppose I could come."

As she got up from the table she smiled and touched his arm, telling him to drink his coffee. Her body was held forward to him, the partially transparent inset of her dress exposing her breast. He was aware of the falling discoloured band of yellow in her intense black hair and it disturbed him again more than anything she had done or said, and as he stared at it she smiled.

"Do I look so awful?" she said. "I haven't combed my hair since I went down to the harbour. I must go and do it now."

He called after her to ask her what she was going to do with herself all day. "You must take it easily. Don't go and exhaust yourself," he said.

"I'll probably swim," she called back from the stairs.

"Be careful of the swell," he said. "It's terribly deceptive. It can sometimes be twenty or thirty feet even on the calmest days." After all he had a certain responsibility for her now. "Don't go out too far."

[4]

The road to the central ridge of mountains wound up through gorges of grey volcanic rock, under steep declivities of pine and eucalyptus closely planted as saplings against the erosion of a sparse burnt soil, red and cindrous, veined yellow here and there by courses of long-dried water. The car crept upward very slowly, beetle-wise, on black setts of blistered rock that gave way, beyond the last windowless white houses, to a track of potholes sunk in grey and crimson sand.

"It was a stroke of genius to bring the cook," she said.

He did not feel that this was flattery. It really was, he thought, rather a stroke of genius on his part to think of the cook. The idea of the cook sprang from his recollection that, at the top of the mule-pass, there was also a rest-house. For practically nothing you could put up there, cook meals and so on and do the thing in comfort. He was very pleased about that. It saved a lot of trouble.

He didn't think he could have come all the way up that hot dreary track otherwise.

The *leste*, after all, had died. The air in the mountains was still hot, but height began to give it, as the car climbed slowly, a thinness that was fresh and crystalline. Objects began to appear so vivid that they stuck out, projected by strong blue lines that were pulsations rather than shadows. In a curious way everything was enlarged by scintillation.

Perhaps it was this that made Manson, sitting at the back of the car with Miss Vane, fix his eyes hypnotically on the black hair of the cook, sitting in front with the driver.

The head of the cook was like an ebony bowl, polished to a sheen of greasy magnificence by brushings of olive oil. Below it the shoulders were flat and square, the erectness of them giving power to the body that was otherwise quite short and stiff, except when it bent in sudden bows of politeness to Miss Vane.

Sometimes the car jolted violently in and out of potholes and Manson and Miss Vane were pitched helplessly upward and against each other, taken unawares. But the shoulders of Manuel, the cook, were never disturbed by more than a quiver and sometimes it seemed to Manson that they gave a shrug.

This hypnosis about the neck of the cook lasted until the car-road ended and the mule-track began, winding away into a thick scrub of wild bay trees and stunted, blue-needled pines. At the foot of the track the mules were waiting, four flickering skeletons brought up by two bare-foot peasants wearing trousers of striped blue shirt material and black trilby hats.

Manuel loaded two osier baskets of provisions, Manson's rucksack and one of Miss Vane's scarlet-labelled too-neat suitcases on to one of the mules, and the peasants began to lead the mules up the hill.

After Manuel had shouted after them the two peasants came back. They both looked down-trodden in protestation and Manuel, standing over them, square and erect, looked more assertive than before.

"What is it, Manuel?" Miss Vane said. "Is something the matter?"

"No, madame." He pronounced his English fully and correctly, elongating the final syllable.

"What is it then?"

"They want to go with us, madame."

"That was the idea, wasn't it?" Manson said.

"It's not necessary, sir. I can manage without them."

"You know the way?" she said.

"Yes, madame," he said. "I've done it before."

After that the taxi driver drove away and the peasants disappeared up the hill. Manuel took the first and second mules, Miss Vane the third, and Manson the fourth. Manson had never been on a mule before and his legs seemed so much too long that he felt gawkily ridiculous. But looking ahead, beyond Miss Vane and the provision mule to the leading figure of Manuel, he was relieved to see that Manuel looked, as he thought, still more stupid.

His preoccupation with the back of Manuel's neck had been so absorbed that he had not really noticed that Manuel was wearing the black suit of a waiter. And as Manuel turned to look back at the column Manson saw that he was wearing the tie, the shirt front and the collar too.

It took three hours to climb through paths among bay tree and pine and tree-heath and an occasional eucalyptus stunted by height to the size of a currant-bush, as far as the rest-house. As the mules marched slowly upward, jerky and rhythmical, the mountains seemed to march rapidly forward, shutting in the heat and shutting out much of the sky. And as the heat developed oppressively Manson called once to Miss Vane:

"You'd hardly think there would be snow up here, would you?"

"There is no snow up here, sir."

"I thought there was always snow. After all, it's six thousand—"

"Not on this side, sir. You're thinking of the Santo Carlo side. There is never snow just here."

Manson did not speak again and it was half an hour before he noticed, glinting in the sun, what he thought were the iron sheds of the power-station framed in a gap ahead.

"I rather think that's the new power-station," he called to Miss Vane. "They had great difficulty in getting the pipes up there—"

"That's not the power-station, sir. That's the old pumping station for the *levadas*. They don't use it now."

"Where is the power-station?" Miss Vane said.

"It's over the other side, madame. You won't be able to see it from this direction."

"And where is the place you can see the two coasts from?" she said. "You know—the sea both sides?"

"You will be able to go there from the rest-house, madame," he said. "It isn't far. You'll be able to climb up there."

Manson stretched out his hand and snatched at the leaves of a eucalyptus tree, crushing it sharply with his fingers and then lifting the leaf to his nose. The harsh oily odour of eucalyptus was unpleasant and irritated him. It reminded him of times when, as a child, his chest had been very bad and he had coughed a lot and he had not been able to get his breath.

He unconsciously kept the leaf in his hand until, at the suggestion of Manuel, they stopped to rest. "We are half way now, madame," Manuel said.

Manuel poured glasses of export beer for Manson and Miss Vane and served them with stiff politeness and then retired to a respectful distance among the mules. From masses of rock above them, studded with pale flat cacti that were like blown roses of delicate green, water dripped in large slow drips, like summery, thundery rain.

"Well, this is marvellous," Miss Vane said and lifted her glass to him, smiling with huge blue eyes in which Manson felt he could see all the summery wateriness and the great scintillation of mountain sky.

He lifted his glass to her in return, re-experiencing a sudden rush of the intimacy he had felt over her dishevelled bed and her handbag and that recurred whenever he looked at the yellow streak in her hair. He had a wild idea that presently, at the rest-house, they might be alone together.

"There's an awful smell of eucalyptus," Miss Vane said.

He flushed, pounding with anger at himself, and said:

"I'm afraid it's me. I crushed a leaf. Don't you like it?—"

"I loathe it," she said. "I can't bear it near me. I hate it. You'll have to go and wash your hands."

He went away in silence and washed his hands among the cacti, under a spilling cleavage of rock. The water was icy in the brilliant, burning air. He washed his hands carefully and then smelled them and it seemed that the smell of eucalyptus remained. Then he washed them again with slow, rejected, clinical care.

It was not until the rest-house came in sight that he emerged from a painful and articulate silence during which he had done nothing but stare at the sweat oozing slowly and darkly down the mule's neck. He was pleasantly startled by hearing Miss Vane call back:

"Hullo there. Asleep?" Her voice was solicitous and friendly once more and was accompanied by a sidelong dazzling smile. "You can see the rest-house. We're nearly there."

"I think it was the beer," he said. "Made me drowsy—"

"Look at it," she said. "It's exciting, isn't it? I'm excited."

"Oh! yes. It's bigger than I thought—"

"Aren't you excited?" she said. "This is really something. This is what I wanted."

The track had widened. She reined the mule and waited for him. Then as she turned the mule half-face to him he noticed the shape of her body, pressed heavily across the dark animal flanks. She had ridden up in a sleeveless thin white dress, the skirt of which was drawn up beyond her knees. He had never been able to make up his mind how old she was and now, in her excitement, her skirt drawn up above bare smooth legs, her eyes enormously shining, he thought she seemed much younger than she had done down in the scorching, withering period of the *leste*, in the town. She seemed to have left her hostile restlessness behind.

"Oh! it's marvellous and it really wasn't far, was it?" she said. "It didn't seem an hour. It was easy after all."

He said he didn't think it had been far either and he was aware suddenly that Manuel had gone ahead. The impossible waiter-suit, mule-mounted, was almost at the veranda steps. A hundred yards separated him from Manson and Miss Vane, and again an overpowering sense of intimacy came over Manson, so that he felt tremulously stupid and could not speak to her.

"Now aren't you glad I made you come?" she said.

"Yes," he said.

"Back there I thought you were mad with me."

"Oh! no."

"Not the smallest piece?"

He shook his head. "Not a little bit," he said.

The smile went temporarily out of her face. The mule jerked nervously ahead. "I really thought you were mad," she said and it did not occur to him until long afterwards that she might have hoped he had been.

[5]

From Manuel, during the rest of that day and the succeeding day, came an almost constant sound of whistling that jarred and irritated Manson like the scrape of a file. The rest-house, neat and clean, with something not unlike a chapel about its bare white-washed coolness, was divided into three parts. In the large central room Manson and Miss Vane ate at a long mahogany table the meals that Manuel prepared in a kitchen that ran along the north side of a large bird-like cage made of gauze. In this cage Manuel kept up the whistling that continued to infuriate Manson even at night time, as he tried to sleep in the third part, composed of his own bedroom and Miss Vane's on the western side.

Miss Vane was a woman who hated trousers.

"I was born a woman and I'll dress like one," she said. So she had ridden astride the mule in a loose cool white dress instead of the slacks Manson thought would have been more suitable, even though he disliked them. And all that day and most of the next, Sunday, she lay in front of the rest-house in a sunsuit of vivid green that was boned so tight to the shape of her body that it was like an extra gleaming skin.

As she lay in the sun Manson was aware of two sorts of feelings about her. When she lay on her back he saw the Miss Vane he had met on the ship; the Miss Vane of the hotel and the town, of the advancing, blistering *leste;* the Miss Vane incorrigibly and restlessly prodding him into coming to the mountains. She was the Miss Vane with the startling, discomforting tongue of yellow across her black hair. She was uneasy and he could not get near her.

When she turned over and lay on her face he could not see the yellow streak in her hair. Her head was one gentle mass of pure black, undisrupted by that one peroxide streak that always set him quivering inside. The black-haired Miss Vane did not startle him. She seemed quiet and untroubled. He wanted to thrust his face down into the plain unsullied mass of her thick black hair and let himself speak with tenderness of all sorts of things.

Always, at the point when he felt he could do this, she turned over on her back, lifting the front of her body straight and taut in the sun. The peroxide streak flared up. The eyes, too blue and too brilliant, flashed with exactly the same sort of unreality, as if she had dyed them too.

"Tomorrow we must do something," she said. "We can't lie here for ever."

"It's very pleasant lying here."

"We must go up to the place where you can see the two coasts. We'll start early and go all day," she said. "By the way, I've been meaning to ask you. You must have come out here very young. How old are you?"

"Twenty-seven," he said.

"I beat you by a year," she said. "It's old, isn't it? We're creeping on. Don't you sometimes feel it's old?—all of it slipping away from you? Life and that sort of thing?"

He could hear Manuel whistling in the distance, in the bird cage, and he could see the paler streak in Miss Vane's hair as she turned and stared at the sky.

"I must say I thought you were older," she said.

He was listening to the inexhaustibly dry, infuriating whistle of Manuel.

"You don't look older," she said, "but I think you act older. But then men of your age often do."

She lifted one hand to shade her eyes from the glare of the sun.

"The sun gets terrific power by midday," she said. "I think I ought to have my glasses. Would you fetch them?—do you mind?"

He got up and began to walk away and she called after him:

"In the bedroom. Probably with my dress. I left them there when I changed."

In the bedroom he remembered the cabin on the ship. He remembered how she liked things to be done for her. But now the bed, neatly made by Manuel, was not dishevelled. It was only her clothes that lay untidily about where she had undressed and thrown them down. He could not find the sun-glasses. They were not with her dress. He picked up her clothes several times and finally laid them on a chair. The glasses were not in her handbag and they were not on the bed.

His inability to find the glasses startled him into nervousness. He approached the bed with trembling hands. He pulled back the coverlet and put his hands under the pillow and let them rest there. He wanted all of a sudden to lie down on the bed. He was caught up in an illusion of lying with her there.

He went quickly out into the sun. From the ledge of short grass, walled by rock, where Miss Vane was lying, he heard voices. And as he came closer he saw that Miss Vane was wearing her sun-glasses.

"It's all right—Manuel found them. I'd left them in the dining-room."

Manuel, in shirt sleeves, without the black waiter's coat, stood stiffly erect, holding a bunch of two or three roses in his hands.

"Don't you think that's amazing?" Miss Vane said. "He even finds roses up here."

"Where on earth do you get roses?" Manson said.

"In the garden, sir. At the back."

"He says there was a wonderful garden here once. An English-man made it. He used to come here for the summer. He was a sugar-planter or something. Wasn't that it, Manuel?"

Manuel's eyes rested thinly and dryly on some point across the valley.

"Yes, madame. He was sugar. He was sugar, wine, sugar-brandy, coal, sardines, water, everything." He spoke slowly. "He took the water from the people and sold it back again."

"You mean he developed the country," Manson said.

"That's so, sir."

Manuel walked away and Manson looked after him. He detected, for the first time, an oddity in Manuel's walk. The right foot, swinging outwardly, stubbed the ground as it came back again. And this weakness, not quite a deformity, suddenly deprived the stocky shoulders of their power.

"Are you looking at his leg?" Miss Vale said. "He was in an accident or something. With his brother. He was telling me before breakfast. Before you came down. Did he tell you?"

"No."

"I feel rather sorry for him," she said.

He sat down in the sun, his mind searching for a change of subject. He stared across the valley, remembering with what thin, dry abstraction Manuel had looked there.

"Oh! I just remembered," he said. "After the *Alacantara* on Wednesday there isn't another decent boat for three weeks."

"No wonder you get a feeling of isolation here."

"Well, anyway I thought you ought to know. It's a long time."

"Would you find it long?"

He wanted to say 'It depends.' He wanted to qualify, somehow, the statement he had already made. He knew that what he had to say and feel depended on Miss Vane and whether Miss Vane caught the *Alacantara*. Already he did not want her to catch it. He was afraid of her catching it. But he could not express what he felt and he said:

"That damned man is always whistling. Can you hear it? He's always whistling."

"I hadn't noticed it."

When they went in to lunch Manuel stood behind her chair, holding it, pushing it gently forward as she sat down.

As he prepared to serve soup she suddenly waved her hands with impatience at herself and said:

"My bag. Would you think I could be such a dim-wit? I leave it everywhere—"

"I will get it, madame," Manuel said.

He hurried out of the room with dignified jerky steps.

"I could have got it for you." Manson said.

"I know you could." The large flashing blue eyes disarmed him. "But he likes doing things. He would be hurt if we didn't let him. That's what he's here for."

Manuel came and put Miss Vane's bag on the lunch-table.

"Thank you, Manuel," she said.

Manuel served soup from a wicker trolley.

"By the way," she said, "we would like to do the climb to the top. How long will it take us?"

"It isn't a climb, madame," Manuel said. "It's just a walk. It takes half an hour."

"You and your inaccessible places," she said to Manson. "Everything is too easy for words."

"What about the Serra?" Manson said. "That isn't easy, is it?"

"I do not know the Serra, sir."

"What is the Serra?" she said.

"It's the high plateau," Manson said. "The really high one. The really lonely one. Isn't that so, Manuel?—it's lonely. People don't like it, do they?"

"No, sir," Manuel said. "People don't like it."

"Why not?" she said.

"I can't say, madame," he said. "I think it's because there's nothing there. People like to have company. They don't like places where there is nothing."

"I think that's where we should go," Manson said. "That would be something worth while."

"I don't think so, sir."

"Oh! I most certainly think so," Manson said. "After all, that's what we came up here for—the high places and the view and that sort of thing."

"If the view is no better," Miss Vane said, "there's hardly any point in going, is there? Is the view any better?"

"I don't think you can see so far, madame," Manuel said.

"Well, there you are," she said.

With irritation Manson said: "I thought you were the adventurous one. I thought you liked it the difficult way."

"Oh! I do," she said. "But if there's no point. I mean if Manuel doesn't think the thing worth while."

Manson waited for Manuel to clear the soup dishes and take them away through the gauze doors that separated the dining-room from his cage at the back.

"I fail to see what Manuel has to do with it," he said. "We can go alone. Manuel isn't obliged to come."

"What is there about this place?" she said.

"He's afraid of it. They're all afraid of it. They're superstitious about it."

"Is there anything to be superstitious about?"

"Not a thing."

"Then why do you suppose they're superstitious?"

"They hate being alone," he said.

"Don't you?" she said.

"Not a bit," he said. "I rather like it—" Abruptly he realized what he had said and he felt his confidence, which had been mounting and strengthening, suddenly recede. Confusedly he tried to retrieve it and said:

"I didn't mean it like that—I meant I liked being alone in the sense that I wasn't frightened of it—"

"Oh! it doesn't mater," she said. "Here comes the food. It looks like a sort of pie—is it, Manuel? Is it pie?"

"Yes, madame," he said. "It is steak and kidney pie. Made in the English way."

After lunch, as they had coffee outside, under a tree he kept telling her was an arbutus, though he was not sure and it was the only way of getting his confidence back, she said:

"About this place. Would you like to go?"

"I'd like to," he said.

Her eyes, always so large and incorrigibly assertive and apparently forceful, seemed suddenly uncertain. She ran her hand across the streak of paler hair and said:

"It isn't one of those evil places, is it? You know—nothing to do with the dead?"

"It's just high and lonely," he said. "It's the crowning point of the island. That's all."

She stared across the valley, to a far glitter of sun on harsh iron rock, and Manson remembered how Manuel had stared across the valley too.

"You'd really like to go, wouldn't you?" she said. "We'd have to go alone, I suppose? Manuel wouldn't come."

He felt an ascendant rush of triumph at the thought of being alone with her.

"I don't think it need bother us," he said. "It isn't that far."

For a moment she did not answer. She had slipped off the dress she had put on to cover her sunsuit during lunch and once again he found himself thinking how taut and mature her body looked, emerging naked and smooth pale brown from the costume of vivid green. If only he could have rubbed out, somehow, the disturbing streak of paler hair.

"You really think it's not one of those evil places?" she said. "Nothing to do with the dead?"

"No more than anywhere else has."

"Only I couldn't bear it," she said, "if it had anything to do with the dead. And it's been so easy so far."

[6]

They arranged to start next morning at nine; but when Manson came out of his bedroom and went out on to the veranda he discovered Miss Vane and Manuel talking at the foot of the steps. Manuel had rigged up a pole on which, at each end, he had hooked a basket for luncheon. As he saw Manson coming he hoisted the pole to his shoulder, balancing the baskets on the curved smooth pole.

With vexation Manson said: "I thought Manuel wasn't coming."

"He's coming as far as lunch," Miss Vane said. "Then if we want to go on farther—"

"Of course we want to go farther, don't we?" he said. "We want to do the whole thing."

"He says that's up to us."

"It's amazing how people fold up when it comes to it," Manson said. "Good God, you might think it was Everest or something."

"Well, it's probably as well he is coming," she said. "We'd only have to carry the lunch baskets and it's going to be awfully hot."

Manuel, who had not spoken, began to walk on ahead. Miss Vane followed him and Manson walked some paces behind her. The sunlight behind him was already so crystalline in its subalpine transparence that it shone in Miss Vane's hair with a remarkable effect of edging it with minute thorns of tawny gold.

Presently, across the steep short valley, he could see the high edge of the central plateau. It surprised him, in that first moment, by having something domestic about it. It emerged as a vast and domestic piece of pumice stone abandoned between two vaster shoulders of naked rock. In the strong sunlight he could have sworn that these rocks, perpendicular and iron-grey and treeless to the foot, shot off a spark or two that flashed like signals across the lower valley.

"That's where we're going," he said to Miss Vane. "See?—up there."

"It looks farther off than I thought," she said.

"We've got all day," he said. "After all it's only Monday—you don't have to catch the *Alacantara* today."

As he spoke of the *Alacantara* he remembered the town: Monday morning, the drawn sun-shutters of the office, the spiritless flat dustiness of rooms shut up for the weekend, the horrible Monday lassitude. A signal from the opposing rocks across the valley shot off with a trick of winking semaphore and expressed his astonished joy at being no longer part of that awful office, watching the cabs on the water-front, the listless boot-blacks rocking on the pavements, the funerals racing away up the hill.

He realized, with a remarkable surge of confidence, that he was free.

"By the way, are you going to catch the *Alacantara*? Have you made up your mind?"

"Not quite."

"I know her captain," he said. "I'd come aboard with you and see that he knew who you were."

She turned and held out her hand suddenly and said:

"There's room for you to walk on the track with me. Come on. I hate walking alone."

A fragment of his hesitation came back.

"Come on," she said. "Come and walk with me. I hate the feeling of someone being just behind me."

She reached out and caught his hand and they walked abreast.

"That's better," she said. "Now I feel you're with me."

Sometimes the swaying coolie-like scales of Manuel's baskets disappeared beyond dark shoulders of rock. Manson felt then that Manuel was not part of himself and Miss Vane. He looked up at the enlarging plateau, assuring himself of its unexciting domesticity, feeling contemptuous of people like Manuel who saw it as a formidable and fearsome thing.

At the same time the feeling grew on him also that Miss Vane was slightly afraid. That was why she wanted him to walk with her; that was why she would ask him now and then if he still wanted to go to the top. He had the increasing impression too that she had something on her mind. Perhaps that was why she was continually so forgetful of things like her handbag.

Half way through the morning one of his shoe-laces came

undone. He had not brought with him very suitable shoes for walking and the best he could find that day was a pair of old canvas sandals, with rubber soles.

As he stooped to tie the shoe-lace Miss Vane stopped to wait for him. He had some difficulty with the shoe-lace and was afraid of breaking it. When he looked up again Manuel had disappeared and Miss Vane was alone, staring at something far down a long spoon-shaped gorge of rock.

His feelings at seeing her there alone gave him a sort of buoyancy. His shoes were soft on the path. He had nothing to do but creep up to her and put his hands on her hair and turn her face to him and kiss her.

Before he could do anything she turned and pointed down the gorge and said:

"There's something down there. Do you see? Right down. A house or something—two or three houses."

"Yes. They're houses," he said.

"I didn't think there were villages up here."

"It's a longish way away," he said. "Probably two or three hours by path."

"We must ask Manuel about it," she said.

His feeling of buoyancy died and when they walked on again he automatically fell into the way of walking behind her until she reminded him about it and held out her hand.

Before lunch, which Manuel laid out in a small clearing of pines, in one of those places where water dripped like summery rain from fissures of cacti-studded rock, Manuel asked her stiffly:

"Would you like something to drink before you eat, madame?"

"I would," she said. "What is there?"

"There's beer, madame," he said. "And gin."

"What gin is it?" Manson said.

"The best, sir." Manuel held up the bottle for Manson to see and Manson said:

"Good. We don't want local muck. I'll have gin too."

He drank the gin rather quickly. Then, looking down over the sliced-out gorges, streamless far below, he used exactly the words Miss Vane had used on the journey up with the mules.

"Well, this is marvellous," he said. The village of obscure white houses seemed of paltry insignificance, far away. "It's absolutely marvellous, I think. Don't you?"

"It's lovely."

"I think it's stunning. How far to the top, Manuel?"

"This is as far as the track goes, sir."

"I don't get that," Manson said. "You can see a path going up there as plain as daylight. I've been watching it. You can see it going most of the way."

"It's probably made by goats, sir."

The remark seemed to Manson to have in it the slightest touch of oblique insolence, and he asked abruptly for another gin. He was very glad that Miss Vane decided to have one too.

But the lunch was good. He awarded absolutely top marks to Manuel for the lunch. A slight breeze blew off the upper mountain and cooled the glare of the sun. He took another gin and was aware of the semaphore spark of signals ignited over the black of distant rocks and he remarked several times, munching on big open sandwiches of red beef and peeled eggs and ham, that food always tasted so much better in the open air.

"What is the village, Manuel?" Miss Vane said.

"That's the village of Santa Anna, madame."

"How far away is it?"

Manuel said: "Several hours. It would probably take more than half a day to get there. Sometimes there are bad mists too. Then it takes more than a day."

With another gin, in which he was glad Miss Vane joined him, Manson felt all the flare of antagonism against Manuel come back. The man was a damn know-all. Too smooth by half. Too smooth. Too knowing. Worst of all too damned right.

"Good God, look—there's an eagle," he said.

A large bird, suspended between the two shoulders of mountain, seemed to hold for a moment the entire sky in its claws.

"That's a buzzard, sir," Manuel said. "There are no eagles here."

Manson stared at the bird that seemed, with motionless deceit, to hold the sky in its claws.

"I'd like another gin," he said. "Would you?"

"I will if you will," she said.

"Good," he said. "That'll get us steamed up for the top."

[7]

During lunch Miss Vane took off her shoes and for some moments after lunch, when she appeared to have some difficulty in getting them on again, Manson felt impatient and disappointed.

"Oh! it's nothing. It's only that my feet ache a bit." He saw her look up at the plateau of rock that spanned and blocked, exactly like the barrier of a dam, the entire western reach of valley.

"It looks awfully far," she said.

"Don't you want to go?"

"It isn't that. I was only wondering about time."

"I thought you were the one with plenty of time," he said. "We ought to have brought the hammock. Then we could have carried you."

He said the words rather breezily, with a smile.

"You think we can make it?" she said. "I mean in the time? Perhaps we ought to ask Manuel?"

"Oh! damn Manuel," he said.

Manuel was washing the lunch things under a small fissure of water that broke from perpendicular rock above the path.

"Manuel—how far is it to the top?" she said. "How long should it take us?"

"You should give two hours, madame."

"There and back?—or just there?"

"There and back," he said.

"Oh! that's nothing," Manson said. "That's no time."

The sight of Manuel deferentially wiping a plate with a tea-cloth, in his shirt-sleeves, so like a waiter who had lost his way, made him feel suddenly superior again.

"You're coming, Manuel, aren't you?" she said.

"No, madame, I'm not coming. I shall wait here for you."

A moment of strained silence seemed to be pinned, suspended, ready to drop, in the immense space of hot noon sky. With irritation Manson heard her break it by saying:

"We've got all afternoon. Won't you change your mind?"

"No thank you, madame."

"Oh! if the fellow doesn't want to come he doesn't want to come. That's that."

"I was simply asking," she said.

A moment later, fired by something between annoyance and exhilaration, he was ready to start.

"If you get tired of waiting," he said to Manuel, "you can start back. We know the way."

The path made a series of regular spiral ascents with growing sharpness, narrowing to a single-line track on which Manson and Miss Vane could well walk together. Disturbed by their feet a rock fell, flattish, skimming like a slate from a house-roof, pitching down, crashing with gunshot echoes into a cauldron of steamy, sunlit haze.

"It's hot, isn't it?" she said. "You don't really want to go to the top, do you?"

"Of course I do. That's what we came for, didn't we?"

She did not answer and he said:

"I don't wonder the English perfected mountaineering. None of these other chaps seem to have the slightest guts for it."

The buzzard reappeared in the sky like a growing speck of dust on glass, but this time below and not above him. He stood for a moment in intent exhilaration, watching the descending bird that was really a hundred feet or so below him now. He was amused to think that he had climbed higher than a bird in the sky, higher than Manuel, higher perhaps than anything but a goat or a goatherd had ever climbed on the island before.

"You know what?" he began to say.

Another rock fell noisily. Its skimming, sliding fall, in clean curvature into hazy space, had the breathless beauty of a ball well thrown. He heard its crash on other rocks below. He listened for some time to its long double-repeated echoes across the valley. Then he realized suddenly that to his half-finished remark there had been no answer.

He turned and saw Miss Vane already forty or fifty feet above him. She was walking steadily. Before he could call she turned and stared back, eyeless in her black sun-glasses, and waved her hand.

"I thought you were the big mountaineer."

"Oh! wait, wait," he said. "We must keep together."

She seemed to laugh at him before going on. He scrambled after her. And although she was not really hurrying it was several

minutes before he reached her. By that time he was glad she was
sitting down.

"My God, it's getting hot," he said.

"You were the one who wanted to do this."

"I know. I'm all right. We mustn't rush it, that's all. It's like
everything else—easy if you keep to a system."

"My system is to lie down at frequent intervals and stop there,"
she said.

As she lay down on the ledge of short dry grass she took off her
sun-glasses. The glare of sun, too harsh for her, made her suddenly
turn and lie on her face, spreading out her arms. Instantly the
sunlight, as it had done earlier in the day, shone on the back of her
hair with the brilliant effect of edging it with minute thorns of
tawny gold.

Suddenly the sensation of uneasy intimacy he had first experienced in the cabin, on the ship, above the dishevelled bed, came
rushing back. It became one with the intoxicating experience of
having climbed higher than the buzzard on the mountain.

He turned her face and began kissing her. He remembered
thinking that that was something he had not bargained for in any
system—would not have bargained for it if he had planned it for a
thousand years. She moved her lips in a series of small fluttering
pulsations that might have been protests or acceptances—he could
not tell. The impression was that she was about to let him go and
then that she could not bear to let him go. The effect was to rock
him gently, in warm blindness, on the edge of the gorge.

He was still in a world of spinning blood and sunlight and tilting
rock when he sat up again. Her eyes were intensely blue under
lowered lids in the sun. In a flash she shut them against the glare,
parting her mouth at the same time.

"That was easy," she said.

"Easy?"

"I mean I didn't expect you to do it like that," she said. "I meant
I thought it would be different with you."

He heard the snapped cry of a bird, like the flap of linen, the only
sound in a vast and burning chasm of silence, somewhere above the
extreme edge of stunted heath and pine.

"Again," she said. "It made me feel better."

Long before the end of that second kiss he was perfectly sure that she belonged to him. He was so sure that he found himself thinking of the rest-house, the dark cover of evening, the way they would be together long after the infuriating whistling of Manuel had died behind the cage. He felt his pride in his confidence leap up through his body in thrusting, stabbing bursts.

"That made me feel better still," she said.

"Better?"

"Happier—that's what I mean."

Suddenly, clearly, and for the first time he found himself wondering why she had bothered to come there at the height of summer.

"Happier?—weren't you before?"

"We ought to have found some shadier spot," she said. "I'm melting. Can you see my bag? Where's my bag?"

He did not bother to look for the bag.

"Were You?"

"No: I wasn't," she said.

"Was that why you came here?"

"Partly."

Her eyes were shut again. In contrast he felt he saw the shape of her breasts, painfully clear under the thin white dress, stir, wake and look wonderfully up at him.

"Only partly?"

"You remember the day I came and I said there wasn't any colour?"

He remembered that. It seemed a thousand years away.

"It was colour I was looking for," she said.

A bird-cry, another break of silence, another suspicion of a whispered echo far away between sun-burnt roofs of rock, was enough to make him uneasy again.

"I don't quite understand," he said. "Colour?"

"Where's my bag?" she said. "Can't you see my bag?"

For God's sake, he thought, the bag. Why the bag? Why did she always forget the bag?

"No, it's not here. You can't have brought it," he said.

"Oh! didn't I?" She sat up, groping in the sun. Her eyes were wide open; he saw them blue and wet, enormous with trouble. Ineffectually he searched for the bag too, knowing it wasn't there.

He knew too what she was going to ask and while he was still groping about the grass she said:

"Would you go back and get it? Would you be a dear?"

He knew suddenly that he was a fool. He was a fool and he would go down and get the bag. He was a fool and he would climb up again. In time she would lose the bag again and he would be a fool and find it once more.

"Must you have it? Do you need it to kiss with?"

"Don't talk like that. I'm lost without it, that's all. You can kiss me anyway."

As she sat upright he kissed her again. He felt her give a great start of excitement, as if all the blood were leaping to the front of her body. Then she broke away and said:

"The bag. Couldn't you get the bag?—would you please?"

"You're not in some kind of trouble, are you?" he said.

"No. No trouble."

"Tell me what it is."

"I'm in no trouble—honest to God I'm not in any trouble."

"What then?"

"I don't know—a sort of hell," she said. "Get the bag and I'll tell you about it. You've made me feel better about it already."

Suddenly where her body had been there was space. Some trick of refraction, a twist in the glare of sun on whiteness, suppressed his power of sight. Instead of her shining body there was a naked gap on the path. As he walked down it to fetch her bag he found he could not see very well. He was aware of groping again, his canvas shoes slithering on scalding dark platters of rock, waking loose stones to curve out on flights of vicious perfection to the steaming haze below.

The infuriating whistle of Manuel brought him back to himself.

"Have you seen Miss Vane's bag?" he shouted.

"Yes, sir. Here it is, sir, with the lunch things."

Manson grasped the white bag and turned to walk back up the path.

"Aren't you going to the top, sir?"

"Mind your own business!" he said. He stopped. "Oh! another thing. I think we'll be starting back tomorrow. You'd better get back and start packing."

"Very well, sir," Manuel said.

High above the mountainside, the sombre hypnotic buzzard had risen again to hold the sky in its claws. It woke in Manson a sudden hatred for the place. The sky of summer seemed to reflect, in a curious harsh and lifeless glare, the depressing slate-like glaze of the high naked edge of plateau. Below, the trees were fired and lost in smouldering ashen dust. From far away a glint of steel in minute winks shot from the mass of pines with the effect of blue glass-paper.

A moment or two later he heard once again that curious sound that was like the dry flap of shaken linen, startling in the thin air. He heard it at the moment of turning the last of the spirals in the path before reaching Miss Vane. And as he heard it and turned his head he lost his sense of focus again, and a rock fell.

It fell this time from under his feet. It seemed to cross, a second later, a shadow that might have been caused by the buzzard suddenly whipping earthwards to kill. Instead he saw that it was another rock. It fell with bewildering swiftness from under his too-smooth canvas shoes, taking with it a black and slaty shower.

This shower was the entire corner of the path. As it fell it seemed to suck him down. For a second or two he was aware of a conscious effort to save himself. Then, clutching with ferocity at Miss Vane's white bag, he fell too.

[8]

His impression of coming death was sharp and instantaneous. It was a flame leaping up to meet him like the uprising ball of sun. Its inescapable extinction was like the extinction of Miss Vane's white body on the path. It was there one moment and then, in a final trick of refraction, was black and void.

He half picked himself up in a shower of slate and slate-dust, at the foot of a pine no taller than a man. His left foot was jammed by rock. His fall had ended in a kind of football tackle, not badly aimed at the feet, by the roots of the pine. He struggled to free his foot, and the tree-roots, under his weight, cracked under the rock and began to come out like slow-drawn teeth, in gristly pain. He thought he was laughing. Then he knew that he was really sucking air, enormous gasps of it, gorging at it, fighting for it in pure fright with his terrified mouth and tongue.

The last of the tree-roots were sucked out and the tree fell over, letting him down. His foot too was free. He laughed and shouted something. He did not know what it was but the very feeling of coherent air across his tongue gave him enormous hope. He felt suddenly as calm and poised as the buzzard above the valley.

He climbed slowly up on his hands and knees, aware of a slight drag in his left leg. It was not important, he thought, and when he reached the path he sat down with his back against rock and kept saying:

"I'm all right. I'm perfectly all right. I'm absolutely and perfectly all right."

"Oh! my God. I'm sick," she said. "Oh! my God—I'm so sick."

"I'll hold you. Lie against the rock," he said.

But he found that he could not hold her. He lay against the rock too, trembling all over. The valley swam below him. Whole waves of dust-bright haze washed over him, drowning him in sweat, leaving him cold.

"I knew I was gone," he said. "I know what the end is like now."

"Let's go down," she said.

His eyes were shut. His sweating face seemed to be glued against a cool bone of projecting rock.

He thought the rock moved. He discovered then that it was her own face, terribly and dryly cool. His sweat was drying too and he shuddered. Then he felt the sun burning his eyeballs through lids that were like dry thin tissue and he knew that if he did not get up and walk he would slide in weakness, like a dislodged stone, off the edge of the gorge.

They were far down on the path, at the place where they had lunched, before she said:

"I never liked heights. I could never bear them. I hate that awful vertigo."

He was glad to see that Manuel had taken him at his word and had started back. He was glad too that the path was at last doubly wide, so that the two of them could walk together.

The idea that something was very wrong with his left foot came to him slowly. The drag of it was heavy and finally it woke into pain.

He found himself at last sitting on the path staring into a shoe half full of blood.

"It was all my fault," she said. "I wanted to go up there."

Half-blindly he poured blood on to the dust of the path and struggled to put on his wet, blackening shoe. Somehow he could not get it back.

Nothing of the kind, he thought. He felt tired and sick. Staring at the blood-stained shoe, he remembered clearly how she had not wanted to go. He recalled his own exultation at rising above Manuel and the bird in the sky. It seemed so ridiculous now that he could only say:

"I didn't want to go either. I hate the damn place."

He sat there for a long time trying to put on his shoe. He could smell the old corrupt dark smell of blood as it dried. The shoe would not go back and there was something sinister and twisted about the swollen shape of his foot. Long before he gave up trying with the shoe he knew somehow that the foot was not going to take him home.

But now, trying to be bright about things, he said:

"They say it's an ill wind. Now you'll probably get an extra day to catch the *Alacantara*."

She did not answer.

"You are going to catch it, aren't you?"

"Yes."

He suddenly wished that something more spectacular had happened back on the path. There was nothing very dramatic after all in cutting a slice or two out of your foot.

"I know her captain," he said. "I'll see that you get fixed up."

"I can understand if you're bitter about me," she said.

"I'm not bitter."

"You sound bitter."

"Perhaps because you kissed me up there."

Strength seemed to drain out of his body and it seemed a long time afterwards before she said:

"Kissing isn't always the start of something. In this case it was the end."

"The end of what?" he said. "Probably me."

"I've been running away from something. That's all. When you kissed me it was the end of running."

He wanted to say something like "Glad to have been of service, Miss Vane." A withering breath of burning rock blew into his face. His foot pained him violently, stabbing in sickening throbs, and he did not answer.

"You've been so sweet to me," she said. "Doing what I wanted."

"Husband," he said, "or what?"

"Husband."

"You must give him the love of a decaying shipping clerk when you get back," he said. "Miss Vane."

"He may not be there when I get back," she said. "That's the point. But I've got to try."

Savagely the heat blew into his face again and the raw weeping soreness of his foot made him sick.

"I'll bet he's a lousy—"

"You might call him that," she said. "But then that's sometimes how it is. Some men are lousy and they get under your skin. You know they're lousy and you can't help it. You can't fight them. But thanks to you—thanks to you I've got it worked out now. I can stop running and go back."

"Good God, don't thank me. That's what I'm for."

He knew it was no use. It was no good, that way of talking. His foot seemed to enlarge and burst like a bloated blister, bringing his head up with a sharp breath of pain. Above him the sky swung round and quivered. A speck that might have been dust or a buzzard or just the shadow of something fell swiftly from it and cut across his sweat-locked eyes.

She saw his pain and said:

"I'll get Manuel. I'll get you back."

"Oh! God no. I can make it."

"I'll get Manuel. It's better."

He tried to watch her figure going down the path. Weakly he tried to call out to her to come back. Then he was alone and it was no use. He was a darkening, dribbling figure, undramatic and strengthless, slipping down from the rock.

The worst of it, some long time later, was the sight of Manuel,

coming to take him away. The correct, oiled, subservient figure. The slight bow. The glance at the foot, the shoe that was black with blood. The cool eyes, the mouth that was so well-shaped, so poised, that it might have ejected at any moment that maddening whistle:
    "I told you so."

[9]

It was morning, about ten o'clock, when Manuel carried him out to the waiting mules. The crushed arch of his foot might have been made of cactus thorns, each thorn a nerve beating nakedly up and down to the thump of blood. His head, like the foot, seemed to have swollen and he felt the great thudding pulse of it rocking outwards, rolling and striking the sides of the valley.
    "I'm going to tie you on to the mule, sir. Just to be safe. In case you feel dizzy."
    "Absolutely all right," he said. "Where's madame?"
    He could no longer call her Miss Vane. It was madame now.
    "She's just getting the last of her things. She's going to ride with you."
    "She's got to catch the *Alacantara*," he said. "What about the car?"
    "I'm going to telephone for it, sir. Then I'll send the hammock back from the top of the road."
    "Hammock? For Christ's sake what hammock?"
    "You'll be better in the hammock, sir."
    He found himself shaking and swaying with sickness, impotent behind the fluttering ears of the mule, the entire valley projected before him in those strong high blue lines that were again pulsations rather than shadow.
    "Much better if you let madame push on. I can manage. Let her push on."
    Presently he was aware of a slow transition of scene: rock and pine looming up, starry walls of cactus leaf dripping past, bright under springs, sunlight firing pine-needles to masses of glass-paper, ashy blue under a sickening sky.
    Heat lay on the back of his neck, in spite of the towel Manuel had put there, like a burning stone. He wondered why there had been

no attempt to escape the heat by starting earlier. Then he remembered not being able to sleep. Great rocks in the valley grating
against each other. A far continuous thunder, a power-house noise,
from across the plateau. Water, a stream somewhere, drowning
him, dragging him under. He remembered falling down. He had
walked out to the veranda, seeing Miss Vane there, in an attempt to
show her that there was nothing wrong with his foot. He vividly
remembered the band of paler hair across the black front of her
head as she turned. He said, "Hullo" and she screamed and out of
the sky at the head of the valley a wing of blackness smothered him.

"The point is that the *Alacantara* is sometimes half a day earlier,"
he said. She was riding twenty or thirty paces in front of him. Her
hair was a mass of pure black, with no other colour but the outer
minute sparkle of tawny fire. It was part of his sickness that his eye
saw the fires of each hair with remarkable clearness, so that he felt
he could touch them with his hands.

He did in fact lift his hands from the saddle. As he did so the
valley swayed. He was no longer part of it. The saddle was not there
to grasp, nor the quivering head of the mule, nor her dark brilliant
hair.

He was lost in emptiness and found himself crying out like a
child. His mouth slobbered as he groped for air. Then the saddle
was there, and the mule, and her head far off, black and unaware.

"It's like everything else," he said. "Never know where you are.
A boat can be two days late. Or half a day early. You never really
know."

If she was listening she showed no sign. For some moments he
was under the impression that she had galloped far down the valley
and disappeared. He shouted something. Masses of tree-heather,
growing taller now as the valley descended, broke apart and
revealed her, drawn up and waiting, only a yard or two away.

"Did you say something?" she said.

"No. All right. Perfectly all right."

"Say when you don't want to go on."

He could not check his mule. He seemed to be pitching forward,
head first, down the track.

"Did you hear what I said about the *Alacantara*?"

"You mustn't worry about that."

"She may be early. She goes out on Wednesday. But you never know—she might be in at midnight tonight. She sometimes is."

"Today is Friday," she said.

He knew that he could not have heard her correctly. He knew that it was only yesterday that he had fallen off the track. It was only an hour or two since he had emptied out his shoe, with its old sour smell of blood, like a dirty beaker.

"You probably won't get a passage for two or three weeks," he said.

She was too far away to answer, a dissolving fragment, under high sun, of pure white and pure black, like a distant road-sign that was the warning of a bend.

"That's the way with this island. It's easy to get here but it's hell's own job to get away."

Some time later he was aware of the undergrowth of pine giving up a pair of stunted figures in black trilby hats. He saw the canopy of a hammock, red-flowered like an old bed coverlet between the poles. He was saying, "Let me alone. Let me walk," and then he was being lifted in. It was rather difficult lifting him in because of his leg and because only one end of the pole could be held up. The other was in the ground, leaving one man free to lift him and set him down.

It was stupid about the leg. As they took him down from the mule he could not feel it at all. Its pain had become self-numbed like the pain of a tooth at a dentist's threshold. All his pain was between his eyes, brightening his vision so that the little flowers of the hammock pattern sprang at him, dancing pink and blue with fire.

"What about you?" he said. "You push on. You've got to go. Anyway the plane is on Saturdays."

"That can wait," she said. "That isn't important. The important thing is to get you down. We ought to have done it before."

"You'd got it all so clear," he said.

The pole straightened. He was lying parallel with the sky. She wiped his face several times with a handkerchief.

"How now?" she said. "Do you feel fit to go?"

"Fit," he said. "Absolutely." And then in a moment of brightness: "Don't forget the handbag."

"I nearly would have done." His impression was that she was

crying. He was not sure. She kissed him gently on the mouth and said: "Take it easy. Easy does it."

"Easy," he said. "That's what you said before."

A few moments later the trilby hats began to carry him slowly, in the hammock, down the path. Easy, he thought, that was it. How easy it had been. A ship, a handbag on a bed, a hotel, a *leste* burning through the town, a rest-house, a track to the top of the sky. Easy: that was her word.

"How do you feel?" she said. "Do you want them to go slower?"

"No," he said. "Aren't you really going now?"

"No," she said. "Not yet. Not now."

Delirium exploded a moment later in stars of pain. There was a smell of camphor from the hammock sheet, anaesthetic, making him gasp for breath; and then, unexpectedly, he was aware of a strange impression.

He stared up at the sky. In the centre of it he could have sworn he saw a shadow, huge and descending, in the shape of the buzzard, holding the sky in its claws.

"Easy," she said, and "Easy" his mind echoed, remembering the shape of her mouth in the sun.

The next moment he began fighting. "I won't go!" he shouted. "I won't go! I won't let it happen to me!" But she did not hear him. The trilby hats did not hear him either, and with calm slowness they carried him forward through the valley, down under the scorning brilliance of noon, towards the sea.

A GREAT DAY FOR BONZO

That July morning when we lay in the corn-loft where the martins were nesting it was so hot and quiet that every breath of chaff-dust falling through the floor-cracks looked like a puff of smoke as it drifted to the stable below. There were just the three of us, myself, Janey and Biff, the boy from the butcher's, lying as still as death on the floor-boards and staring through them to where, in the stable, we could see a man knotting a rope with his hands.

"He's making a lasso," Janey whispered.

"That's not a lasso," I said. "It's a halter. It's like my grandfather goes to fetch the horse with."

"No. It's a lasso," she whispered. "I know it's a lasso."

Biff, the only one who didn't speak because he had enough to do keeping the martin's eggs safe in his cap, always wore the same big brown cap, with a proper peak, like a man's, and it was just right for putting eggs in. He couldn't see much either because he hadn't got his glasses. Whenever he climbed trees or barn-roofs or hedges to look for nests Janey and I always had to hold his glasses for him in case he broke them. Without them his eyes looked funny, not only boss-eyed, but naked somehow, as if they had peeled.

Janey was still holding his glasses while the man got busy with the rope and all Biff could do was to lie there groping with his hands and trying to squint with his boss-eyes at what was happening below. I think I really liked Biff so much because he was boss-eyed. It made him look funny and friendly at the same time. He was a wonderful tree-climber too and one day, when we were grown up, we were going round the world together, and afterwards Janey was going to marry one of us. Neither of us knew which one and nor, at the time, did she. Sometimes I thought it would be Biff because he was the best tree-climber and then sometimes I thought it wouldn't because he was boss-eyed.

Presently the man undid the big slip-knot he had made and then made another and pulled it tighter. After that he hung the rope over his shoulder. Then he looked up. That was the first time I ever saw his face and it made me very surprised. It was a kind, nice face, I thought, but it had a dark savage bruise under one cheek-bone and it looked thin and tired. His hair was short and grey and his chin the colour of pumice stone and his moustache was the same kind as my grandfather's. It curled out and then hung loosely down and I remember wondering if, like my grandfather's did, it ever got into his tea.

After he had looked up he took the rope off his shoulder and then started to sling it over a cross-beam. I couldn't think why he wanted to throw it over the cross-beam. It wasn't very easy to see all that was happening in the stable because the door was closed and the windows were hung with old bits of harness and horse-collars with frayed check linings and an old tin lantern with a lump of staring candle inside.

I think he threw the rope up three or four times before he realized the beam was too high. After that I saw him walk up and down the stable several times, trying to find another place.

After about a minute he came to the manger. Above the manger were wooden racks for hay. One of the racks had an iron ring in it and I saw him look up at it for a time. Then he climbed on to the manger, balanced himself on it and then started to thread the rope through the ring.

I began to wish I wasn't there. My throat felt tight and parched. I think Janey began to wish she wasn't there too because suddenly she started whimpering. I don't think Biff was frightened because he still couldn't see very well. All he did was to grope about on the floor, knocking chaff-dust through the cracks and not knowing it was puffing out in little clouds.

About half a minute later the man had the rope tied to the ring. He gave it a hard wrench or two with his hands. Then he did a thing that made my throat feel tighter and more parched than ever and I wished again I wasn't there.

He suddenly put the rope round his neck and then turned away from the wall and shut his eyes. By that time I was getting frightened. I didn't like to see him there with his eyes shut, his legs crouching a little, just as if he was going to jump off the manger on to the floor below.

Janey was already whimpering again and I was ready to cry myself when suddenly, from outside the stable, a dog started barking and scratching madly at the door. For some minutes I had heard something making thin shrill sounds out there but I thought it was simply the sound that house-martins make when they fly backwards and forwards or sit and talk to each other in the summertime.

As soon as he heard the dog barking the man stood bolt upright gain. He snatched the rope from his neck and started yelling.

"Go on, damn you! Git off—go on, damn you, git off back!"

I think the dog must have leapt as high as the top of the stable door when it heard the voice of the man calling to it from inside. I heard its claws slide down the woodwork, scratching madly. It howled too with that terrible moaning wail that dogs give when they're trapped or tied up too long or unhappy. When the man shouted again it made no difference. The dog wailed and leapt higher than ever at hearing his voice and it was even worse to hear it the second time because there was a sort of overjoyed panic in the way it was fighting to get in.

Then the dog hurled itself bodily against the door. I heard its skull actually hit the bottom of the door and then it was scratching madly, trying to tear a hole in the bricks of the step.

The man jumped down from the manger. He jumped down so suddenly that I had forgotten the rope was still not round his neck and I think Janey and Biff had too. Janey started crying openly and Biff stumbled to his feet, scraping the floor-boards and sending a mass of chaff-dust through the cracks in bigger clouds.

When the man saw the dust he stopped suddenly and looked up. His face was dead white now and more drawn. Outside the door the dog was still howling and scratching and whimpering and the man seemed undecided for a moment whether to let the dog in or come to us upstairs.

He let the dog in. It flew at him, wailing. Then it went round and round in circles, rolling on the floor. It was a small white dog, a cross between a wire-haired terrier and something else, and it had brown-black marks on the side of its face that were very like the bruise on the face of the man.

"Down," he said. "Git down! Damn you—how did you git out?"

The dog lay on the stable floor. Its pale pink tongue was like a piece of quivering india-rubber. As it cowered there I thought for a moment the man would kick it but instead he made a heavy, loose sort of gesture with one hand, trying to calm it. That was the first time I noticed how big his hands were. They were so big that they looked sadly naked and helpless, more naked and helpless than Biff did without his glasses, and he said:

"Down, boy. Down. All right, boy, quiet now."

A moment later he started to come up the wooden stairs to the stable loft. I began to think of the eggs in Biff's cap. I knew that none of us ought to have been there and I felt sick and started shaking.

At the top of the stairs was a trap-door. We hadn't come in that way because it was more fun to climb the wall of the bullock-yard outside and then push each other up and get through the window. None of us knew that the trap-door was there and the sudden sight of the floor-boards opening and the man's big grey head coming up through it made Janey give a little yelp, something like that of the dog.

"Who are you kids? What are you up to?" the man said. "Come on down. Come on—come on down."

Biff was the first to go down, with Janey following him and saying, "Biff, wait for your glasses. Here's your glasses, Biff," and then to the man: "Don't you hit him will you? He can't see very well without his glasses."

The funny thing now was that Janey was calmer than either of us. She was the shortest of the three, even smaller than I was, although I was the youngest, but she was thick and sturdy, with dark brown hair made into two short pig-tails tied with thin white ribbon and bright dark eyes.

"Don't you hit him," she said. "He can't see very well. If you hit him I'll tell the policeman."

Then Janey gave Biff his glasses back and he started to huff on them, in the way he always did before he cleaned them up, and I noticed he stood aside. I knew then that he was only afraid of being hit because of the eggs in his cap. At the same time I knew I was afraid of everything, more than afraid: I was terrified about the eggs, the thought of the policeman, the man who stood there so white and tired, with his huge helpless hands, and even of the dog.

"You kids no business up there," he said. "You know that. What were you doing up there?"

"Nothing," I said. I was sick and trembling. "Nothing."

"Up to no good," he said, "I'll bet. Up to no good."

"We were studying birds," Janey said."We have to study birds."

"Birds' nesting, eh?" he said. "Pinching eggs? Trespassing? The policeman can get told about that as well."

"If you tell the policeman I shall tell the policeman," Janey said. "I shall tell him what you were doing up there."

She pointed to the manger. The rope still dangled from the hook. We all looked at it, the man more drawn-faced than ever, alert and startled. I wasn't sure if Janey knew what the rope was for. I wasn't very sure myself. But the sudden way she pointed at it, her mouth tight, her little pig-tails stiffened out and her eyes as bright as black marbles, all at once created in the man a strange change of attitude.

"Here," he said. "Here. I'll tell you what."

His voice had become soft and husky. All its tiredness seemed to rise to the surface of his throat in an enormous indrawn sigh. At the same time he bent down, snapped his fingers and thumb together and called the dog. It came over to him almost sliding on its belly. In its exhaustion it looked even wearier than he did himself and at last it lay down in front of him, its head on its paws, panting.

"Like him? You go on home now and you can have him. I'm going to part with him," he said.

We stood in front of him with open mouths. Biff had his glasses on again and now they looked like moons.

"Go on," he said. "Take him. Call him Bonzo. That's his name."

At the sound of his name the dog lifted his head.

"You want a bit of string on his collar, so you can lead him," he said, "that's all."

"Bonzo! Bonzo!" Biff said.

The dog leapt to his feet, tail up, his tongue quivering, and from that moment I was no longer so afraid.

We were about a quarter of a mile down the road, going past the pond where we always found moorhens' nests on the fallen branch of willow, when Biff said he thought it was his turn to lead the dog.

Up to that time Janey had been leading him. We had arranged to lead him in turns, each having him five minutes, with me taking the second turn because I was the smallest one. We had no idea of time but Biff said the best thing was to change over every time we counted five hundred. Neither Janey nor I could count up to five hundred and nor, in fact, could Biff. But he could count up to one hundred, he said, and do it in one minute, which meant that it was five minutes every time he counted a hundred five times.

We were just standing by the pond, arguing about whose turn it was, with Biff saying he wouldn't get the dog a bone from the shop if I didn't let him take second turn, when suddenly the dog gave a snatch with his head, whipped the string from Janey's hand and started back up the road.

We all ran after him and were about a hundred yards behind him when he reached the bullock-yard. At one time there had been a farmhouse on the far side of the yard. Now it wasn't a house any longer but was used instead as a barn for storing straw. The windows never had any glass in them and straw stuck out of the holes in the same way as it does out of the holes in a scarecrow.

Now too there were only bullocks in the yard in winter and never any horses in the stables except perhaps at hay-time or harvest when a man put his team there at dinner time because it was the coolest place in the heat of the day.

So as we ran across the yard to the stable beyond the only moving things about the place were ourselves, the dog and the house-martins flying high in the sun. Just outside the stable stood a big sycamore and the shade of it was so black that the dog, flashing under it all doubled up with excitement, looked like a rolling snowball.

Biff could always climb trees better than I could, but he was on the fat side and I could run much faster. Janey was always bold and clever but she couldn't run at all. So I was first across the bullock-yard and first under the sycamore and the dog himself wasn't so very far ahead of me as I reached the open stable door.

I don't know what I expected inside the stable but when I reached the stable door I stopped. It was terribly quiet inside and the stable seemed to be empty. The shade of the sycamore helped to make it dark too and my eyes, coming out of the brilliant morning sun, were dazzled.

Then I heard the dog. He seemed to be somewhere far inside the stable, towards the end of the manger, and he was whimpering. I started calling "Bonzo! Bonzo!" and then I went inside.

Suddenly I saw the dog crouching in the shadows behind the staircase that went up to the loft and beside him was the man. He was just sitting on the floor with his big hands flat on his knees, staring in front of him.

"He got away," I said. "He broke the string and we couldn't stop him. We couldn't help it. Is it all right to have him back?"

He didn't answer. There was a funny look on his face and I felt he hardly knew I was there. I remembered seeing much the same look on the face of Miss Burgess, who lived alone in the street next to us, the day a black van came and took her away.

Just at that moment Janey and Biff came in, both of them shouting "Bonzo! Bonzo!" and then stopping suddenly, just as I had done, because it was dark inside and their eyes were dazzled.

"Come on, Bonzo," I said, "come on, boy," and I reached out to take him by the collar.

He started to back away. He didn't exactly show his teeth but his lips stretched like a catapult and quivered back again.

"Where is he?" Biff shouted.

"He's here," I said. "He won't come with me."

Then Janey and Biff came up to where I stood, watching the man and the dog.

"I'll make him come," Biff said and he started to say, "Bone—big bone, Bonzo—fat bone—me find big bone, Bonzo. Come on, Bonzo," but the dog stretched his lips again and backed away.

"Why won't he come?" Janey said.

She was talking to the man but again he didn't move or answer.

"Doesn't he know you said we could have him?" she said.

"Perhaps he didn't hear you say," I said. "Perhaps you ought to tell him again."

"Bone, Bonzo," Biff said. "Big bone, Bonzo."

Slowly, after a moment or two, the man raised his head. He had been simply staring straight in front of him, cold and glassy, as if none of us were there.

"Where do you kids come from?" he said. "Where do you live I mean?"

"We all live in the same street," Janey said. "Biff and me live opposite each other. Biff lives at the butcher's shop. His father's the butcher."

"I work at the butcher's sometimes too," I said. "Saturdays. Making sausages. I turn the handle of the sausage machine while Biff puts the meat in."

"We brought our dinner out for the day," Biff said, "but we've eaten it."

The man seemed to think about this. His mouth fell open a little as he sat thinking and once he put one of his big hands up to his cheek, touching the bruise on it gently.

"Butcher's?" That was all he said, but I know he hardly knew what we were talking about. He spoke the word very slowly, like someone who couldn't spell or pronounce properly, and then went on staring again, unaware of either us or the dog.

"You tell him," I said. "You tell him and he'll come."

"Yes, you tell him," Janey said.

"We're going to lead him five minutes each," I said. "Then each one's going to keep him a week at a time."

Once again he raised his head. Every time he raised his head the dog looked up, always slowly but somehow sharply, fixing his eyes on him. It was a very curious thing, but I got the impression, each time, that the dog knew what the man was thinking.

"Here, boy," he said and I thought at first he was talking to the dog. But then I saw that he was speaking to Biff. "He might come better if you went and got that bone."

"All right," Biff said. "All right."

"Bring it with some meat on it," the man said, "if you can. And a bit o' bread too. He likes a bit o' bread."

"Janey's uncle sells milk," I said. "Does he like milk?"

"Dogs never eat milk," Biff said. "Cats eat milk. Dogs eat bones and bread."

"We had a little dog once and he ate milk," Janey said. "I could get some milk if he eats it."

"He eats it," the man said. "He eats anything. What sort of sausages have you got?"

"We don't have sausages Tuesdays," Biff said. "We have polonies though. And scratchings."

"He likes scratchings," the man said. "You bring him a bit o' polony and a few scratchings and he'll do anything for you."

"Will he beg?" Janey said.

"He'll beg. You'll see," he said. "You got to make friends with him first though."

"We'll go," Janey said to me. "You stay here."

I started to feel a little frightened again at the thought of being left alone there with the man staring so oddly in front of him and the dog who seemed to be able to read his thoughts and I said:

"Doesn't he like cake? My mother could give me a piece of cake if he likes it. Caraway. We had some on Sunday."

"He don't like cake much," he said.

A moment later Janey and Biff started to run out of the stable and I was all alone with the dog and the man and there was no sound except his heavy breathing as he stared in front of him and the thin whistle of the house-martins across the yard outside.

We sat for a long time alone together, not speaking. Once I remembered the rope and looked round and saw it still hanging by the hook above the manger. But for most of the time I sat staring through the open stable door, out to the black pool of sycamore shade and beyond it to where morning sunlight burned down on big green bunches of elderberry, part of a rusty hay-drag and an occasional swooping bird.

I wasn't really frightened; his face was too kind for that; I only wished that Janey and Biff wouldn't be gone too long and that sometimes the man would talk to me instead of staring in front of his big loose hands.

I thought of several things to try to make him talk but at first he either never answered them or wasn't interested.

"Do you play jacks?" I said.

"Play what?"

"Jacks," I said. "Jack-stones. You have five stones—Janey plays. She's better than anybody. She can do all-ups and grabs and anything. Can you?"

He didn't answer again; I could see he wasn't interested in jack-stones.

"Where do you live?" I said.

He didn't answer that either. I saw a martin come down and

settle on the wall against the elderberry tree, his tail quivering dark
in the sun. I watched him until he flew up again, snapping at
something in the hot still air, and then I thought of something else
to say.

"Have you got a horse?" I said.

Whether he had a horse or not I never knew.

"My grandfather's got a horse," I said. "A white one. We had
another white one before that but it wasn't well and we had to
shoot it. Then they came and took it away and made currant jelly of
its hooves."

Sometimes the dog stirred but mostly, when the man was quiet,
the dog was quiet too, lying on its belly, motionless, its head on its
paws.

"Do you like Janey?" I said.

He wanted to know who Janey was and I told him, explaining at
the same time:

"She's either going to marry me or Biff. I don't know which yet.
We shall have to wait and see."

Suddenly, for the first time, he turned on me quite fiercely.

"Married?" he said. "Don't you have nothing to do with that
caper."

He must have seen that I looked quite startled at his fierceness
because abruptly his face altered. It seemed to lighten and broaden
and suddenly, to my enormous relief and surprise, I saw him smile.

A moment later he actually turned and laughed at me.

"What was that you said about horse's hooves?" he said. "What
sort o' jelly?"

"Currant."

"God alive," he said, "currant?" He even laughed a second time.
"You sure it wasn't apple or summat?"

"No: currant," I said. "Red. Like you have with hare."

That seemed to put him in a much better humour and I said:

"Which do you like best? Hare or rabbit? I like hare. My
grandfather catches hares with a bit of string and a wire and a bit of
stick in the hedgerows."

"Never?" he said.

I was thinking up something else to say when he laughed outright
again. It almost seemed as if the dog was laughing too and while he

was still in that state of good humour I decided to ask him something that had been troubling me for a long time.

"What were you going to do with the rope?" I said.

He went back at once into his brooding, uneasy, groping stare, not answering, and again I felt terribly sorry for him because of his huge helpless hands.

"You weren't going to lasso yourself, were you?" I said.

His voice was suddenly short and fierce again.

"You keep your mouth shut about that," he said. "Keep your mouth shut."

He spat on the floor as straight as you shoot out of a pea-shooter and then stared at the blob of spittle for a long time, again as if I wasn't there.

"You never see me up there, did you?" he said.

I started to say I had seen him up there.

"No you never," he said. "You never see me."

I was going to say a second time that I had seen him but he shook his head slowly and said:

"No you never. You never see me and you ain't never goin' to tell nobody you did. Are you now?"

"No," I said.

"What you don't see you can't talk about, can you?" he said.

"No," I said.

"If you don't tell it nobody can't hear it, can they?"

"No," I said.

"That's right," he said.

We sat for a little while longer, not talking much, and then I said:

"Shall I go and find some jack-stones? Then Janey can show you how to play when she comes back."

What I really wanted was the chance to get outside to see if there was a sign of Biff and Janey coming back and I was glad when he said:

"That's it. You go out and find your jack-stones. And see if you can find a little tin or summat and a drop o' water and bring the dog a drink while you're there."

I went outside. It was hot and still in the sun. From the top bar of the gate in the bullock-yard I stood and looked across the fields and the road for a sign of Biff and Janey. The road and the fields were empty. In the distances, above the hedgerows, across the flat blue-green ears of corn, waves of heat were shimmering and dancing just like water.

Then I got over the gate and began to look in the cart-track for jack-stones. Already the track was hard and baked from summer and bits of blue chicory were flowering in the disused cart-ruts, with a lot of silver-weed and shell-pink sunshades. Where the track was barer I found five stones, one almost a pure white one, about the size of a robin's egg, and then three brown ones and a bluey-grey one with red veins in it, all scribbled about, just like a writing-lark's.

Then I got back over the gate and went round behind the building that used to be a house but was now a straw-barn. An old gas-tarred water-barrel stood under the eave, by the doorway, and in the nettles beside it I found an old enamel saucepan, blue outside and white inside, with a hole in it that had been plugged up with a piece of sack.

I climbed up on the barrel and looked down at the water. It was very black and about half-way up the barrel and I could see tiny red worms in it, wriggling like hairs. I started to try to catch the worms in the saucepan and at the same time I could see my face, with its smooth, almost white hair, reflected in the blackness of the water below.

I've no idea now how long I was fishing there in the water-barrel; I lost count of time. But suddenly, side by side, with the reflection of my face in the water, there was his face. It seemed suddenly to fall out of the sky and float there without a sound.

"Give us that," he said. "I'm as dry as a fish," and he took the saucepan from me and started drinking.

I was too surprised and startled to be frightened. His big gloomy face staring up at me out of that black water-barrel froze the back of my neck. I wanted to start running. I actually slipped down the side of the barrel, catching my bare knee in one of the hoops, and in another second or two I should have been away, my legs melting, across the fields.

Then I saw him drinking. He was drinking like a horse, his mouth and most of the front of his face buried in the saucepan. He made a sucking desperate sound just like a horse and after he had emptied the saucepan once he filled it a second time and then a third.

What fascinated and terrified me about all this was the thought of the worms. I knew you should never drink water out of water-barrels. If you did the worms would grow inside you and swell up and poison you and make you die. I knew there were three sure ways you could die. One was by not eating; the other was by not breathing; and the third was through drinking water out of water-barrels where there were worms.

When he had finished his third saucepan of water I looked up and stared at him and said:

"You'll die, drinking that water. The worms will swell up inside you and you'll die and they'll put you in the bury-hole."

That was the worst thing I could imagine, being put in the bury-hole. That was the most terrible, awful thing in the world, I thought, but he didn't seem either impressed or frightened.

"That wouldn't come amiss, would it? Not to some folks. Not to me, chance it."

"You don't want to die, do you?" I said.

"Die?" he said. "Very like they'll come a time when you'll want to die."

"No," I said. "No."

"Ah! but you never know, do you?" he said. "That's it. You never know."

I was too puzzled to answer. On his wet, stubbly face the sun shone down fierce and brilliant, making the skin seem glassy and jagged. He actually started to take another drink of water. Then he changed his mind and doused the rest of the water over his face, wiping it off with big swabbing jabs of his coat-sleeve.

"Where's the dog?" I said. I suddenly remembered the dog. "Where's Bonzo?"

"Tied him up," he said. "We got to take him some water."

He dipped another saucepan of water from the barrel.

"Why do you want to give him away?" I said.

"He's nothing but a plague to me," he said. "He plagues me to death. I'll be glad and thankful to be shut on him."

"He's a nice dog."

"He's all right. He plagues me though. I wish he was some-where."

We took the saucepan of water and started to walk back to the stable.

"Soon as them other kids get back you can hop it," he said, "and give me a minute's peace. You can take him with you and I'll get some peace for a change."

The dog was tied up at the foot of the stairs. When we gave him the water, he lapped at it without stopping for breath. "Drier n' me," the man said and I was just beginning to feel dry myself and wondering whether I should quench my thirst by sucking one of the pebbles, like my grandfather did in the harvest field, when I heard the voices of Biff and Janey coming back across the yard.

For a few seconds I thought the eyes of the man would drop out of his head when he saw what Biff had brought.

"That's all right," he kept saying. "That's good."

Biff had brought a shin-bone of beef, a red polony sausage, and a good big handful of scratchings, all wrapped in newspaper. Janey had nearly a pint of milk in a can. In one pocket Biff had a pork pie wrapped in grease-proof paper and in the other three rounds of bread.

He unwrapped the shin-bone first and then started to spread the newspaper on the floor, but the man grabbed it out of his hand.

"That ain't today's, is it?" he said.

He began to peer at the newspaper, his eyes bulging and close to the page. There were still beads of moisture on his face but I couldn't tell if they were sweat or water. His big hands made the pages crackle as he turned them over and then suddenly he folded the paper up and gave it back to Biff.

"Yesterday's, ain't it? Yesterday's," he said. "What's the date there?"

"The twenty-ninth," Biff said. "That's the day before."

"Twenty-ninth," he said. He sat thinking, again in the same huge, helpless groping way as when we had first seen him. "Twenty-ninth—what day are we now?"

"Tuesday," Janey said. "We told you before."

"Tuesday, eh? What date was Saturday?"

"Twenty-sixth," Janey said.

Janey was always quicker than any of us but that time I was quick too.

"Have you been here all that time?" I said.

"Get the grub out, get the grub out," he said.

He picked up the shin-bone. For a moment I thought he would start gnawing and tearing it with his hands. By now the dog was on his feet, straining at the string that still tied him to the stairs.

"Here, Bonzo, Bone. Bone," Biff said and the dog started whimpering. "Come on, boy—bone. Here boy, here—"

As the dog gave a great straining pull at the string, rushing forward and then choking himself back, whimpering again, the man raised the shin-bone with a menacing swing and said:

"Don't start harbourin' him in bad habits. Git back there!—go on, git back."

"He's got to have the bone, hasn't he?" Biff said.

"All right," the man said, "but not all of a minute. The bone's to get him to go with you, ain't it? That's what you brought it for."

It must have been past midday by that time. As Biff started to unwrap the pork pie I began to feel hungry. We had eaten our dinner at half-past ten and I think Biff and Janey were hungry too. Biff started to get out his shut-knife, ready to cut the pie, but the man said:

"Hold hard a minute. What are you cutting that for?"

"It's for us," Biff said.

"What about me? Don't I git no dinner?"

"If you like," Biff said. "You can have some polony if you like."

He grabbed the polony, tearing the top skin off with his teeth. Then he held it in his fist like a big scarlet ice-cream cone, gnawing and licking the sausage out of the top of it. Biff held out a slice of bread and he grabbed that too. All the time he never spoke a word. Once or twice the red skin of the sausage got gnawed loose but it made no difference to him: he tore it with his teeth and ate that too.

"You can have some milk if you like," Janey said.

With his mouth full of sausage he buried his face in the milk-can, drinking out of it in the same sucking, slopping way as he had drunk water from the saucepan in the yard.

"How are the scratchings?" he said. He began to eat the scratchings, throwing them into his mouth, then crunching them like nuts. Scratchings are the bits of pork leaf you get left over when lard is made. They're a brown-golden colour and crisp and they're better with salt on them. I thought perhaps he would ask for salt but it never seemed to occur to him as he threw the scratchings into his mouth and crunched them madly down.

"What about the dog?" I said suddenly. Everybody had forgotten the dog. "I thought we got the scratchings for Bonzo."

He threw a few scratchings on the stable floor, not speaking. The dog went for them as madly as he had done, licking the floor for crumbs.

"What about the bone?" Biff said. "Can't he have the bone?"

"Lotta meat on that bone," the man said.

It was true there were skinny bits of meat with a few bluish sinews left on the bone, but I hardly thought he would eat them. Then I heard his teeth grate on the bone, gnawing at flesh. It made queer cold shivers run across the small of my neck to see a man eating raw meat like a dog and once more I felt sorry for him and I know by the way Biff and Janey sat there staring, forgetting the bread and the pork pie, that they were sorry too.

Suddenly, for the first time, he seemed to become really aware of us sitting there. His eyes rolled about for a few seconds, white and big and watery. He spat up a piece of gristle that had got caught in his throat. This seemed to wake him still more and after he'd taken another drink of milk he said:

"You kids can bunk off now. Tie the string tight round your hand this time so he don't git loose. It's no use if you don't tie him tight. He'll only git loose again."

"Like a piece of pie?" Biff said. I think we were all a little sick at the thought of the pie. After seeing him tear the flesh from the bone like that we none of us had much heart for the pie. "You can have some if you want to."

He started wolfing the pie. Sometimes a piece of the crust, with trembling bits of jelly, fell out of his hands or his mouth on to the floor below but again it made no difference. He always picked it up, cramming it into his mouth without wiping the dirt from it or even bothering to look at it at all.

"Anybody down the road when you come back?" he said suddenly to Biff.

"No. Nobody," Biff said.

"There was a man across a field hoeing wezzles," Janey said.

"One says yes, one says no," he said. "Make up your minds."

"There was a man," Janey said, "but he was right across the field."

"All right, all right," he said. "If he's there when you go back don't say nothing—don't talk to him. If he sees you just look slippy."

"All right," we said.

He was still finishing the pie and we were still sitting on the floor, staring at him, when I remembered something I wanted to ask him.

"You've got a big bruise on your face," I said. "Did you know? If you'd have thought of it Biff could have brought a piece of meat for it. A piece of meat on a bruise makes it better."

To my surprise he completely ignored the question of the bruise. I might never have asked it. Instead he looked at each one of us in turn and then said:

"Who's going to lead him this time?"

"It's my turn," Biff said.

"Who led him last time?"

"Janey started."

"All right. You lead him," he said to Biff. "Now git hold of him tight. No half-larks. And one on you walk in front with the bone. Who's going to walk with the bone?"

"I want to," I said.

"All right," he said, "you walk in front of him with the bone. Then he'll follow you till bull's noon. All you got to do is keep in front with the bone."

"I will," I said.

By the time we left he was lying down on the stable-floor staring upward.

"Now perhaps I can git a minute's peace," he said. "Perhaps I can git some peace now."

Outside, across the bullock-yard and down the cart-track where I had found the jack-stones, it was hotter than ever. The sun was straight and blinding. A few thistles were already seeding by the hedgerow but there was hardly a breath of air to blow the down away.

When we got to the gate leading out to the road we stopped a moment and something made me get up on to the top bar of the gate and look back along the cart-track, with its blue stars of chicory and sunshades in the sun and tufts of bearded thistledown to where, by the sycamore, the stone walls of the stable were almost white in the sun.

"He's come out to watch us," I said.

From the gate we could see him at the door of the stable, looking round. The queer thing was that, after all, he did not seem to be looking at us. He reminded me of someone who was looking round for intruders, just to satisfy himself before locking up a house, for the last time, at night.

Suddenly he disappeared. A second later we all heard the big bolt of the stable door slam back inside. In the hot still air it was like the sound of a rifle bolt being snapped in, hard and steely, in readiness to fire.

The dog, I thought, seemed to have heard it too. Almost at once he started whimpering and scratching under the lowest bar of the gate, trying to get through.

"Start running with the bone," Biff said. "Give him a smell of the bone and then start running."

We got him about three hundred yards beyond the pond, almost to the point where the road forks, about a mile from the town, when he suddenly doubled back, wrapped the string round Biff's legs and started back up the road.

At that moment I was ten yards or so ahead with the bone and as soon as I saw him turn I turned too and began to run after him. I realized at once that I should never catch up with him, and the only way I could think of stopping him was to throw the bone.

I threw it as hard as I could and it bounced behind him with a thump on a pile of stones at the side of the road. As soon as he heard it fall he stopped, turned and made a grab for it. The bone was nearly as big as he was and it looked like a big red table-leg as he stood there on top of the pile of stones, wagging his tail and looking for the first time very pleased with himself and very sharp and cheeky.

"Drop it! Drop it!" I said.

"Shut up!" Biff said. "Now he's got the bone he'll come as easy as pie. Won't you, Bonzo? You'll come now, won't you?" He started slapping his knees with his hands and looking appealingly at

Bonzo through his big moon spectacles, at the same time approaching him gently, calling his name and sometimes whistling. "Come on Bonzo boy. Come on, boy, come on—"

The dog actually dropped the bone on top of the pile of stones and then stood with his mouth open and his tongue out, laughing.

"Good boy, Bonzo," Biff said. "That's a boy—"

He suddenly rushed forward to grab his collar but in a second Bonzo picked the bone up and dived back into the tall grasses along the roadside and then through a blackthorn hedge and into the field beyond.

At that point the blackthorn hedge was too thick and prickly for the three of us to get through but there was a gate thirty or forty yards up the road and in a few seconds we were climbing over it into the field. The oats growing right up to the gate and the hedgerow were twice as tall as us and were a soft pink-yellow colour, ripe for cutting. There was no sign of the dog. I watched for the oat-stalks to start moving but nothing stirred and there was no sound except the sound of grasshoppers whirring in the heat of noon and a yellow-hammer singing the same few notes over and over again on another side of the field.

"Bonzo! Bonzo!"

We called him over and over again but he made no answer. I got on my knees and tried to look through the rows of oat-stalks but on the headland they were running the wrong way and it was like looking into a forest of pink-yellow straw all tangled with thistle stalks, pink convolvulus and little flowers of scarlet pimpernel.

Then Janey, who was always so quick, thought she heard him farther down the hedgerow. We all listened and I thought I heard him too, panting softly.

"Let's track him," Biff said. "Get down. Start tracking."

We started to go off in Indian file down the hedgerow. Biff leading, Janey next and I coming on behind. Every few yards we stopped, crouched down and listened. Sometimes there was a sudden faint stirring down the rows of oat-stalks but it never went on for long and it might have been only a rabbit, or field-mouse or a bird.

"He must be in the other field," I said. "Let's look in that."

"I know where he is," Janey said. "He's gone back to the barn."

"No," Biff said, 'he's in here, I know he is, I can smell the bone."

He turned round from where he was crawling on his hands and knees and looked back at us with his funny eyes that always seemed to be swimming out of one side of his thick watery spectacles and said: "You can smell it. You smell. You can smell the bone."

For a minute we all stopped and smelled. Perhaps Biff was more used to the smell of meat than I was but I couldn't smell anything except the ripe oats, the seeds of grasses and the clay earth turned dry and dusty by days of sun.

"I can't smell anything either," Janey said."I'll go back to the barn if you like and see if he's there."

"No," Biff said."I can smell it. It's over there."

I suppose we had crawled about a quarter of the way round the field before, as we stopped for the tenth or eleventh time, we heard another sound. It was a harsh, crisp, swishing sound, regular and steady, and neither Biff nor Janey knew what it was.

But I knew what it was.

"It's a man with a scythe," I said. "He's mowing round the field."

All three of us lay down in the grass by the hedgerow, listening, not daring to breathe. Then after a few moments I moved over towards the oats and parted some of them with my hands and looked down the rows. The rows were very straight there and this time they ran parallel with the hedgerows so that, some distance down them, I could actually see the scythe swinging and biting into them and just behind them the trouser legs of the man, his boots summer-dusty, the legs of the trousers tied up with bits of string.

Suddenly the man stopped mowing. I saw the blade of his scythe flash white as he laid it down on the stubble. Then he moved away and I could not see him for a moment or two but presently I heard him spit once or twice and after that there was a sound of water trickling by the hedgerow. Biff started laughing into his hands and then I saw the man come back. He laid his jacket on the last swathe of oats he had mown and then sat down on it and began to unpack his dinner, a lump of bread-and-cheese, some onions and a big blue can of tea, from out of a round straw dinner bag. Before he started to eat he spread his handkerchief on his knees and took out a big clasp-knife and wiped it on his trousers. The handle of the knife was thick crinkly bone and the handkerchief was red with big white spots on.

All that time none of us dared move and then, down the rows and a little to the left, between myself and the man, I caught sight of something else.

It was Bonzo, lying in the rows of oats with his feet on the bone. As soon as I saw him I was so excited that I forgot everything else: the man, Janey and Biff, where we were and how we were not supposed to be there and what might happen to us if we were found. I was so excited that before I could stop myself I was calling him by his name.

"Bonzo!" I said. "Bonzo—"

I hadn't called him more than twice before he bolted. He went straight forward, crashing through three or four yards of oats and then leaping clean past the man eating his dinner on the stubble beyond.

The man let out a yell as the dog leapt past him and I think he was more frightened than we were as we turned and started running. The last I saw of him was a glimpse of his brown bald head as he snatched off his cap and threw it at the dog.

A moment or two later we were crashing through a gap in the hedgerow, out into a pasture field beyond and skulking and scurrying down the ditch like terrified leverets, panting for breath.

When we reached the road there was no sign of Bonzo. You could see the empty white curve of the road quivering at each end with shimmering waves of heat and again there was no sound in the hot midday air but the whirr of grasshopper and the short tinkling song of yellow-hammers along the hedgerows.

"He must have gone across the fields," Biff said. "That way."

"I bet he didn't," Janey said. "I bet he went to the barn. He *wants* to go to the barn—can't you see?—that's where he *wants* to go."

Biff thought the field and Janey thought the barn. I couldn't make up my mind where he would go. I was really thinking about the man with the scythe and how he would probably chase us. All I really wanted was to be able to find the dog, take him back home and start making a kennel for him and teach him to fetch stones, but Biff said:

"All right. I'll go across the field and look and Janey go to the barn and look. And you," he said to me, "stop here."

"I don't want to stop here—"

"You stop here," he said. "You guard the road. You be sentry."

I didn't want to be sentry. I was five and a half, but Janey was six and a half and Biff was over seven. Whenever there were things they felt I was too young to do they always made me sentry.

"You sit on top of the stones and keep your eyes skinned," Biff said.

"And if he comes," Janey said, "catch him and hold him by the collar and tie him to a tree."

I don't know why, but I felt uneasy and queer as soon as Janey went up the road and I hadn't been sitting long on the pile of stones before I began to wish we had never let her go back there all alone. Somehow I couldn't get out of my head the picture of the man with the rope, how he had drunk the water with worms in it and eaten raw meat off the bone and how, above all, he just sat there with his uneasy groping stare and his enormous helpless hands.

"Janey," I thought, "if you're not back soon I'll count a hundred and if you're not back then I'll come and look for you."

I don't know how long I sat on the pile of stones all by myself, between the high blackthorn hedges that already had their little grey-green sloes on them, in the hot still sun, waiting for Janey and Biff to come back. All the time there was no sign of Bonzo and once I started to play jack-stones, but after a time I gave it up because the stones were too big for my hands. Then I began looking among the bigger stones, turning them over, and finally I found a long flat one that had a lot of wonderful things underneath it: a rain-beetle, a lot of pigs that rolled themselves up in balls, a devil's coach-horse and a big fat brown slug that I thought at first was a toad.

Then I started to count up to a hundred because Janey wasn't back. I couldn't really count up to a hundred. I could only count up to twenty and then, as I always did at hide-and-seek, skip and pretend the rest.

"*Twenty*. One, two three—*thirty*. One, two, three, four, five—*fifty*. Fif-one, fif-two, fif-three—*seventy*. Nine-two, nine-three, nine-four, nine-five, nine-six, *a hundred*!"

I didn't know until afterwards that all the time I was sitting there playing with the stones, looking underneath them and pretending to count up to a hundred, something strange was happening to Janey in the stable.

When she got back to the stable the door was open. After a few moments she went inside and looked about her but neither Bonzo nor the man was there. Then she went outside and stood for a moment under the big sycamore, listening.

After a time she thought she heard a sound. It seemed to come from the direction of the building that had once been a farmhouse. She went across the bullock-yard towards the house and presently she saw the man standing by the water-barrel, muttering to himself.

"Have you seen the dog?" she said. "Have you seen Bonzo? We've lost him again."

He turned on her, startled. She told me afterwards how his eyes looked strange and green. I never really believed that. Nobody's eyes could ever look green, I thought, but I believed her when she said:

"Don't you remember how Arthur Burgess looked when he thought he'd eaten the poison-berries? He looked like that. He looked bad as if he was going to die."

I knew what was really the matter with him. I knew that he was going to die because he'd drunk water with worms in it. That was a sure way to die, as sure as stopping breathing or not eating food. Anybody ought to know that was the way to die.

Then before she could say anything else he turned on her and said:

"You get outa here—go on, git out on it. Allus vapourin' round, you kids—git out on it. Leave me be."

"We want Bonzo," she said. "I think he came back here. Did he come back?"

He didn't answer. She said he seemed to go faint suddenly and gave a big shiver, standing there in the sun. His face was terribly pale, she said, and the bristles on his face stood out like stiff grey prickles.

Then he started to wander back towards the stable, groping his way. She followed him, saying a few things, asking questions, mostly about Bonzo, which he never answered.

At last he was in the stable and once more he lay down on the floor. He lay with his face away from her for a time, muttering, half-speaking things with little groans. She sat down on the floor beside him, sorry for him, and asked him several times if he felt bad and once if he wanted water.

At the mention of water he turned and looked at her as if he were seeing her there for the first time.

"Do you go to school?" he said.

"Yes," she said.

"Why ain't you at school today?"

"We just started holidays," she said.

He stared at the stable floor and then got himself up on one elbow and said:

"Can you write?"

"Yes, I can write," she said. "I'm nearly seven. Miss Jackson says I'm a good writer."

He didn't speak for a time. Instead he fumbled in his pockets until finally he brought out a stub of pencil and then a piece of paper.

"You know where Blackland Spinneys are?" he said.

"Yes," she said. "We sometimes go primrosing there."

He started to give her the piece of paper and the pencil as if he were going to ask her to write something down. But suddenly he changed his mind and put them back in his pocket. It was hard to know what he meant by these sudden changes of mind but it was harder still when he said:

"Do you read the Bible at school? Do you say prayers and all that?"

"Yes," she said.

"Say something."

She didn't know what he meant by that and she saw him lie back on the stable floor, flat on his back, with closed eyes.

"Say what?" she said.

"What you say at school."

She had no idea what to say. The first thing that came into her head was *The Lord is my Shepherd*.

"Shall I say that?" she said.

"If you like," he said. "That'll do."

"*The Lord is my Shepherd*," she said. "*I shall not want. He maketh me to lie down in green pastures*."

"God," he said, once or twice. "God. Oh! God."

It was all a mystery to her. All the time she was talking she kept her eyes on his face. It was very quiet in the stable in the coldish shade, out of the sun, but she was never frightened. And the reason why she was never frightened, she told us afterwards, was because the strange, funny, cold-drawn look on his face gradually went away as she sat there. He lay quiet and tranquil, as if after a long and terrible tiredness he had started to drop to sleep.

He spoke to her in fact only once or twice more and then with his eyes still closed.

"Don't you come back here no more, you kids," he said. "Hear that? Don't you come back no more—I shan't be here."

"Supposing Bonzo comes back?"

"He won't come back. He'll only come back if he knows I'm here. And I shan't be here. I'll be gone for good in a minute or two."

She stood for a few moments longer before he finally asked her to go, saying, "Shut the door." Then as she stood at the stable door, just before shutting it, she remembered something.

"What about Blackland Spinneys?" she said. "Is that where you live?"

He didn't answer.

"Do you feel better now?" she said.

He didn't answer that either.

"Thank you for Bonzo," she said.

By the time she came down the road again to where I was waiting on the pile of stones Biff had come back too. There was no sign of Bonzo.

Then when Janey began to tell us all that had happened in the stable and the bullock-yard, how the eyes of the man were green and how ill he looked, as if he were going to die, I began to get more and more excited.

"He's going to die!" I said. "He's going to die. I saw him drinking the water with the worms in it. That's the way you get poisoned. That's the way you die."

"Die?" Biff said. "You're not sharp. You can't die from drinking water."

"You can," I said. "You can. Water out of ditches. Water with worms in it."

"Then," Biff said, "how is it dogs don't die? How is it birds don't die? They drink water out of ditches. How is it cows don't die? They drink water with newts in it. And frogs. How is it they don't die?"

"Sometimes they do."

"Yes, but not next minute. They don't drop down dead next minute."

"Let's go and catch newts," Janey said. "We can paddle too. It's hot."

"We haven't got Bonzo," Biff said, "have we? We can't go without Bonzo."

We sat there for a few minutes longer trying to decide what to do when suddenly a man pushed his head over the gate farther down the road and said:

"You kids!—is this your dog? I nearly cut him a-two—you want to get him killed? Why'n't you take him home and chain him up somewhere?"

It was the man with the scythe. He had Bonzo gripped tight by the collar.

"He's all covered in burrs and thistles," the man said. "Got one or two in his foot too I fancy. That'll stop him capering off too far. Now you just git off home and take him with you."

As we went down the road we were all so happy that we forgot completely, for the first time, about the man in the stable. And this time too everything went right with Bonzo. Biff held him really tight by the string. And, as the man said, there were thistles in his foot and sticky burrs all over his body, so that he limped a bit, looking almost, I thought, like a plum-pudding dog.

He looked a little sorry for himself too, I thought, sometimes hopping on three legs and holding the other in the air. The thistles in his foot were just what we wanted. We knew, with them, that he couldn't run very far.

Just before we got home we stopped for a few moments by a stone-mason's yard to decide who should have Bonzo first and how long each should keep him. Under the stone-mason's shed two men were sawing a lump of white stone and the air was full of hot dry dust from the saw. When the men saw us standing there with the dog they suddenly stopped sawing and one of them, wiping his neck with a sweat-rag, looked at Bonzo and grinned.

"That's a bit of a clanger you got there," he said, "ain't it? What run up the entry?"

The second man laughed too and said:

"Sausages goin' t'ave black and white skins this week, Biff?" They both laughed then. "Or is he goin' into the pigs' puddens?"

They both seemed to think that that was very funny, but none of us laughed and Biff said:

"He's our dog. He's all right."

"So long as he ain't mine," the second man said. He was the funniest of the two and he blew his nose with his fingers. "Does he have fits?"

We said he didn't have fits; we said he was a good dog and could run fast and you could teach him to beg. But the men didn't seem impressed by this and the second one spat and laughed again and said:

"If he starts gittin' fits you feed him on pigeon's milk. That'll cure 'im."

"Pigeons don't have milk," Biff shouted. "But donkeys do!"

After that the men didn't seem to want to talk any more. So presently we decided that Janey, because she was a girl, should have Bonzo first and keep him for one week from that very afternoon.

Janey's father worked on the railway. Sometimes he worked on night-shift. You went up to Janey's house by a brick entry where her mother hung out the washing on wet days and beyond the entry was an asphalt yard and then a little garden where her father grew rows of onions, big clumps of red and yellow dahlias and a few potatoes. When he wasn't working on day-shift Janey's father would sit in the middle of his garden, on a broken kitchen chair, in a tiny square of grass that he clipped with scissors, and stare at his plants with pride and wonder.

Sometimes he put his plants into flower-shows and that afternoon I thought he would explode when he saw Janey leading the dog down the ash-path between the onions and potatoes.

"Get that dog out of here!" he shouted. "Who brought that in? Who let that out? Go on!" he yelled. "Get out—get out of here!"

He began to pick up stones.

"He's ours," Janey started to say. "Biff's and mine and—"

"Take him back where he belongs!" her father bellowed. "Get him out of here!"

After that we led him slowly across the street to our house. I knew my mother didn't like dogs; I knew my father didn't like dogs either. But it was in my mind to ask if Bonzo could live with my grandfather, who was a very nice, genial, easy-going man who kept a little farm where, at threshing-time, thousands of rats came out from under corn-stacks. In another month or two it would be threshing-time and Bonzo would be able to kill the rats and soon everybody, like us, would know how wonderful he was.

In the house it was very hot, the blinds were drawn and my mother was asleep in the sitting-room.

I went out into the street again and told the truth to Biff and Janey. "My mother's asleep," I said. "I daren't wake her."

Biff was glad.

"My father likes dogs," he said. "We always had dogs. Once we had a dog called Blinder. He could see in the dark. We had a big rat in the cellar and it got into a corner and its eyes had red flames coming out of them but Blinder killed it."

"My grandfather has rats too," I said. "They live in the corn-stacks. Bonzo'll kill them."

"I bet he's a good ratter," Biff said. "My father'll like him if he's a good ratter."

Janey and I stood outside the butcher's shop while Biff went into the shop with Bonzo. Blue and white striped awnings covered the windows of the shop and there was a queer faint sickly smell of meat in the hot air.

Biff's father was a fat stocky man with red cheeks and ears, a bluish bald head and a funny way of being nice to you one day and not speaking to you the next. My mother said it was the smell of the meat; it made him liverish. Sometimes if I helped in the shop, with Biff, he gave me pig's-tails. I liked pig's-tails. There isn't much meat on a pig's-tail but what little there is is very tasty. I was always overjoyed when I got a pig's-tail, just as I was always downcast, when, for days on end, Biff's father wouldn't speak to me. But that was how he was, my mother said. You never knew how the man was going to be, five minutes together. That was how butchers were: the smell of the meat made them moody and fat and tatchy.

"Well, look on his collar!" we heard Biff's father shouting. "Haven't you got sense enough to look on his collar? He belongs to somebody, doesn't he? There must be a name on the collar!"

In another moment he came outside with Biff, dressed in his blue and white apron with the big steel hanging from his waist, dragging Bonzo by the scruff of the neck. I could see he was in one of his liverish tatchy moods. He was purplish-hot in the face and he almost lifted the dog off the ground as he dragged it on to the pavement and said:

"Here, what does it say there? What does it say on the collar?"

Biff squatted down and turned Bonzo's collar round and then read out:

" 'Bonzo. J. Slater. High Farm. Blacklands Spinneys. Evensford.' "

"Well, now you know," his father said. "He belongs up at Blacklands. Take him back there."

None of us knew what to say.

"Go on—take him back. He's strayed. Take him back there—or else down to the police station. One of the two—but I don't want him here. I won't have a moocher like that about the place."

We led him down the street. He was still limping from the thistle in his foot and I thought he looked tired and thirsty. I was getting a little tired and thirsty myself and Janey said:

"Perhaps my uncle would have him. He could help get the cows in."

But it was no use: her uncle said dogs were bad for cows. They worried them something chronic; they made their milk go sour. But he was a friendly easy man and he gave us all a drink of milk from a churn. The milk was cool and fresh from standing all day on the stone flags of the dairy and we gave Bonzo a drink of water from a tap in the yard. Then Janey's uncle gave us a pear each. They were small honey pears, soft and yellow and very sweet, the first pears of the summer, and they were so nice that all of us ate the cores.

"You start off now and take him back," Janey's uncle said. "That's your best tip. You don't want a policeman to see you, do you?"

That was the last thing we wanted. We remembered what the

man in the stable had said. Up to that time we hadn't thought much
more about him but now Biff said:

"Perhaps we ought to take him back to the stable. Shall we?"

"He said we were never to go back there," Janey said. "Never.
He wanted to get a little peace, he said, and we wasn't to go back."

"All right," Biff said. "We'll have to take him back to this farm.
At Blacklands."

Then Janey remembered something. The word Blacklands reminded her of the time she had sat in the stable with the man and
how he had taken a piece of paper and a stub of pencil from his
pocket and had said to her suddenly: "Can you write?" and then
"Do you know a place called Blacklands Spinneys?" as if he were
going to ask her to write it down.

"It's the same place," she said.

"All right," Biff said. "I expect that's his home. Let's go up
there."

After we had been walking some time—they way to the spinneys
was all up-hill and the road was white with heat and we rested
several times—I remembered something too.

"I wonder if he's dead yet," I said.

"He can't die," Biff said, "not from drinking water. Act sharp—I
told you."

"Perhaps he'll die in the night," I said. "People always die in the
night."

"That they don't," Biff said. "I had an aunt what died at tea-
time."

"If you die," I said, "can you come alive again?"

"No," Biff said. "It's just like meat. Meat can't come alive again,
can it? Nobody can come alive."

"Jesus did," Janey said.

Janey was always so quick and clever and this time Biff couldn't
answer.

After that I couldn't make up my mind whether people could
come alive again or not and I began to be worried by the thought of
the man in the stable and what we had seen there. I wondered if he
died whether, when we went to look for martin's nests again, we
might not find him there, under the manger perhaps, where it was
dark, still staring upward.

"I want to go home," I said.

"Oh! don't be a kid," Biff said. "Don't be wet."

"You catch hold of my hand," Janey said. "When we get to the farm we'll see some hens."

I don't know why but perhaps it was the thought of the hens, as we began to walk in the shadow of the spinneys, where the road was like a thin white tunnel between thick hornbeam and hazel boughs, that began to comfort me. Gradually I forgot the thought of the man who might be lying dead under the manger, below the old horse-collars and the lamp with its staring candle, and once I said:

"I like hens. My grandmother's got a hen that talks."

"Hens can't talk," Biff said. "How can they?"

"This one can," I said. "You give it maize and corn and it eats it and then starts talking."

"Nobody can talk only people," Biff said, "can they, Janey?"

"Parrots can talk," Janey said, "and sometimes jackdaws."

"Let's catch a jackdaw and see if it talks," I said.

"Come on," Biff said. "Don't *drag*. When do you think we'll get there?"

Perhaps it was not more than a mile up that road, between the woods dark and thick with summer, the birds in them quiet in the still afternoon and the primrose leaves burned in the ditches by the heat of July, but the road was straight and white and hot and it seemed much further.

Once we came to a pond and we stopped for a few moments to let Bonzo drink in it. All round the pond were thin tall reeds like dark, green spears, with a few bulrushes among them and pink sprays of willow-herb. On the far side stood a clump of elder-trees and it was shady there. Part of the water was thick with water-lilies and between the leaves little circles kept springing up and dying away.

"Look," Janey said. "Fish. Coming up to breathe."

"Fish can't breathe," Biff said. "If they breathe they die."

"No they don't," Janey said. "They have to have air like people."

"You don't know anything," Biff said.

"Nor do you," Janey said. "Boys don't know everything. They think they do."

I thought it was nice by the water, with the tall cool reeds, the shade of the elder-trees, the flat shining water-lilies, the water with its little spreading circles and hardly a sound in the air but the dog lapping water as he drank at the edge of the pond.

"Let's stop and catch fish," I said. "Or else newts, or tadpoles."

"It's too late for tadpoles," Biff said. "You don't know anything."

"We'll stop and paddle when we come back," Janey said, "shall we?"

"It's too deep to paddle," Biff said. "We'd all get drownded."

After a time we walked on again, slowly, tired now in the heat, even the dog flagging, and I was just beginning to wonder if we should ever get there and if Biff perhaps wasn't after all something like his father, moody and tatchy because the smell of the meat got into him, when suddenly Janey said:

"There's the house. There's the farm. There it is."

We all stopped. The house stood in a clearing of the wood. It was a house that you might have thought had been a church at one time. Its windows were long and narrow and rounded at the top. In the half-circle at the top of the window the glass was blue and yellow, with sometimes a piece of green. The window frames were painted a dirty reddish-brown and over the front porch, which had sections of coloured glass in it too, fell drooping masses of ivy, like a dusty dark green rug hung out to dry. The house was built of brick and at the back of it were a few brick out-buildings, all of them roofed in corrugated iron that shone brown with rust in the sun. Underneath them stood bits of machinery, rusty too, with old barrows, a water-cart, a hay-rake and several cans and churns.

What made you think of a church too were four big yew-trees that flanked the path leading down to the road. I didn't like these trees; they made me feel unhappy. I didn't like the way the road ended just beyond them either, the white line of it cut off by a gate, and how the woods beyond it, dense and taller now, went on and on, unbroken.

"Let's go back," I started to say and then I noticed something terribly strange about the dog.

"He's shamming dead," I said.

The dog was lying flat on his side, with his eyes closed and all four legs crooked and limp, as if he had broken them.

"Come on," Biff said and began trying to pull him to his feet by the collar.

Bonzo didn't get up. All that happened was that Biff pulled him about a foot along the grass and then dropped him in the same position.

"Perhaps he's hurt," I said. "Perhaps it's the thistle in his foot."

Even Biff didn't think that was silly and we spent some time trying to clean his feet of thistles. Each time we lifted a foot it dropped back again as if it was dead.

"Now you can come," Biff said. "You're all right now, Bonzo. Come on now—come on, boy."

Biff pulled hard on the string in a sudden jerk and Bonzo actually got to his feet. A moment later he started to behave like a mule. He dug his hind legs into the grass and showed a thin slip of his teeth and hardened the muscles of his chest so that Biff couldn't drag him.

"Come on," Biff said. "You've got to come. Push him. Push him from behind."

The first moment we pushed him he let out a growl. It was the first time he had growled at us all day. It was guttural and hard. I didn't like it. Then I remembered suddenly that if dogs bit you you went mad and then you died.

"He won't bite us, will he?" I said.

"Not if you're not *frit* of him," Biff said. "If you're frit he'll bite you. He knows you're not master if you're frit. You've got to be master. Come on, Bonzo. I'll show you who's master."

Biff went on for about another five minutes trying to show Bonzo who was master. It was very hot trying to lug Bonzo to his feet and soon Biff's eyes began to look more and more like jelly beans and his glasses were misty with sweat. All the time Bonzo dug his legs into the grass, like a mule, and wouldn't budge. Once or twice he let out another growl and once he lay down again, his feet crooked and stiff and his eyes closed.

Then Janey tried with him. She lifted one of the lids of his eyes and peered into it. "Why won't you come, Bonzo?" she said. "Bonzo, look at me," but she might have been peering into an empty buttonhole.

"We'll just have to go in and tell the people we've got him out here," she said.

"Who's going?" Biff said.

"You go," Janey said.

"I've done all the pulling and tugging," Biff said. "You go."

"You're the biggest," she said.

I was suddenly afraid they would send me because I was the smallest and I began to feel cold in my neck, my hair tingling like little watch springs.

"I'm fagged out," Biff said. "I want to lay down and get my puff back."

"If somebody doesn't tell them we'll have to go to the police station," Janey said.

"Don't let's go to the police station," I said. "You know what the man said."

"They might lock us up," Janey said. "They might say we stole the dog."

That seemed to impress Biff and he started hesitating. After he had hesitated a moment or two Janey said:

"Go on, Biff. You're the bravest. You always are."

I think Biff liked that. He didn't look half so fagged out after that and he said:

"I've got to clean my specs first though. You hold him tight while I clean my specs."

Then he took off his glasses and huffed on them and started polishing them on his handkerchief, sometimes squinting through them, so that he looked funnier and more boss-eyed than ever. I thought he spent a little more time on his glasses than usual and sometimes you might have thought he was a soldier, polishing his kit before going on parade.

Then he stood up. He pulled his big brown cap lower over his eyes and said:

"Hold on to him hard. Both of you. One of you take his collar and the other hold the string."

"All right," we said and we crouched down low in the grasses, holding Bonzo down.

Then Biff walked down the road to the house. I was glad I didn't have to go to that house, with its queer churchy windows, the black yew trees that made me unhappy and the way it seemed to stand neglected and isolated, in a gap in the woods, at a dead end.

When Biff got to the house he went round the back of it and knocked on the kitchen door. The farm-yard was empty. He told us afterwards he knocked three or four times and that no one answered. Then he thought he heard sounds from somewhere farther along that side of the house and he thought they seemed to come from an out-house, a wash-house or a dairy, at the end of the path.

He went along the path until he got to an open door. It was in fact just a sort of out-house and inside it was a girl. She was sitting on a chair, plucking a chicken, and she was wearing a black pinafore.

Somehow, by the way she looked up at him, big-eyed and startled, he knew that she was frightened. He was half-frightened himself and he started to ask her if her name was Slater. As he said that she gave a sudden start, half-getting up from the chair, so that before she could prevent it the half-plucked chicken slipped from her lap and she just grabbed it in time, by one leg, before it fell to the floor.

"What made you ask that?" she said. "Who are you? Where did you come from?"

"I've got your dog," Biff said. "I've got Bonzo."

She stood up, still holding the chicken by its leg, loose and naked, at her side. She was a tall girl, with a lot of heavy black hair, and no colour in her face except brown smoky circles under her eyes. Biff thought she looked about nineteen or twenty. He couldn't tell. Perhaps she was more, perhaps twenty-five. He hadn't time to think much about things like that before she suddenly grabbed him and pulled him into the out-house and started jabbering questions.

"What made you think my name was Slater?" she said. "Where did you find the dog?"

She jabbered so fast, her mouth loose and quivering, that he never got the break of a second to answer a single question until she had been talking for several minutes. Then she seemed to think of something. For a moment she actually stopped talking and looked out of the door quickly, up and down the yard.

Then he said: "We got him from a man. In a barn. He said we could—"

"What barn? Where? What barn?"

She suddenly knelt down and gripped him by the hands.

"Tell me what barn. Where? Where is it? Tell me where it was."

He began to try to tell her where it was but she interrupted him again, shaking him backwards and forwards nervously, her eyes big and close to his face.

"What was he like?" she said. "Had he got grey hair? Were his hands big? What was he doing there?"

"He was acting funny," Biff said.

"How? How do you mean? Where? How do you mean he was acting?—funny? How?"

Biff started to tell her how we had seen the man drink the barrel water and gnaw raw meat off the bone but again she didn't let him get very far. Again she smothered him with questions. Then at last she suddenly dropped the chicken on the chair and seized hold of his hands and said:

"Where did you say you had the dog? Where?"

"Just down the road," he said. He hadn't told her before. She hadn't given him a chance and now he thought she would cry as he told her.

"How far down the road?" she said.

"A little way—"

"You go back," she said. "You go back now and start walking down the road. You start walking. Start walking, don't speak to anybody and in a minute I'll catch up with you."

A moment later, and before he could move to go, she was standing bolt upright. At the same time she made a grab for the chicken. She actually started plucking at it with her free hand, not looking at it. All the time she was staring at the doorway and when Biff turned he saw what she was looking at.

In the doorway was a man. He was tall too and thin, with straight black trousers held up by a belt. Biff took particular notice of the belt because it was like one his father used on him sometimes when the meat got into him and he was liverish and tatchy.

The man was slightly hump-shouldered too, in the sort of way that men get when they work on the land, stooping, and there was something peculiar about his eyes. Biff said he thought at first he was cock-eyed, like himself, and then he saw that the lid of one eye had been cut badly and hadn't healed properly, so that one side of it was screwed up by a dark scar, giving it a leer.

"Catch up?" he said. "Catch up with who?"

She didn't answer. Her eyes looked frozen while her hands darted about the chicken, plucking it.

"Who's this?" the man said. His voice was hollow, crabby and grating. "Who's he?"

Then before the girl could stop him Biff said:

"I brought a dog back. Is your name Slater?"

"Who?" The man turned on him sharply and swiftly. The shadow of an arm hooked over and the girl jabbered:

"Don't tell him nothing. Don't tell him nothing. Don't tell him."

"What dog? What dog?" the man said. Biff tried to step backwards out of the out-house but the man put his foot in the doorway and said: "No you don't. What dog? Who sent you here?"

"Don't tell him!" the girl shouted.

"Shut your mouth!" he said to her. "I'm talking—"

"Run," she said. "Run. You run now."

"Nobody's running," the man said. "Not him and not you. The only one who's running ain't here and ain't likely to be—"

"Run," she said. "You run now."

She made a sudden imploring gesture with her hands, forgetting the chicken. It slipped out of her grasp, falling to the floor.

Before she could move to pick it up the man stooped and grabbed it by the legs. For a moment Biff thought he would hit her with it. He actually swung it in the air and the girl actually put her hands to her face to protect herself, saying:

"You hit me. Go on. Hit me. You hit me again and see. You hit me once before—I thought you'd learnt that lesson—"

"I'm your father, ain't I?" he said. "I ain't your father for nothing, am I?"

"You can hit me a thousand times," she said, "and it won't make no difference. I want him and I'll have him—chance what you say—"

He suddenly threw the chicken down on the table. She didn't flinch this time. She stood her ground, Biff said bolt upright, her eyes staring. The man made a guttural sound in his throat—it might have been that he was going to spit at her, Biff thought—and then he seemed to realize, for the first time, that Biff had heard all that was going on and he said:

"You git outa here. Go on. Make yourself scarce and don't come nosin' round folk's back-doors another time. Go on!" He started shouting suddenly. "Go on—!"

Biff was frightened and started running. He hadn't gone more than half a dozen steps down the path before she sprang to the door and screamed after him:

"His name's Slater. That man—the man in the barn. Tell him it's all right—tell him to come here—"

"You tell him no such thing!" the man yelled. "Git out on it afore I limb you—you and the dog too!"

The girl broke free and started to run down the path. After a few paces the man caught up with her and after that all Biff could hear was his voice, shouting:

"He thought he'd killt me, didn't he? How many more times do I have to din it into you? It's all over and done with, I tell you, it's finished. Get that into your daft miserable head! Any more from you and I'll shoot you and him and the dog too."

At the gate of the yard Biff's fingers were trembling so much that, for a moment, he couldn't undo the latch. And as he stood there trembling and fumbling he thought he recognized a familiar sound; the swish of a strap and the sound of a buckle beating.

I suppose we had been sitting by the pond for ten minutes or so, resting in the shade of the elder-trees, behind the thick tall lines of reed, when the dog began to behave queerly for the second time.

This time he didn't lie down and stiffen himself and pretend to be dead. He suddenly stood up, looked in the direction of the woods and cocked his ears. Then his throat began to quiver, giving out a low rumble, like a toy dynamo. Then suddenly his tail went up and you could feel him bristling.

"I think he can smell a rabbit or something," I said.

"He can *hear* something," Biff said. All about us there was nothing but the deep soundless calm of afternoon, stretching far away through long woods, hot and without a breath of air. "Dogs can hear things people can't. Listen!"

We lay and listened. With my face in the grass I held my breath, hearing nothing but the tiny whirr of insects in the heat, hidden somewhere among grass and reeds. Then suddenly I couldn't hold my breath any longer. I gulped and a puff of grass seed seemed to get into my mouth, so that I choked and started coughing.

"Shut up!" Biff said.

"I can't help it—"

"Shut up," he whispered.

We lay for a few moments longer, listening. This time I lay on my side and the grasses looked like a gold forest, the tallest stalks like trees, the bits of totty-grass trembling like ferns above red-yellow tufts of egg-and-bacon flowers. There was still nothing I could hear except the click and whirr of insects about the pond and then Biff said:

"You keep hold of Bonzo. I'm going to look out on the road."

We watched him squirm on his belly round the pond. He looked like an Indian tracking animals. As I watched him I wished I was an Indian too and we had a wigwam to sleep in, with Janey as our squaw. Then Biff disappeared behind a hawthorn bush and I couldn't see him for a time.

But presently I saw his face in the grasses, turning to come back to us. Whenever Biff was specially excited his spectacles slipped a bit—they were really always too big for him and sometimes he wound bits of wool round the bridge to keep them on his nose a little better—and his eyes started groping and getting bigger and bigger as they tried to look through the lenses and not over the top.

By the time he crawled back to us his spectacles were almost on the end of his nose.

"It's the man," he said. "The one from the house. He's coming down the road with a gun."

As we slipped down the bank and lay still further in the reeds I could still hear nothing but the sound of insects clicking and whirring in the hot afternoon. The dog had stopped his grumbling. Now we made him lie down too and Biff unbuttoned his jacket and wrapped it over his head.

After we had been lying there like that for a minute or two, the dog not moving now or making a sound, I began to hear the footsteps of the man coming down the road between the woods. The road was not more than ten or fifteen yards away from us and the footsteps were slow and shuffling on the dry loose stones.

It seemed hours before they stopped. All the time I was afraid I would start choking again and I kept my hands over my mouth, pressing my head against the hard clay bank of the pond and shutting my eyes. I opened them only once, just for a second, and I saw that Janey had her eyes closed too. But her lashes were quivering and she was biting her bottom lip hard on one side.

Soon the man started walking again. At first I couldn't tell if he was walking farther down the road or if he had turned now and was walking back again, towards the house. In the middle of wondering I thought of the house and how dark it was, with the big yews and the strange churchy-coloured windows, and how it seemed cut off from everywhere, isolated in the clearing of the woods, at the beginning of nowhere.

Then after a long time I couldn't hear the footsteps. It was not only quiet in the afternoon. The air was tingling everywhere and it made you tremble in your veins. At the same time I couldn't be sure if the man had walked away altogether or if he was still there, somewhere on the road, behind a hawthorn bush, watching and waiting for us to move.

I think we might have gone on lying there until darkness if it hadn't been, once again, for the dog. All of a sudden he struggled out from under Biff's jacket, stood on his feet and shook himself from head to foot with a shudder.

After that he went down to the edge of the pond and started drinking. The sound of him lapping the water was like somebody clapping their hands.

"Were you frit?" Biff said.

"No," I said.

"No," Janey said.

The three of us were lying there with him, at the foot of the bank, not drinking but dabbling our hands in cool water and then splashing it over our faces and our hair.

"I think Bonzo was a bit frit though," Biff said.

"I wasn't frit until Bonzo was," I said.

"Nor was I," Janey said. "I wasn't frit till he was."

"Good old Bonz," Biff said. "Good old boy. Good Bonz."

"What are we going to do with him now?" Janey said.

"That's it," Biff said."What are we going to do with him? What are we going to do with you, Bonz, eh?"

Biff stroked Bonzo on the back of his neck. The dog took a last lap of the pond-water and then hopped up the bank and started to walk towards the road. Our faces and hands were still wet as we followed him.

"Where shall we take him?" Janey said.

"We'll stop at the end of the road," Biff said, "and have a pow-wow. You haven't tried your house, yet," he said to me.

After that we took another look up the road, at the long dusty white slit of gravel narrowing away between parched summer woods, empty in the straight sunlight, and then started running.

We were still running, the dog in front of us, when about half a mile down the road a figure suddenly came running out of the woods to meet us.

It was the girl and she hadn't even washed the blood from her arms.

She was carrying a bag now, a sort of oil-cloth bag, black and shining, with a string handle, just like the one my grandmother used for bringing tea to us in the harvest field. You could see bits of clothing and newspaper sticking out of the top of it, as if she hadn't had time to pack it properly. She also had a comb in her free hand and two hair-pins in her mouth, but when she stopped she pushed the comb into the bag and started to fix the pins in her hair.

"Where's that man?" she said. "The one you saw? The one you told me about? All right, Bonzo, all right. Down now, Bonzo, down."

We started to tell her that the man was in the stable but the dog was so excited, whimpering and crying, jumping up against her skirt and twisting his body to and fro in excitement, that I don't know if she heard us or not.

All she said was: "Could you take me there? Could you show it to me, please?" and she said this several times, still trying to fix the pins in her hair with one hand. Once or twice she looked back up the road but there was no sign of anyone there and Biff said:

"That man started coming. He was coming down there with a gun in his hands."

"That's all right. That doesn't matter," she said. "You tell me where the other man was. Where was he?"

The dog was a little quieter by that time. She was able to hear what we said about the stable.

"You get to it by a track," we said. "Across fields. Nobody lives there."

"Take me," she said. "Show me, will you? Is there a short cut there?"

"We can go by the brook," Janey said.

"There isn't a bridge that way," I said.

"We can paddle over in the shallow place by the spring," Biff said. "Where the sticklebacks are."

"Do we have to go through the town that way?" the girl said.

"No," Biff said. "No. Nowhere near the town."

"That's good," she said. "That's good. I don't want to go near the town."

Except that she had to stop once and put down the bag, and refix the pins in her hair because they had fallen loose again she hardly changed her pace as we went with her through the fields, by the short cut, along by the brook where we sometimes fished for sticklebacks and occasionally saw a kingfisher shooting down through the willow-herb and the reeds.

There was a kingfisher there that afternoon. It came swooping downstream in such a flash of blue and copper, crying thinly, that I was startled and Janey let out a little cry. But the girl either didn't see it or didn't give it a second thought if she did. She just kept walking, not so very fast, as it seemed, but with long strides, springing on her heels and swinging her long scarred arms. All the time her head was slightly down. Her thick hair kept falling into her neck and sometimes partly on to her shoulders.

At one of the stiles we had to climb she turned on us without really stopping and said:

"When did you first see him? How long ago was that?"

"In the morning," Biff told her. "A long time ago."

You like some people the first time you see them, even if they're not very happy. I could see that she was not happy. I didn't know why, but her eyes were dark and the way she kept trying to pin up her hair was troubled and restless and queer. But I knew I liked her and because I liked her I felt there was something she ought to know.

"I think he'll be dead by now," I said. "I think he was going to die—"

"What makes you say that?" she said. She turned on me with big scared eyes, walking sideways, all twisted, her hair falling over one side of her face. "Die?—why?—why would he die?"

"Because he drank water," I said. "Water with worms in it. Out of a barrel. If you do that you die."

She laughed. Biff said I was only half-sharp. Janey laughed at me too and I felt hurt and ashamed at what I had said. But the girl laughed again, longer this time, the sound almost happy, and then suddenly she ruffled her hand in my hair and said:

"You'll do. You're all right. You keep me laughing, won't you?"

A few moments later we crossed the stream. It was only two or three inches deep there and full of flat white stones. There were always sticklebacks there and minnows that came darting out from under the shadow of the stones and I remembered how once we had caught crayfish under a stone and didn't know what it was.

The first to go through the stream was Bonzo and then after him the girl. She went over with the same long springing strides as she had used all the way up through the fields and now she seemed completely unaware of the stones. She went straight through the water up to her ankles, slopping forward, her shoes oozing water as she climbed the bank on the other side.

"How much farther?" She turned and almost shouted at us, as if we were still some distance behind.

"You got your feet all wet," I said. "Look at your shoes—"

She didn't look at her shoes. Instead she looked up at the sky and I saw the sun shine flat into her large dark eyes with their heavy under-bruises, and in the steely forks of the pins that she still hadn't fixed properly into her hair.

"How much farther now?" she said. "Is it far?"

"You can almost see it now," Biff said. "You'll see it when we get to the top of the field."

At the crest of the slope that went up from that side of the stream ran a line of hawthorn trees with cow-worn trunks, where that afternoon sheep were lying, panting in the shade. These trees cut off, until you got near enough to see through them, the view over the fields towards the bullock-yard, the stable and the barn.

She reached the trees, with Bonzo, half a minute before us. She didn't seem to see the sheep, any more than she had seen the stones in the brook. She simply went blundering under the trees without stopping, making the sheep stumble up on their knees and then herd away together, bunting and alarmed, disturbed by the dog, into deeper shade.

After that we didn't try to catch her. By the time we got to the bullock-yard she had disappeared through the door of the stable, which was open now.

All I could see was the white shape of Bonzo, squatting on the threshold, a white splash that looked no bigger than a bird-dropping in the black covering shadow of the sycamore.

If it had seemed an hour or so while we waited by the pond for the man with the gun to move away it seemed like a whole afternoon while we waited, sitting on the gate of the bullock-yard, for someone to come out of the stable and into the yard.

Once I thought of the man being dead from drinking water. I even thought I wanted him to be dead. Then Biff and Janey would know that I was right and wouldn't laugh at me any more.

"I think he's died," I said. "I think he's dead from the water."

"Oh! What the pipe," Biff said. "Everybody's always dead with you. You always imagine things. Sit still. You'll make me drop my glasses. We shan't bring him next time, shall we, Janey? It'll be just me and you next time, won't it, Janey?"

"I think he's dead too," she said. "If he's not, why is she so long in there?"

After that Biff didn't say so much. He went on huffily polishing his glasses over and over again, taking them off and then squinting through them and putting them back on his nose again.

Suddenly I knew that Janey was frightened. She jumped down from the gate and started to walk away.

"Let's hide," she said. "I don't want to see any dead people. They have their eyes open and they never shut them."

That was too much for me too. I knew the man must be dead now. I jumped down from the gate too, and then Biff jumped down. Then we all looked through the bars of the gate but there was still nothing to be seen outside the stable but the white shape of Bonzo in the open stable door, in the great dark shade of the sycamore.

"Where shall we hide?" I said.

We ran some distance along the cart-track. Then we hid behind a bush of elderberry. We sat there for a long time without speaking, smelling the rank deep odour of elderberry stems, waiting for something to happen, and then Janey, who was always so quick, said:

"I heard the gate click. Didn't you hear?"

A minute or so later the man and the girl walked past us, down the track. I noticed the girl had washed the blood from her arms and had combed and pinned her hair. Only a second or two later Bonzo came after them, ten or fifteen feet behind. The man was carrying the black oil-cloth bag now and the dog seemed to fix his eyes on it, his nose close to the ground. With his other hand the man had taken the girl by the shoulders, and his hand kept moving across her shoulder, smoothing it down.

"Bonzo," we whispered. "Here. Good Bonzo. Here, Bonz, old boy—here."

He went straight past us without looking at the elderberry tree. His eyes were simply fixed on the feet of the man, the wet shoes of the girl and the oil-cloth bag. We whispered after him once or twice again but he took no notice. The last we saw of him was when he squirmed through the gap of the hedge and turned, following the girl and the man down the road.

"Come on," Biff said. "Let's see where they go."

Twenty minutes later we were standing on the high iron railway bridge that spanned the single-track line at the little branch station on that side of the town. We had to wait about ten minutes for the signals to change for the train. During all that time the man and the girl, with Bonzo, stood on the platform, below us and about thirty yards away.

I noticed they didn't talk much. Sometimes the man looked up and down the track in the evening sunshine. His face, I thought, didn't look so old any longer. It didn't look so grey and prickled and drawn as before. He even smiled once or twice. And once I saw the girl stare quickly down at the platform, biting her lips, rather as if she couldn't bear it if he smiled.

Then the train came in, making clouds of smoke, as it went under the bridge where we were looking through the ironwork. By the time the smoke had begun to clear away the train had stopped in the station, doors were opening and shutting, and in another moment or two the man and the girl were in the train.

For a moment or two Bonzo was alone on the platform. Then Biff put his fingers into his mouth and gave a quick sharp whistle and the dog looked up. It seemed, for a second or two, as if he had heard us and knew we were there. Then there was another whistle, this time from the guard of the train, and in another second the dog jumped into the train.

"Good old Bonz," Biff said. The train began to draw out of the station, its smoke dark yellow against the sun. "So long, Bonz."

"So long, Bonz," I said.

"So long, Bonz," Janey said. "Goodbye."

That night it was still light when I went to bed. It was hot in the bedroom and I was still excited. But I was not so excited about Bonzo, the man with the gun, and what a great and wonderful day it had been as about another thing.

"You said you could die," I told my father, "if you drank water out of a barrel. But there was a man today, he had a dog named Bonzo and he drank water with worms in it and he didn't die."

"Go to sleep now," my father said. "Never mind about that. I said you would die *after it*. That's all. Go to sleep now."

But I couldn't sleep. For a long time I lay awake, staring at the summer sky as it darkened, pale yellow to orange and then to the dusky colour of the smoke from the train. After the long day I was tired but not sleepy and I wasn't frightened any more. Now I knew that you didn't always die when you thought you would and that often, after all, there was no need to be afraid.

I began to think instead about the martin's eggs. We had four eggs. Biff had two, Janey one, and I had the other. In the morning I would make two pin-holes in my egg, blow it into a cup and then hang it in my bedroom on a string.

DEATH OF A HUNTSMAN

Every weekday evening, watches ready, black umbrellas neatly rolled and put away with neat black homburgs on carriage racks, attaché cases laid aside, newspapers poised, the fellow-travellers of Harry Barnfield, the city gentlemen, waited for him to catch—or rather miss—the five-ten train.

As the last minutes jerked away on the big station clock above wreaths of smoke and steam the city gentlemen sat with jocular expectation on the edges of carriage seats or actually craning necks from carriage windows, as if ready to check with stop watches the end of Harry Barnfield's race with time.

"Running it pretty fine tonight."

"Doomed. Never make it."

"Oh! trust Harry."

"Absolutely doomed. Never make it."

"Oh! Harry'll make it. Trust Harry. Never fluked it yet. Trust Harry."

All Harry Barnfield's friends, like himself, lived in the country, kept farms at a heavy loss and came to London for business every day. J.B. (Punch) Warburton, who was in shipping and every other day or so brought up from his farm little perforated boxes of fresh eggs for less fortunate friends in the city, would get ready, in mockery, to hold open the carriage door.

"Action stations." J. B. Warburton, a wit, was not called Punch for nothing. "Grappling hooks at ready!"

"This is a bit of bad. Dammit, I believe—" George Reed Thompson also had a farm. Its chief object, apart from losing money, was to enable him to stock a large deep-freeze every summer, with excellent asparagus, strawberries, raspberries, spring chickens, pheasant, partridges, and vegetables, all home-raised. "Harry's going to let us down—!"

"Nine-ten, nine-fifteen." Craning from the window, Freddie Jekyll, who was a stockbroker and rode, every spring, with great success at local point-to-points, would actually begin to check off the seconds. "Nine-twenty—"

"Officer of the watch, keep a sharp look-out there!"

"Aye, aye, sir."

"All ashore who are going ashore."

"Aye, aye, sir."

"A firm hold on those grappling hooks!"

"Dammit, he's missed it. I make it eleven past already."

Sometimes a whistle would blow; sometimes a final door would slam with doom along the far hissing reaches of the waiting express. But always, at last, without fail, the city gentlemen would be able to raise, at first severally and then collectively, a joyful, bantering cheer.

"Here, Harry, here! Here, old boy!"

Cheering, signalling frantically from windows, thrusting out of it malacca handles of umbrellas as if they were really grappling hooks, they would drag Harry Barnfield finally aboard.

"Five-nine point twelve," they would tell him. "New world record."

Panting, smiling modestly from behind sweat-clouded spectacles, Harry Barnfield would lean shyly on the handle of his umbrella, struggling to recover breath. Laughing, the city gentlemen would begin to unfold their papers, offering congratulations.

"Well run, Harry. Damn near thing though, old boy. Thought you were doomed."

But that, they always told themselves, was the great thing about Harry. You could always rely on Harry. You could always be sure of Harry. Harry would never let you down.

What a good sport he was, they all said, Harry Barnfield. There were no two ways, no possible arguments about that. There was no shadow of harm in Harry Barnfield.

[2]

All his life Harry Barnfield, who looked ten years more middle-aged than forty-three, had been fond of horses without ever being a good rider of them.

His body was short and chunky. It had the odd appearance, especially when he rode a horse, of having had a middle cut of six or seven inches removed from between ribs and groin, leaving the trunk too short between legs and shoulders. It was also rather soft, almost pulpy, as if his bones had never matured. This pulpiness was still more noticeable in the eyes, which behind their spectacles were shy, grey, protuberant and rather jellified, looking altogether too large for his balding head.

All this gave him, in the saddle, a floppy, over-eager air and, as the black tails of his coat flew out behind, the look of a fat little bird trying hard to fly from the ground and never quite succeeding. Riding, he would tell you, was awful fun, and his voice was high and squeaky.

Every evening, ten minutes before the arrival of the train that brought him back to the country with his friends the city gentlemen, he started to give a final polish to his spectacles, the lenses of which were rather thick. For five minutes or so he polished them with scrupulous short-sightedness on a square of cream silk that he kept in his breast pocket, huffing on them with brief panting little breaths, showing a pink, lapping tongue.

The effect of this scrupulous preparation of the spectacles was to make his face seem quite absurdly alight. Smiling from behind the glittering lenses, calling good night to his friends, he came out of the station with wonderful eagerness, head well in front of the chunky body, black umbrella prodding him forward, attaché case paddling the air from the other hand, bowler hat tilted slightly backward and sitting on the loose crimson ears.

Once out of the station he sucked in a long deep breath—as if to say: ah, at last, the country! The short little body seemed transformed with eager exhilaration. Fields came down almost to within reach of the fences surrounding the station coal-yards and on late spring evenings the greening hedges were brilliant and thick as banks of parsley. Primroses and sprays of pale mauve lady-smocks sprang lushly from damp dykes below the hedgerows and along the roads beyond these were black-boughed cherry orchards in white thick bloom. A few weeks later apple orchards and great snow mounds of hawthorn came into blossom and in the scent of them he could taste the first milkiness of summer just as surely as he tasted winter in the first sweet-acid tang of the big-toothed Spanish

chestnut leaves as they began to swim down from the trees in
November, haunting the dark staves of baring copses.

Then, as he drove home in his car, much of his eagerness
vanished. He gradually took on the air of being calm and free: free
of the dusty odours of city offices, city termini, free of his friends
the city gentlemen in the smoky train. His body relapsed completely into quietness. His big eyes stopped their agitation and
became, behind the bulging lenses of the spectacles, perfectly,
blissfully at rest.

It took him twenty minutes to drive out to the big double-gabled
house of old red brick that had, behind it, a row of excellent stables
with a long hay-loft above. He had been awfully lucky, he would
tell you, to get the house. It was absolutely what he wanted. The
stables themselves were perfect and at the front were four good
meadows, all flat, bordered by a pleasant alder-shaded stream.

The fields were about twenty acres in all, and from three of them,
in June, he gathered all the hay he would need. Then in early
autumn he took down part of the fences and put up a run of four
brushwood jumps and over these, on Saturdays and Sundays, he
started practising jumping. Sometimes, too, in the same inelastic
way that never improved during the entire hunting season, he
practised jumping the brook. Then by late November the alders lost
the last of their leaves; the hazels, the willows and the sweet
chestnuts became naked too and presently he could feel the sting of
frost in his nostrils as he brought his horse in through the blue-grey
twilights across which the sound of croaking pheasants settling to
roost clattered like wintry frightened laughter.

"That you, Harry? I hope to God you didn't forget the gin?"

"Yes, it's me, Katey."

If it had not been that he was almost always blinking very slightly,
with a sort of mechanical twitch, behind the glasses, it might have
seemed that he had never lost the habit of surprise as his wife called
to him, her voice somewhere between a croak and a cough, from
the kitchen.

It might also have seemed, from the snap in her voice, that she
was not very tolerant of forgetfulness. But fortunately neither
surprise nor forgetfulness were habits of his. He was never surprised
and he never forgot the gin.

"On the hall table, Katey," he would tell her. "Any message from Lewis? I'm just hopping across the yard."

His inquiry about Lewis, his groom, was never answered, except by another cough, and this never surprised him either. His only real thought was for his horses. In summer he had only to whistle and they came to him from across the meadows. In winter he walked quietly across the courtyard to the stables, let himself in, touched for a moment the warm flanks of the two animals, said good night to them exactly as if they were children and then, almost on tip-toe, let himself out again. Outside, if there were stars, he generally stopped to look up at them, breathing over again the good country air. Then he stiffened, braced his short pulpy body and went back into the house again.

"Where the hell did you say the gin was? Every bloody evening you slink off like a badger and I'm left wondering where you dump the stuff."

"I told you where it was, Katey." From the hall table he would quietly pick up the gin-bottle and take it to the kitchen. "Here. Here it is."

"Then why the hell couldn't you say so?"

"I did say so."

"You talk like a squeak-mouse all the time. How do you expect me to hear if you talk like a damn squeak-mouse?"

His wife was tallish, fair and very blowsy. She looked, he always thought, remarkably like some caged and battered lioness. Her hair, which she wore down on her shoulders, had passed through several stages of blondeness. Sometimes it was almost white, bleached to lifelessness; sometimes it was the yellow of a ferret and he would not have been surprised, then, to see that her eyes were pink; sometimes it was like coarse rope, with a cord of darker hair twisting through the centre. But the most common effect was that of the lioness, restless, caged and needing a comb.

"Any news, Katey?" he would say. "Anything been happening?"

"Where, what and to whom?" she would ask him. "To bloody whom? Tell me." The fingers of both hands were stained yellow with much smoking. Her lips were rather thick. She had also mastered the art of getting a cigarette to stick to the lower, thicker one without letting it fall into whatever she was cooking. She was

very fond of cooking. The air, every evening, was full of odours of
herbs, garlic, wine vinegars and frying onions. The smell of frying
onions invariably made him ravenously hungry but it was always
nine o'clock, sometimes ten, occasionally still later, before she
would yell across the hall to where he sat sipping sherry in the
drawing-room:

"Come and get it if you want it. And if you don't want it—" the
rest of the sentence asphyxiated in coughing.

Sometimes, so late at night, he did not want it. Excellent though
the food often was, he found himself not hungry any more. He sat
inelastically at table, ate with his fork and sipped a glass of claret,
perhaps two. She, on the other hand, more than ever like the
lioness, ravenous far beyond feeding time, ate eyelessly, no longer
seeing the food, the table or himself through mists of gin.

"Forgot to tell you—Lewis saw that kid riding through the place
again today. Rode clean through the courtyard, by the cucumber
house and out the other side."

"Good Heavens, didn't Lewis choker her off?"

"Gave her hell he says."

"And what happened? What did she say?"

"Said she'd been told it was perfectly all right. You'd never
mind."

"But good grief," he said, "we can't have that. We can't have
strangers riding through the place as if it's their own. That won't
do. That simply won't do—"

"All right," she said. "All right. You tell her. I've told her. Lewis
has told her. Now you tell her. It's your turn."

She lit a cigarette, pushed more food into her mouth and began
laughing. A little stream of bright crimson tomato sauce ran down
her chin. A shred or two of tobacco clung to her front teeth and
there was actually a touch of pink, the first bloodshot vein or two,
in the whites of her eyes.

"But who *is* she?"

"Search me. *You* find out. It's *your* turn—"

Open-mouthed, she laughed again across the table, the cigarette
dangling this time from the lower lip as she mockingly pointed her
glass at his face.

He knew that this gesture of fresh derision meant that she no longer saw him very well. Already the eyes had begun their swimming unfocused dilations.

"All right," he said. "I'll speak to her."

"Good," she said. "That's the brave Harry. Brave old Harry."

As she threw back her head, laughing openly now, letting the cigarette fall into her plate of half-eaten food, revealing relics of her last mouthful smeared across her lips and her tongue, he did not ask himself why he had ever married her. It was too late for asking that kind of question.

"When does she appear?" he said.

"Oh! off and on. Any time. On and off—"

"I'll try to catch her on Saturday," he said. "Or Sunday."

Derisively and deliberately she raised her hand, not laughing now, in a sort of mock benediction.

"Now don't be rash, Harry dear. Brave old Harry," she said. "Don't be rash. She might catch you."

[3]

On the following Sunday morning, as he walked up past the cucumber house to where a path led through two wicket gates to the meadows beyond, a light breeze was coming off the little river, bringing with it the scent of a few late swathes of hay. The glass of the cucumber house, with its dark green under-tracery of leaves, flashed white in the sun. The summer had been more stormy than fine, with weeks of August rain, and now, in mid-September, the fields were flush with grasses.

He stopped to look inside the cucumber house. Under the glass the temperature had already risen to ninety-five. Thick green vines dripped with steamy moisture. Columns of cucumbers, dark and straight, hung down from dense masses of leaves that shut out the strong morning sun.

The cucumbers were his wife's idea. She was very imaginative, he had to admit, about cucumbers. Whereas the average person merely sliced up cucumbers, made them into sandwiches or simply ate them with fresh salmon for lunch in summer, his wife was acquainted with numerous recipes in which cucumbers were cooked, stuffed like aubergines or served with piquant sauces or

high flavours such as Provençale. Harry Barnfield did not care much
for cucumbers. More often than not, cooked or uncooked, they
gave him wind, heartburn or chronic indigestion. But over the years
of his married life he had learned to eat them because he was too
good-natured to deny his wife the chance of surprising guests with
dishes they had never heard of before. He well understood her
cucumbers and her little gastronomic triumphs with them.

That Sunday morning, as he stood under the steaming shadowy
vines, he thought he saw, suddenly, a bright yellow break of
sunlight travel the entire length of the glasshouse outside. The
leaves of the cucumbers were so thick that it was some moments
before he grasped that this was, in fact, a person riding past him on
a horse.

Even then, as he discovered when he rushed out of the cucumber
house, he was partly mistaken. The horse was merely a pony,
blackish brown in colour, with a loose black tail.

With impatience he started to shout after it: "Hi! you there!
Where do you think you're going? Don't you know—?" and then
stopped, seeing in fact that its rider was nothing more than a young
girl in a yellow sweater, jodhpurs, black velvet cap and pigtails. The
pigtails too were black and they hung long and straight down the
yellow shoulders, tied at the ends not with ribbon but with short
lengths of crimson cord.

The girl did not stop. He started to shout again and then, quite
without thinking, began to run after her.

"Young lady!" he called. "Young lady!—one moment, young
lady, one moment please—"

It was thirty or forty yards farther on before he caught up with
her. By that time she had stopped, bent down and was already
lifting the catch of the first of the wicket gates with the handle of
her riding-crop.

"Just a moment, young lady, just one moment—"

As he stopped he found himself short of breath and panting
slightly. She turned very slightly in the saddle to look at him. Her
eyes were brown, motionless and unusually round and large. They
seemed, like his own, rather too big for her face.

"Aren't you aware," he said, "that this is private property?—this
path? It's private property!"

She did not move. She looked, he thought, fifteen, perhaps sixteen, not more than that, though rather well developed for her age. The sleeves of the yellow jumper were half-rolled up, showing firm brown forearms that glistened with downy golden hairs. Her face was the same golden brown colour, the lips without make-up, so that they too had a touch of brown.

"You really can't ride through here like this," he said. "You've been told before. You really can't, you know."

Again she did not move. He did not know if the large motionless eyes were utterly insolent or merely transfixed in frightened innocence and he was still trying to make up his mind about it when he noticed how straight but relaxed she sat on the pony. He had to admit, even in vexation, that she sat very well; very well indeed, he thought.

"It's very tiresome," he said, "all this. You simply can't ride rough-shod over other people's property like this."

"Rough-shod?"

Her voice surprised him very much by its deepness. It almost seemed, he thought, like the voice of a woman twice her age.

"Do you really think," she said, "I'm riding rough-shod?"

The eyes, still holding him in enormous circles of inquiring innocence, disarmed him with sheer brightness.

"That's neither here nor there," he said. "The simple fact is that you cannot ride when and how you please over other people's property."

"I was told I could."

"Told? By whom?"

"My mother."

At this moment his spectacles began to mist over. For the next second or two she seemed to melt away and become lost to him.

Uneasily he thought to himself that he ought to take his spectacles off, polish them and put them back again. He began to feel inexplicably nervous about this and his hands groped about his face. Then when he realized that if he took off his spectacles he would, with his weak, short-sighted eyes, be able to see her even less well he made the unfortunate compromise of trying to look over the top of them.

She smiled.

"Your mother?" he said. "What has your mother to do with it? Do you mean I know your mother?"

"You *knew* her."

"Oh! and when pray would that be?"

He hadn't the slightest idea why he should ask that question and in fact she ignored it completely.

"My name is Valerie Whittington."

"Oh! yes. I see. Oh! yes," he said slowly. "Oh! yes." He was so intensely surprised that, without thinking, he at once took off his spectacles and rubbed the lenses on his coat sleeve.

"Is the colonel—?"

"He died last year."

Again he polished the lenses of the spectacles quickly on the coat sleeve.

"We've taken the gamekeeper's cottage at Fir Top. I don't suppose you know it," she said.

"Oh! yes."

Something made him keep the spectacles in his hand a little longer.

"I can ride down through the park and along by the river and then back through the woods across the hill," the girl said. "It's a complete circle if I taken the path through here. If not I have to go back the same way again and you know how it is. It's never so nice going back the same way."

He murmured something about no, it was never so nice and then put on his spectacles. Clear, fresh and with that remarkable blend of insolence and innocent charm, she stared down at him, making him feel a baffled, fumbling idiot.

"So it was your mother told you about the path?"

"She just said she was sure you wouldn't mind."

Why, he wondered, did she say that?

"She said you were the sort of man who never did mind."

Again he felt baffled and stupid.

Then, for the first time, the pony moved. Up to that moment she had kept remarkably still and it was in fact so quiet, standing erect in the hot September sun, that he had been almost unaware that it was there until now, suddenly, it reared its head and shuddered.

Instinctively he put one hand on its flank to calm it down. It quieted almost immediately and she said:

"I'm afraid he's really not big enough for me. But he's the best we can afford for the time."

She ran her hand down the pony's neck, leaning forward as she did so. He saw the muscles of the neck light up like watered silk. At the same time he saw the flanks of the girl tauten, smooth out and then relax again.

"Does your mother ride now?" he said.

"No," she said. "Not now."

"She used to ride very well."

"Yes. She said you'd remember."

Again he felt baffled; again he groped towards his spectacles.

"Well," she said. "I suppose I must go back."

She started to turn the pony round. He found all his many uncertainties stiffen into astonishment.

"I thought you wanted to go on?" he said—"over the hill?"

"You said you didn't want me to."

"Oh! yes I know, but that was—I admit—Oh! no—well I mean—" He found himself incapable of forming a coherent sentence. "By all means—it was simply that I didn't want—well, you know, strangers—"

"I ought to have come and asked you," she said. "I know now. But you were never at home."

"Oh! no, no, no," he said. "Oh! no."

The pony was still facing the cucumber house, uneasy now. Sunlight was catching the angle of the roof panes, flashing white glare into the animal's eyes in spite of the blinkers, and Harry Barnfield put his hand on its nose, steadying it down.

"I'll be putting up jumps next week," he said. "In the meadows there." The touch of the animal brought back a little, but only a little, of his assurance. "You could—well, I mean if you cared—you could use them. I'm never here weekdays."

She smiled as if to begin to thank him but a flash of light from the cucumber house once again caught the pony's eye, making it rear.

"You'd better turn him round," he said, "and take him along. It's the sun on the cucumber house."

"I will," she said.

He moved forward to unlatch the gate for her. The pony also moved forward. A new wave of uncertainty ran through Harry Barnfield and he said:

"Remember me to your mother, will you? If she would care—Oh! I don't suppose she would like a cucumber? We have masses. We have too many cucumbers by far."

"We neither of us care for them," she said, "but I'll tell her all the same."

She rode through the gate. He shut the gate after her, leaned on it and watched her ride, at a walk, up the path. After forty or fifty yards the path began to go uphill to where, against the skyline, clumps of pine grew from browning bracken hillocks before the true woods began. The morning was so clear that he could see on the tips of these pines the stiff fresh crusts of the light olive summer cones. He could see also the brown arms of the girl below the rolled sleeves of the yellow sweater, the flecks of white on the short legs of the pony and the knots of red on the pigtails.

He was suddenly aware that there was something disturbing about her without being able to say what it was. In that insolent innocent way of hers she rode very well, he thought, but the pony was quite ridiculous. Her body and the pony simply did not fit each other, any more than her body and her voice seemed part of the same person.

"Edna should get her a horse," he said aloud and then, with sweat breaking out again from under his misty spectacles, began to walk back to the cucumber house.

There he was overcome by embarrassment at remembering how he had been stupid enough to offer the girl a cucumber; and in remembering it forgot completely that he had called her mother by name.

[4]

Soon after that he began to come home on late September evenings to a recurrence of mild gin-dry quips from Katey. He did not really mind being quipped; the city gentlemen made him used to that sort of thing.

"Your girlfriend was jumping again today. Here most of the morning and back again before I'd swallowed lunch. Stayed till five. I'd have offered her a bed but I wasn't tight enough."

"I wish you wouldn't call her my girlfriend."

"Best I can think of, Harry. You put her up to this game."

Presently she began to use his jumps not only on weekdays but on Saturdays and Sundays too. Sometimes he would wake as early as eight o'clock, look out across the meadows and see the yellow sweater dipping between the barriers of brushwood.

He saw it also as it faded in the twilights. And always he was baffled by the ridiculous nature of the pony, the pigtails and the long impossibly dangling legs of the girl as she rode.

"Your girlfriend certainly works at it. Lewis tells me she was here at six the other morning. He was mad. The animal kicked up his mushrooms."

"I do wish you wouldn't call her my girlfriend. She's fifteen. Sixteen if she's that."

"From the day they're born," Katey said, "they're women. Never mind their age."

At first he found it an embarrassment, slight but uneasy, to join her at the jumps. He supposed it arose from the fact that in his inelastic way he often fell off the horse. That did not matter very much when he jumped alone but it was awkward, even painful when people were watching.

In this way he began to ride more cautiously, more dumpily, more stiffly than before. For two weekends he did not jump at all. At the third he heard a clatter of pony hooves on the stable yard, looked up to see her long legs astride the pony and heard her deep voice say:

"I thought you must be ill, Mr. Barnfield, because you weren't jumping. Mother sent me to inquire."

Her voice, deeper than ever, he thought, startled and disturbed him; and he fumbled for words.

"Oh! no, oh! no. Perfectly all right, thank you. Oh! no. It's just that the countryside has been looking so lovely that I've been giving the jumps a miss and riding up on the hill instead. In fact I'm just going up there now."

"Do you mind if I ride that way with you?" she said.

Some minutes later they were riding together up the hillside, under clumps of pines, along paths by which huge bracken fronds were already tipped with fox-brown. Late blackberries shone pulpy and dark with bloom in the morning sunlight and where the bracken cleared there ran rose-bright stains of heather, with snow-tufts of cotton-grass in seed.

"You can smell that wonderful, wonderful scent of pines," she said.

He lifted his face instinctively to breathe the scent of pines and instead was distracted, for it might have been the fiftieth time, by her incongruous legs scratching the lowest tips of bracken fronds as she rode.

"My wife and I were having a slight argument as to how old you were," he said. "Of course it's rude to guess a lady's age but—"

"Oh! I'm ancient," she said, "Positively and absolutely ancient."

He started to smile.

"And how old," she said, "did you say?"

"Oh! fifteen," he said at once, not really thinking at all. "Perhaps I'll give you sixteen."

"Give me sixteen," she said. "And then seventeen. And then eighteen. And then if you like—"

She stopped. Looking up from the pony she turned on him the enormous circular eyes that appeared so often to be full of naïve insolence and then waited for him, as it were, to recover his breath.

"And then nineteen. And then if you like, next month, you can come to my twentieth birthday."

He was too staggered to bring to this situation anything but absolute silence as they rode to the hill-top.

"I think you're surprised," she said.

"Oh! no. Oh! no," he said. "Well, yes and no, in a way—"

"Don't you think I look twenty?"

"Well, it's not always absolutely easy—"

"How do you demonstrate age?" she said and he rode to the crest of the hill-top without an answer, his head sweating under his close tweed cap, his spectacles misting and turning to a premature fog-bound landscape the entire valley of morning brilliance below.

He was temporarily saved from making a complete and disastrous fool of himself by hearing the pony breathing hard, in partial distress.

"I think you should give him a blow," he said. "It's a pretty long drag up here."

She thought so too and they both began dismounting. Then, as she swung to the ground, he had a second surprise.

This, he suddenly realized, was the first time he had actually seen her when not on the pony. Standing there, at his own level, she seemed to enlarge and straighten up. He was aware of a pair of splendid yellow shoulders. Riding had made her straight in the back, throwing her breasts well forward, keeping her head erect and high. She was also, he now discovered with fresh uneasiness, slightly taller than he was.

He turned away to tie his horse to a pine. When he had finished he looked round to see her walking, with surprisingly delicate strides for so tall a girl, towards the ridge of the hillside.

Finally she stopped, turned and waved to him. For a single moment he thought she had in her hand a flower of some kind and it looked, he thought, like a scarlet poppy. Then he saw that it was one of the cords she had snatched from her pigtails.

"Come over and look at the view," she called.

By the time he joined her she was sitting down in a patch of bracken. He sat down too: looking, not at the view below him, the map of copse and pasture and hedgerow flecked already with the occasional pure bright chrome of elm and hornbeam, the dense oaks and grass still green as summer, but at the sight of the girl now unplaiting and combing out the mass of bright brown hair into a single tail.

"You look surprised," she said. "But then I notice you always do."

She started to let her hair fall loosely over her shoulders, until it half-enclosed her face. Then she put her hand in the pocket of her jodhpurs and pulled out a powder compact, a lipstick and lastly a small oval mirror with a blue enamel back.

"Do you mind holding that?" she said.

He held the mirror in front of her face. Once or twice she stretched forward, touching his hand and moved the mirror to one side or the other.

In silence, for perhaps the next five minutes or so, he watched her make up her face. He saw the lips, freed of their dull brownness, thicken, becoming very full, almost over-full, in redness. He saw her smooth with the powder-pad the skin of her face, giving it a tone of milky brown.

Finally she threw back her hair from her shoulders and he had time to notice that the enlargement of the lips, so bright now and almost pouting, had the effect of bringing into proportion the large brown eyes.

"How do I look?" she said.

His immediate impression was that the make-up, the loosened hair and the fuller, brighter lips had softened her completely. It was very like the effect on parched grass of warm and heavy rain.

At the same time he could not help feeling desperately, awkwardly and embarrassingly sorry for her.

"Now do I look twenty?" she said.

It was on the tip of his tongue to say "More—older" and afterwards he knew that it would have pleased her very much if he had, but he said instead:

"What made you do that just now?—just here?"

"Oh! God!" she said and the sepulchral wretched cry of her deep voice shocked him so much that his mouth fell open, "I'm so miserable—Oh! God! I can't tell you how miserable I am."

She turned suddenly and, not actually sobbing but with a harsh choke or two, lay face downwards in the bracken, beating her hands on the ground.

Pained and discomforted, he started to move towards her. She seemed to sense the movement and half-leapt up.

"Don't touch me!" she howled.

It was the furthest thing from his mind. He stood for a moment with his mouth open and then started blunderingly to walk away.

"Where are you going?" she moaned.

At that second sepulchral cry he stopped.

"I thought you'd rather have it out by yourself."

"I don't want to have it out!" she said. "I don't want to have it out! I don't want to have it out!"

It was beyond him to understand and he wished unhappily that he were back home, jumping or talking to Lewis or having a glass of sherry with Bill Chalmers, his neighbour, or with Punch Warburton, who sometimes came over and talked horses and weather and general gossip before Sunday lunchtime.

"Then what do you want?" he said.

"God only knows," she said quietly. "God knows. God only knows."

By that time she was really crying and he was sensible enough to let her go on with it for another ten minutes or so. During that time he sat on the ground beside her, mostly staring uneasily across the bracken in fear that somebody he knew would come past and see him there.

That would be a miserable situation to be caught in, but as it happened, nobody came. There was in fact hardly a sound on the hill-top and hardly a movement except an occasional late butterfly hovering about the blackberries or a rook or two passing above the pines.

When she had finished crying she sat up. The first thing she did was to begin to wipe off the lipstick. She wiped it off quite savagely, positively scrubbing at it with a handkerchief, until her lips again had that dry brownish undressed look about them.

Then she started to plait her hair. When she had finished one plait she held the end of it in her mouth while she tied it with the cord. Then she did the same with the other. Finally she tossed the two plaits back over her shoulders and, with a rough hand sweep, straightened the rest of her hair flat with her hands.

"There," she said bitterly, "how will that do?"

The bitterness in her voice profoundly shocked him.

"It can't be as bad as all that," he said, "can it?"

Her eyes stared at him, blank and sour.

"As bad as all what?"

"Well, whatever—can't you tell me?"

"I've never told anybody," she said. "I wouldn't know how to begin."

He started to say something about how much better it was if you could get these things off your chest when he saw her standing up. Once again, for the second time that morning, he was aware of the splendid yellow shoulders, her tallness and the contradiction of the ridiculous scarlet-fastened pigtails with the rest of her body.

"I'd better get back," she said, "before she starts creating hell at me."

"She?"

"Mother," she said. "Oh! and by the way. I almost forgot. She sent a message for you."

"For me?"

"She says will you be sure to come along on Tuesday evening for a drink? She's having a few friends in. About seven o'clock."

He began to say something about his train not always getting in on time, but she cut him short:

"I think you'd better try and make it if you can. She said to tell you she positively won't take no for an answer."

"Well, I shall have to see—"

"You won't," she said. "You know mother, don't you?"

"I did know her. Years ago—"

"If you knew her then," she said, "you know her now."

He started to feel uneasy again at that remark and said something about he would do his best and did it include his wife, the invitation?

"Nothing was said about Mrs. Barnfield."

A few minutes later, at the crest of the hill, he was holding her foot in the stirrup while she mounted the pony. There was really no need for that piece of help of his, since she could almost have mounted the animal directly from the ground, but she seemed touched by it and turned and gave him, without a word, a short thankful smile.

This touched him too more than words could possibly have done and he mounted his horse in silence. After that they rode, also in silence, for two hundred yards along the hill-top to where the path forked and she said:

"This is my way back. Thank you for everything. Don't forget Tuesday. I'll get it in the neck if you do."

This again was beyond him and he said simply, raising his cap:

"I'll do what I can. Good-bye."

Then, turning to ride away, she gave him an odd miserable little smile and once again he found himself appalled by the ridiculous sight of her sitting on the pony. Somehow the picture was not only fatuous. It struck him as being infinitely lonely too.

"And no more crying now," he said. "No more of that."

She turned, rested one hand on the rump of the pony and stared, not at him but completely and far past him, with empty eyes.

"If you listen carefully," she said. "you'll probably hear me howling across the hill in the nighttime."

[5]

It was past half past seven and already dark, the following Tuesday evening, when he drove up to the old keeper's cottage on the opposite side of the hill. There were lights in the narrow mullioned windows of the little house but, much to his surprise, no other cars.

Edna Whittington herself came to the door to answer his ring, holding in her left hand a half-empty glass and a cigarette in a bright yellow amber holder.

"Sweet of you, Henry. Absolutely and typically sweet."

As she leaned forward so that he could kiss her first on one cheek and then the other he caught an overpowering fragrance, sickly in the night air. He did not fail to notice too how she called him Henry.

"But come in, Henry, come in, come in, you sweet man. Let's look at you."

He went in and, inside, discovered that the house was empty.

"I'm sorry I'm so late," he said.

With magenta-nailed fingers she took his black homburg hat and umbrella and laid them on a window sill. "The train lost time." He looked round the room to make perfectly sure, for a second time, about its emptiness. "Has everybody gone?"

"Everybody gone?"

"I thought it was a party."

"Party?" she said. "Whoever said it was a party?"

"Valerie."

"Oh! my little girl," she said. "That little girl of mine. My silly little girl."

He started to say that he thought the girl had been pretty emphatic about the party but Edna Whittington laughed, cutting him short, and said:

"She never gets it right, Henry. Never gets anything right, the silly child, just never gets it right."

"Isn't she here either?"

"Out to a little birthday party," she said. "Just a teeny-weeny affair."

She poured him a glass of sherry. Her voice was husky. It was nearly twenty-five years since he had seen her before and he remembered, in time, that the voice had always been husky.

"Well, cheers, Henry," she said. "Resounding numbers of cheers. Lots of luck."

She raised her glass, looking at him with chilled, squinting, remarkably white-blue eyes. Her hair was bluish too and there were shadows of blue, almost violet, in the powder on her face. Her chest, flattish, was steely and bare, except for a double row of pearls, to the beginnings of the creased pouches of her breasts, and her face had a strange bony prettiness except in the mouth, which twisted upward at one side.

"Come and sit here on the sofa and tell me all about yourself. Tell me about life. Here, dear man—not there. Just the old Henry—afraid something will bite you."

He did not think, he said, as he sat beside her on the settee, that he had anything very much of himself to tell; or of life for that matter.

"Well, I have," she said. "Here we've been in the neighbourhood six months and not a bleat from you."

"I honestly didn't know you were here."

"Then you honestly should have done. It was in all the papers. I mean about the colonel. Didn't you read about that?"

He had to confess, with growing wretchedness, that he hadn't even read in the papers about the colonel, who had dropped down of thrombosis a year before. Nevertheless he was, he said, very sorry. It was a sad thing, that.

"He'd got awfully fat," she said. "And of course marrying late and so on. He was a man of forty-five before Valerie was born."

He knew that it was not only the colonel but she too who had married very late. He sat thinking of this, sipping his sherry, watching a meagre fire of birch logs smouldering in the round black grate, and she said:

"Yes, I call it pretty stodgy, Henry. Two miles away and not a single lamb's peep out of you. The trouble is you live in a stew-pot."

"Now here, I say—"

"Well, don't you? Up to town with *The Times* in the morning. Down from town with the *Standard* in the evening. If that isn't stew-potism tell me what is. Doesn't anything else go on in these parts?"

"Oh! blow it," he said. "It isn't as bad as that."

"Isn't it?" she said. "I think it's absolutely fungoid."

He suddenly felt very slight incensed at this and went on to explain, as calmly as he could, how you sometimes held parties, had people to dinner, went in spring to the point-to-points and, damn it, in winter, hunted quite a lot. He didn't think you could call that stew-potism, could you?

"There's the hunt ball in a month's time too," he reminded her finally. "You can chalk that up for a whale of a time."

"I would," she said, "if anybody had invited me."

Before he realized what he was saying, he said:

"I'll invite you. Both of you. Delighted."

"Oh! the child could never come."

"No?"

He could not think why on earth the girl could never come.

"She's a mere infant, Henry. Hardly out of the shell. She never does these things. Besides, I'd never let her."

"Why?"

"Oh! Henry, she isn't fledged. She's only half-grown. She isn't fit for that sort of thing. You know what these hunt affairs are too. Wolk-packs. Those gangs are not hunts for nothing."

In his direct, harmless, simple way, the way in which, as everybody always said, there was never any malice, he said:

"But you'd come, wouldn't you?"

"Like a lamplighter, Henry. Absolutely adore to."

He began to murmur something in polite satisfaction about this when she added:

"That's if Katey wouldn't explode."

"I don't think Katey would mind."

That, he always thought, was one nice thing about Katey. She was a good sport, Katey: never jealous in that way.

"And how," she said, "is Katey?"

He shrugged his shoulders: as if there were nothing of very great moment to tell of Katey.

"Tell me about her, Henry," she said. "You can tell me."

There was nothing, he thought, that he possibly wanted to tell.

"I'm sorry," she said, "have I boobed? I simply thought—well, people talk and you know how it is. Somehow I got the impresh— well, you know the impresh one gets—that you and Katey weren't pulling all that steamingly well in harness."

He was roused by the increasing absurdity of her language. She was like a piece of iced-cake that one finds in a silvered box, in a forgotten drawer, among silver leaves, thirty years after the voices at the wedding have faded away. The brittle archaisms of the language were like the hard tarnished silver balls left on the cake. They had seemed so magnificently bright in his youth but now—Good God, had he and Edna and the rest of them really talked like that? If it hadn't been for that absurd, husky clipping voice of hers he would never have believed they had.

As if her thoughts were running in the same direction she said:

"We had some great times, Henry. You and I and Vicky Burton and Freddie Anstruther and Peggy Forbes and Carol Chalmers and Floaty Dean—he was a bright moonbeam, Floaty—do you ever hear anything of any of the crowd?"

"I'm afraid I've lost touch with all of them."

"Well, not all, Henry. Don't say that. You haven't lost touch with me."

Here, as so often in the conversation, she smiled, played with the pearls above the thin steely bosom or extended, to its full length, the arm holding the dying cigarette in its yellow holder.

"Do you remember a day on the river at Pangbourne?"

He pretended not to remember it while, in reality, remembering it very well. That day she had worn her pale yellow hair in a bob and a hat like a round pink saucepan. Her white dress had been short and waistless, revealing round and pretty knees below the skirt.

There was no doubt in his mind that she too had been very pretty and she said:

"But you remember coming home, through the woods? You

wanted to go with Carol but I wanted you to come with me. All the rhododendrons were out, big white and pale pink ones so that you could see them in the dark, and I made an honest man of you."

She laughed distastefully.

"You *surely* don't forget, Henry, do you?" she said. "After all, it was the first time with you and me, even if it wasn't the last, and you know how—"

"Look, Edna, we were all a bit crazy at that time and I don't think we have to drag it all—"

He was relieved to hear the sound of car brakes in the road outside. Then he heard a car door slam and the sound of feet running up the path outside.

A moment later Valerie Whittington came in. She was wearing a blue gabardine school mackintosh and a plain grey felt hat and white ankle socks above her plain flat shoes. The mackintosh was too long for her by several inches and when she started to take it off he saw that underneath it she was wearing a plain dark blue dress that was full and bushy in the skirt. It too was too long for her.

"Well, there you are at last, child. Say good evening to Mr. Barnfield before you go up. I know you know him because he was kind enough to let you use the path."

"Good evening, Mr. Barnfield."

He said good evening too and knew, as he did so, that she had the greatest difficulty in looking at him. He tried in vain to catch the big, brown, too-circular eyes.

"Well, up you go now, child. It's late. It's past your time. Say good night to Mr. Barnfield.

"Good night, Mr. Barnfield."

He nodded. He thought she made a sort of timid, half-urgent effort to protest but she turned away too quickly, leaving him unsure. The last visible sign of what she might be thinking was a shudder of her lower lip, hard and quite convulsive, just before she turned, opened the door and went out without a word.

"I must go too," he said.

"Oh! not yet, Henry. Have another sherry—"

"No, no," he said. "Really, no, no. Katey will have dinner—"

"Give her a ping on the blower and say you'll be another half hour. We've hardly exchanged the sliver of a word—"

"No, honestly, Edna," he said. "Honestly I must go."

She came with him, at last, to the door. In the light from the door she stood for a moment gauntly, thinly framed, a piece of silver cardboard, and he thought again of the wedding cake. Then she half closed the door behind her. The October air was mild and windless but as she stretched out long fleshless arms to say good-bye he said hastily:

"Don't come out. Don't get cold. I'm perfectly capable—"

"Good night, Henry," she said. "Sweet of you to come. And that's a date, then, isn't it?—the ball?"

"That's if you'd care—"

"Oh! Henry." She laughed huskily. "Care?"

She offered her face to be kissed. He made as if to inflict on it, somewhere between cheek and ear, a swift dab of farewell. The next moment he felt her thin fingers grasp him about the elbows. Then they moved up to his shoulders and suddenly she was offering her mouth instead.

"You can do better than that, Henry, can't you?" she said. She laughed with what he supposed she thought was tenderness. Her voice crackled on its rising note with a brittle snap. "I know you can. From what I remember of the rhododendrons. And not only the rhododendrons."

"Look, Edna, I've already told you. That's all over long since," he said, and escaped, leaving her mouth in air.

[6]

He was surprised, the following Sunday morning, to see no sign of the yellow sweater among the brushwood jumps in the meadows.

"Your girlfriend has passed you up," Katey said. "She hasn't been near all week, so Lewis says."

After breakfast he rode out to the meadow and jumped for half an hour in cool exhilarating air, across grass still white-wet from frost. In the hedgerows leaves of maple and hornbeam were growing every day more and more like clear light candle-flame and up on the hill the beeches were burning deeper and deeper, fox-fiery beyond the pines, against ice-blue autumn sky.

The hill was irresistible and finally he rode up, slowly, in bright sunshine, about eleven o'clock, through acres of dying bracken and birches that were shedding, in pure silence, after the night frost, the gentlest yellow fall of leaves.

One or two people were walking on the crest of the hill but no one except himself was riding and he was half in mind to turn the horse, ride down the opposite hillside as far as *The Black Boy* and treat himself to a whisky there at twelve o'clock, when he suddenly saw walking across the bracken a tall figure in a black skirt and a puce-pink blouse.

It was a pigtail-less, hatless, horseless Valerie Whittington, waving her hand.

"I thought it must be you," she said and even he was not too stupid to know that she must have been waiting for him there.

"Where's your pony?" he said.

"I've stopped riding."

'Oh?"

It was all he could think of to say as he raised his cap, dismounted and stood beside her.

He saw at once that she was wearing lipstick. She had also managed to bunch up her hair into thick brown curls and to make an effort to match the colour on her face to the puce pink of the blouse. Except for the evening at the cottage he had not seen her in skirts before and now he saw that her legs were long, well-shaped and slender.

"Given up riding?" he said. "How is that?"

"I've just given up riding," she said.

"Even from the tone of this remark he saw that she had changed a great deal. Like her voice, her face was grave, almost solemn. Her eyes seemed queer and distant.

"Have you time to walk a little way?" she said.

He said yes, he had time, and they walked slowly, in cool sunshine, he leading the horse, to where he could see once again the entire valley of oak-woods and pasture below. In a few weeks he would be hunting across it, drinking the first sharp draughts of winter.

"I'm afraid I behaved like a fool up here the other day," she said, "and I'm sorry about the other night."

He said he couldn't think why.

"Well, it's all over now," she said, "but I just wanted to say."

Exactly what, he asked, was all over now?

"Me," she said. "I'm leaving home. I'm going away."

It was instantly typical of him to ask her if she thought that was wise.

"Wise or not," she said, "I'm going."

Everybody wanted to run away when they were young, he said, but it was like measles. You got over it in time and you were probably all the better for having been through the wretched thing.

"Yes, I'm better," she said. "Because I know where I'm going now. Thanks to you."

He couldn't think what he possibly had to do with it and she said:

"I like being with you. I grow up when I'm with you. Somehow you never take me away from myself."

This odd, solemn little pronouncement of hers affected him far more than her tears had ever done and he glanced quickly at her face. It was full of another, different kind of tearfulness, dry and barren, with a pinched sadness that started dragging at his heart.

"You know what I've been doing since last Sunday?" she said.

"No."

"Coming up here."

"Yes?"

"Every day," she said. "Walking. Not with the pony—I haven't ridden the pony since that day. Just walking. I think I know every path here now. There's a wonderful one goes down past the holly trees. You come to a little lake at the bottom with quince trees on an island—at least I think they're quince trees."

If he had time, she went on, she wanted him to walk down there. Would he? Did he mind?

He tethered his horse to a fence and they started to walk along a path that wound down, steeply in places, through crackling curtains of bracken, old holly trees thick with pink-brown knots of berry and more clumps of birch trees sowing in absolute silence little yellow pennies of leaves.

At the bottom there was, as she had said, a small perfectly circular lake enclosed by rings of alder, willow and hazel trees. In the still air

its surface was thick with floating shoals of leaves. In absolute
silence two quince trees, half-bare branches full of ungathered
golden lamps of fruit, shone with apparent permanent candescence
on a little island in the glow of noon.

"This is it," she said.

Neither then, nor later, nor in fact at any other time, did they
saw a word about her mother. They stood for a long time without a
word about anything, simply watching the little lake soundlessly
embalmed in October sunlight, the quince-lamps setting the little
island half on fire.

"I don't think you should go away," he said.

"Why not?"

He answered her in the quiet, uncomplex way that, as everyone
so often remarked, was so much part of him, so much the typical
Harry Barnfield.

"I don't want you to," he said.

She started to say something and then stopped. He looked at her
face. He thought suddenly that it had lost the dry, barren tearfulness. Now it looked uncomplicated, alight and free. The big
glowing brown eyes seemed to embrace him with a wonderful look
of gratitude.

"What were you going to say?" he said.

"Nothing."

"You were."

"I was," she said, "but now it doesn't matter."

All at once she laid her hands on his shoulders, drawing them
slowly down until, quite nervously, she plucked at the lapels of his
jacket. In shyness she could not look at him. She could only stare at
her own fingers as she drew them slowly up and down.

Suddenly she let them fly up to his uncertain, spectacled, honest
face with a breaking cry.

"Oh! my God, hold me," she said. "Hold me—just hold me, will
you?—for God's sake please just hold me—"

In a stupid daze Harry Barnfield held her; and from across the
lake the sound of a duck's wing flapping somewhere about the
island of quinces reached him, long afterwards, like the echo of a
stone dropping far away at the bottom of a well.

[7]

Soon, as the autumn went on, his friends the city gentlemen began to notice a strange, unforetold change in his habits. No longer was it possible, several days a week, to wait with expectation and cheers to put the grappling hooks on Harry Barnfield as he ran, spectacled and panting, to catch the evening train.

The reason for this was a simple one: Harry Barnfield was, on these evenings, not there to be grappled.

By the time the train departed he was already away in the country, saying good-bye to the girl on the hillside or, in bad weather, as they sat in his car by the road. A train at two-thirty gave him an hour or more before, at six o'clock, he watched her, with a dry twist in his heart, walk away into twilights filled more and more with storms of blowing leaves.

Earlier in the afternoon they walked by the little lake. As late as the first week in November the lamps of the quinces hung miraculously suspended from the grey central islands of boughs and then gradually, one by one, dropped into the frosted reeds below.

By the middle of November there remained, on the south side of the island, where the sun caught it full in the early afternoons, one quince, the last of the autumn lanterns, and as Harry Barnfield and the girl came down the path through thinning alder trees she got into the way of running on ahead of him to the edge of the lake, always giving the same little cry:

"Look, Harry, our quince is still there!"

For about a week longer they watched, as if it were some marvellously suspended planet glowing above the wintry stretches of water where thin ice sometimes lingered white all day in the thickest shadow of reeds, the last remaining quince, suspended bare and yellow on frost-stripped boughs.

"When it falls I shall feel the summer has gone completely," the girl said.

Soon Harry Barnfield felt as she did: that this was the last of summer poured into a single phial of honey. When it fell and split at last he knew he would hear, dark and snapping, the breath of winter.

By the fifteenth day of the month the quince, looking bigger and more golden than ever in an afternoon of pure, almost shrill blue sky already touched on the horizon by the coppery threat of frost, still remained.

"Look, Harry!" the girl said, "our quince is still there!"

For some time they walked slowly by the lake. In the breathless blue afternoon the one remaining globe of fruit glowed more than ever like the distillation of all the summer.

"It's nearly two months now," the girl said, "since we first came down here. Have you been happy?"

He started to say that he had never been so happy in his life but she cut him short and said:

"What made you happy?"

He could not think what had made him happy except, perhaps, that he had been freed, at last, from the shackles of his daily ride in the train, the banterings of the city gentlemen and above all from the evening crackle of Katey's voice calling that she hoped to God he hadn't forgotten the gin. But before he had time to reply the girl said:

"I'll tell you why it is. It's because you've made someone else happy. Me, in fact."

"I'm glad about that."

"You see," she said, "it's like shining a light. You shine it and it reflects back at you."

"But supposing," he said in his simple, straightforward way, "there's nothing to reflect back from?"

"Oh! but there is," she said, "there's me."

He smiled at this and a moment later she stopped, touched his arm and said:

"I wonder if you feel about it the same way as I do? I feel in a wonderful way that you and I have been growing up together."

He hadn't a second in which to answer this odd remark before, across the lake, the quince fell with a thud, almost a punch, into the reeds below. The sound startled the girl so much that she gave a sudden dismaying gasp:

"Oh! Harry, it's gone! Our quince has gone—oh! Harry, look, it's empty without it!"

He stared across to the island and saw that it was, as she said, quite empty.

"Now," she said, "it's winter."

He thought he caught for the briefest possible moment a colder breath of air rising from the lake, but it was in fact her shadow crossing his face, shutting out the sun, as she turned and looked at him.

"The quince has gone and it's winter," she said. "The week has gone and tomorrow it's Friday. Have you forgotten?"

"Friday?" he said. "Forgotten?"

"Friday," she said, "is the Hunt Ball."

"Good God, I'd forgotten," he said.

Now it was her turn to smile and she said:

"Whatever you do you mustn't forget. You simply mustn't. You're coming to fetch us. Will you dance with me?"

"If—" He was about to say "If your mother will let you," but he checked himself in time and said, "If you don't mind being trodden on. It's some time since I danced, especially to modern things."

"I've a new dress," she said.

There crossed his mind the picture of her coming home, as he vividly remembered it, from the birthday party: the dress long, straight and blue under the blue school mackintosh; and he felt his heart once again start to ache for her, afraid of what she would wear.

"Nobody has seen it," she said.

It was on the tip of his tongue to say "Not even—" when he checked himself again and she said:

"I hope you'll like me in it. Nobody knows about it. I bought it alone, by myself. It's the colour of—No, I won't tell you after all. You'll see it tomorrow and then you can tell me if it reminds you of something."

Suddenly she stretched up her arms in a short delightful gesture.

"You will dance with me?" she said, "won't you? A lot?"

"I warn you—" he said, and then: "I'm pretty awful."

For the second time she held up her arms. She put her left arm lightly on his shoulder and he took her other hand.

"I'll hum the tune," she said. "Listen carefully."

She started humming something but although he listened carefully he could not recognize at all what tune it was.

"You'll have to guide me," she said. "My eyes are shut. I always dance with my eyes shut. And by the way next week I'm twenty. Ancient. Had you forgotten?''

He had forgotten about that too.

"You dance nicely—very nicely—we go together—nicely—very nicely together—"

She started to sing the words to the tune she was humming, the tune he did not recognize, and as he danced to it, steering her about the frost-bared path along the lake, he remembered the sound of the quince dropping into the reeds, the last vanishing phial of the summer's honey, filling his mind like a golden ominous echo.

[8]

When he called alone at the keeper's cottage next evening about half past eight he saw at once that all his fears were justified. It was she who opened the door; and already, as he saw, she was wearing the blue school mackintosh. He even thought he caught, as she turned her head, a glimpse of two pigtails tucked inside the half-turned-up collar at the back.

Nervously picking first at his silk evening scarf and then his black homburg hat he stood in the little sitting room and wished, for once, that Edna was there.

"Mother will be a few minutes yet," the girl said. "She always takes an awful time. She said I was to give you sherry. Or is there something else you'd rather have?"

He was about to say that sherry would suit him perfectly when she smiled, leaned close to him and said:

"This, for instance?"

She kissed him lightly. Her lips, not made up, with that curious undressed brownish look about them, rested on his mouth for no more than a second or two and then drew away.

"How many dances," she said, "are you going to dance with me?"

"Well—"

"Dance with me all evening."

"I shall have to dance with your mother—"

"Dance one dance with mother and then all the rest with me."

Again she kissed him lightly on the lips. "All night. For ever. Dance with me for ever."

Miserably, a few moment later, he took the glass of sherry she poured out for him.

"I'm not allowed to drink," she said. "But I'm going to. Mother will be ages."

With increasing wretchedness he saw her pour another glass of sherry, hold it up to him and say:

"Do you know what I used to say when I was a child and wanted to describe something that was very, very good?"

"No."

"I used to call it the bestest good one." She laughed with large shining eyes and drank half the sherry in a gulp. "Here's to our evening. May it be the bestest good one in the world."

All this time she kept the blue gabardine school mackintosh closely buttoned at the neck. He would not have been surprised to see that her stockings were black, though in fact they were flesh-coloured, and once he found himself looking down at her black flat-heeled shoes.

"Oh! that reminds me," she said. "Would you hide these in the car for me? They're my dancing shoes."

He took the brown paper parcel she gave him and went out to the car and put the parcel on the back seat. The night was starry and crisp, with a half moon in the west.

Immediately, as he got back to the house, he heard the husky voice of Edna Whittington asking where he was.

In the sitting room she greeted him with outstretched thin bar arms, fingers crooked.

"Henry. I thought you were leaving us, trotting out there in the cold. I thought my little girl wasn't looking after you."

She was wearing a skin-tight dress that looked, he thought, as if it were made of silver mail. It made her look more than ever like a sere cardboard leaf left over from a wedding cake. Her long finger nails and her lips were a sharp magenta and the skin of her chest and face was powdered to a rosy-violet shade.

"No Katey?"

Her voice was full of petulant mock regret.

He apologized and said that Katey was, on the whole, not a great one for dancing.

"Poor Katey. Well, anyway, all the more luck for me."

In the intervals of talking and, he thought, smiling too much, she poured herself a glass of sherry and then filled up his own. All this time the girl stood apart, schoolgirlish, meek, hands in pockets of her mackintosh, not speaking.

"Henry," Edna Whittington said, "it's terribly sweet of you to take us to this thing and it's mean of me to ask another favour. But would you?"

"Of course."

"What time does this affair break up?"

"Oh! hard to say," he said. "Three or four. I've known it to be five."

"Shambles?"

"Quite often," he said. "Well, it's the Hunt Ball and you know how people are."

"I know how people are and that's why I wanted to ask you. Would you," she said, "be an absolute lamb and bring Valerie back by one o'clock? I've promised her she can come on that one condition."

"If you think—"

"I do think and you're an absolute lamb. She doesn't mind being alone in the house and then you can come back for me and we'll stay on to the end."

The girl did not speak or move. Her large brown eyes were simply fixed straight ahead of her, as if she actually hadn't heard.

Ten minutes later the three of them drove off, Edna Whittington sitting beside him at the wheel, wearing only a white long silk shawl as a wrap, the girl at the back, motionless and obliterated in the darkness, without a word.

"Oh! look! they've floodlit the mansion! The whole place looks like a wedding cake!"

As he turned the car into tall high park gates Edna Whittington's voice ripped at the night with a husky tear. At the end of a long avenue of bare regiments of chestnuts a great house seemed to stare with a single candescent eye, pure white, across black spaces of

winter parkland. And as the car drew nearer he thought that it
looked, as she said, like a wedding cake, just as she herself, thin,
shining and silver, looked more than ever like a leaf of it that had
been long since torn away.

Less than ten minutes later he was inside the long central hall of
the mansion, bright with chandeliers and crowded already with
dancers, many of them his acquaintances of the hunting field, some
his friends the city gentlemen, hearing Edna Whittington say with a
smile of her bony once pretty magenta mouth:

"It's over twenty years since I danced with you, Henry, and I
can't wait to have a quick one. What are they playing? What are
you looking at?"

"I was wondering," he said, "where Valerie had—"

A moment later, before he could complete the sentence or she
could answer it, he felt himself pressed to the thin sheer front of her
body and borne away.

[9]

It might have been half an hour, perhaps only twenty minutes,
when he turned in the middle of the second of his dances with Edna
Whittington and became the victim of exactly the same kind of
momentary illusion that he had suffered one brilliant Sunday
morning in the cucumber house.

For a second or two, out of the corner of his eye, he thought he
saw a strange but remotely recognizable fragment of yellow light
cross a far corner of the room and disappear behind a triangular tier
of pink chrysanthemums.

He was suddenly stunned to realize that this was Valerie Whittington, wearing a remarkably long pale yellow dress and long black
gloves that showed her pale bare upper arms and her completely
naked back and shoulders. He was so numbed by this appearance
that only one thought raced through his head, in reality the rapid
recollection of something she had said by the lake on the previous
afternoon:

"Nobody knows about it. It's the colour of—No, I won't tell
you. You'll see it tomorrow and then you can tell me if it reminds
you of anything."

Instantly he recalled the quinces and how the lamp of summer had gone out.

Somehow he got through the rest of the dance without betraying that he was in a turmoil of fright and indecision. He had broken out already into a cold and sickening sweat but as the dance ended he had presence of mind enough to mop his forehead with his handkerchief and say:

"It's awfully hot in here, Edna. My glasses are getting misty. Do you mind if I go and clean them? And wouldn't you like a drink? Can I bring you something—gin and something?—would you?—by all means, yes—"

He escaped, spent five minutes in an empty back corridor breathing on his spectacles, polishing them and then in sheer fright breathing on them again. After that he worked his way to the corner of the bar and restored himself with a whisky, saying desperately at the last moment:

"No, a large one, large one please."

Then he took the drink back into the corridor. He had hardly leaned against the wall and had actually not lifted the glass to his lips when he looked up and saw Valerie Whittington suddenly appear at the far end of the corridor as if she had in some miraculous way come up through a trap door.

She started to walk towards him. She walked quite slowly, upright, shoulders square and splendid, the motion of her legs just breaking the front of the dress with ripples. And across the vision of her walking slowly down towards him he caught for the flash of a second the former vision of her in the gabardine mackintosh, schoolgirlish, tense and obliterated, the pigtails tucked into the collar at the back.

A moment later she was saying:

"I know what you're thinking. You're thinking did I have it on under the mackintosh, aren't you?"

"Partly that—"

"I hadn't," she said. "It was easy. I got the shop to send it here. I'd hardly a thing on under the mackintosh."

She started to smile. Her lips were made up, a pale red, and she had managed once again to pile her hair into a mass of curls. She did not speak again for a moment or two. She continued to smile at

him with the large circular brown eyes that so often seemed to
embrace him with tenderness and then at last she said:

"Does it remind you of anything?"

"Of course," he said.

To his surprise the two words seemed to move her very deeply
and he saw that there were sudden tears in her eyes.

"You're the bestest good one in the world," she said and she
pressed her face against his own.

He too found himself very moved by that. He wished he had
nothing to do but take her by one of the long black gloves and into
the dark spaces of parkland outside the house, but he remembered
Edna Whittington.

Some of his anxiety about this must have crossed his face because
almost immediately she said:

"I'll tell you something else you're thinking too, shall I?"

Harry Barnfield, only too well aware of what he was thinking,
could not answer.

"You're thinking you've got to dance with me."

"Well—"

He inclined his head a fraction down and away from her. When
he looked up at her again he was struck by a wonderful air of
composure about her face, the wide bare shoulders and especially
the hands, black in their gloves, clasped lightly before the waistline
of the yellow dress. She could not have looked more composed if
she had been wearing the dress for the fiftieth instead of the first
time but he knew, somehow, in spite of it all, that she was
frightened.

"It's got to be done," she said, "and I can't do it without you."

He tried not to look into her eyes. They were no longer wet with
even the suspicion of tears. They gazed back at him, instead, with
an almost luminous composure and now, at last, she stretched out
her hands.

"Come along," she said. "Take me."

If there had been no other person on the dance floor as he led her
on to it some moments later he could hardly have felt more pained
and conspicuous. It was like dancing in some sort of competition,
naked, in the middle of an empty field, before a thousand
spectators.

The amazing thing was that whenever he looked at the face of the girl it was still alight with that astonishing luminous composure.

"Look at me," she said once. "Keep looking at me."

Whether she was thinking of her mother, as he was the whole time, he did not know. He could not see Edna Whittington. But as he danced he became more and more obsessed with the haunting impression that she was watching him from somewhere, evilly and microscopically, waiting for the dance to end.

When it did end he turned helplessly on the floor, arms still outstretched, very much like a child learning to walk and suddenly deprived of a pair of helping hands. The girl, composed as ever, started to move away, the skin of her back shining golden in the light of the chandeliers. The dress itself looked, as she had meant it to do, more than ever the colour of quinces and he saw on her bare arms a bloom of soft down like that on the skin of the fruit.

Then as she turned, smiled at him with an amazing triumphant serenity, holding out her arm for him to take, he saw Edna Whittington.

She was standing not far from the tier of pink chrysanthemums. She did not look, now, like a piece of silver cardboard. She looked exactly like the perfectly straight double-edged blade of a dagger rammed point downwards into the floor: arms perfectly crossed, feet close together, thin body perfectly motionless under the tight silver dress, small microscopic eyes staring straight forward out of a carved white face, fixed on himself and the girl as they crossed the dance floor.

Suddenly he was no longer uneasy, self-conscious, or even disturbed. He began to feel strangely confident, almost antagonistic. And in this sudden change of mood he felt himself guide the arm of the girl, changing her course across the dance floor, steering her straight to Edna Whittington.

Suddenly the band started playing again. The girl gave a quick little cry of delight, turned to him and put her hands on his shoulders. A moment later they were dancing.

Then, for what was to be the last time, she spoke of her mother.

"Is she looking?"

"Yes."

"Tell me how she looks," she said. "You know I dance with my eyes closed."

"There's no need to think of her."

Whether it was because of this simple remark of his he never knew, but suddenly she rested her face against his and spoke to him in a whisper.

"You don't know how happy I am," she said. "Oh! don't wake me, will you? Please don't wake me."

She spoke once more as they danced and it was also in a whisper.

"If I told you I loved you here in the middle of this dance floor would you think it ridiculous?"

"That's the last thing I would ever think."

"I love you," she said.

At the end of the dance a frigid, pale, supernaturally polite Edna Whittington, holding a glittering yellow cigarette holder in full stretched magenta fingers, met them as they came from the floor. Rigidly and antagonistically he held himself ready to do some sort of brave and impossible battle with her and was surprised to hear her say:

"You did book our table for supper, didn't you, Henry?"

"Of course."

"You should have told me where it was," she said. "Then I could have sat down."

Throughout the rest of the evening, until one o'clock, this was as sharp as the tone of her reproach and resentment ever grew. She regarded himself, the girl, the dancing, and even the dress, with the same unmitigated calm. When he danced with her, as he did several times, she talked with a kind of repressed propriety, saying such things as:

"It's a most pleasant evening, Henry. And not noisy. Not a brawl. Not half as crowded as I thought it would be."

"The Hunt's going through a difficult patch," he said. "Rather going down, I'm afraid. There isn't the interest. There aren't the chaps."

"You seen to know a lot of people, even so."

The more polite and calm she grew the more unreal, he thought, the night became. Alternately he danced with herself and the girl. Friendly and bantering from across the floor came exchanges of manly pleasantry with friends like Punch Warburton, Freddie Jekyll, and George Reed Thompson, the city gentlemen, from odd acquaintances like Dr. Frobisher, Justice Smythe, and Colonel Charnly-Rose: stalwart chaps, the solid backbone of the Hunt.

Away somewhere in the distance lay the even greater unreality of Katey: Katey drowned throughout the years of his marriage in mists of gin, Katey the tawdry lioness, Katey with her garlic-raw, smoke-stained fingers, calling him a squeak-mouse.

He felt himself left, over and over again, with the one reality of his life that had ever meant anything. All the rest had shrivelled behind him like black burnt paper. Nothing made any sense in any sort of way any more, except the voice of the girl imploring him with the tenderest, most luminous happiness:

"Oh! Don't wake me, will you? Please don't wake me."

It would be the best possible thing now, he thought, to get it over quickly: to go straight to Katey, in the morning, and tell her what had happened and how, because of it, he could not go on with the old, damnable, dreary business any longer.

He had arrived at this, the simplest of decisions, by midnight, when Edna Whittington, the girl, and himself sat down to supper. To his relief and surprise it was a remarkably pleasant supper. He poured champagne and the girl, unreproached, was allowed to drink it. He fetched, with his own hands, as she and her mother expressed their fancy, plates of cold chicken or salmon, frozen strawberries and ice-cream, mousse and mayonnaise.

"Did I see someone with pineapple gateau, Henry?" Edna Whittington said and he went dutifully to search for it, pursued by a voice of unbelievably husky-sweet encouragement: "And be a lamb and find cream, Henry, if you can. Dancing makes me hungry."

In the next hour the wine, the food and the utter absence of malignity in all that Edna Whittington said or did had lured him into a state where he was no longer apprehensive or uncertain or even ready to go into brave and antagonistic battle against her.

In consequence he was as unprepared as a rabbit sitting before a stoat when, at one o'clock, Edna Whittington looked at her watch, then at the girl, then at himself and said:

"Child, it's time for you to go home. Henry, are you ready to take her?"

[10]

The girl did not move. He felt the ease of the evening shatter with an ugly crack. His nerves upheld his skin with minute pin-pricks of actual pain.

"I said it was time to go home, child. Get your things. Put your coat on. Mr. Barnfield will take you."

The girl still did not move or speak. Looking at her, he was reminded of the first morning he had ever met her. The innocent insolence had come back to her face again and he understood it now.

"Valerie."

Edna Whittington waited. He lifted his glass, drank some champagne and waited too. The girl still did not move. She sat with black gloves composed and crossed on the table in front of her. Her eyes, not so wide and circular as they often were, looked half down at her hands, half at the dance floor. Just above the cut of the yellow dress her breasts started to rise and fall rather quickly but otherwise she did not stir.

"I am not in the habit of telling you twice," Edna Whittington said. The voice was icy. "Get your things at once and go home."

The band had begun playing. He clenched the stem of his glass, then relaxed his fingers and looked straight at the icy-grey microscopic eyes of Edna Whittington.

"She's not going home," he said.

"Will you please mind your own business?"

He found himself drawing on remarkable reserves of calm, backed by the echo of a voice which kept saying "I feel in a wonderful way that we've been growing up together."

"Child—"

"I have told you, Edna, that she is not going home."

"Will you kindly mind your own business!"

He lifted his face, pushed his glass aside and looked straight into the eyes of the girl.

"Shall we dance?" he said.

She hesitated for a fraction of a second. He thought he saw at the same time an indecipherable shadow run across her face, as if she were actually in a turmoil of indecision. And for a moment he was in horror that she would fail, break down, and go home.

Instead she smiled and got up. As the skirt of the yellow dress moved into full view from below the table he remembered the shining lamp of the solitary remaining quince burning in the blue November glassiness above the lake on cooling crystal afternoons, the last phial of the summer's honey, and he knew that now, at last, there was no need to doubt her.

A moment later they were dancing. They danced perhaps twice round the room before she even looked or spoke to him. Then slowly she lifted her face, staring at him as if she could not see him distinctly.

"You're the bestest good one," she said. "The most bestest good one in the world."

And as she spoke he found, suddenly, that he could not bear to look at her. Her huge brown eyes were drowned in tears of happiness.

[11]

It was nearly three o'clock when Edna Whittington said to him in a husky discordant voice that betrayed, at last, the first snap of anger:

"If you feel you've enjoyed yourself enough I should like to go home."

"I'm ready whenever you are," he said. "Shall I take you alone or shall we all go together?"

She paused before answering; and he thought for a moment that she was going to laugh, as she sometimes did, distastefully. Instead she picked the minutest shred of tobacco from her mouth, looked at it and then flicked it away.

"We'll all go together," she said. "I want to talk to you."

"As far as I'm concerned there's nothing to talk about."

"She's my daughter," she said, "and I want to talk to you."

"Very well, Edna," he said. "Talk to me."

"I'll talk to you," she said, "at home."

They drove home in frosty darkness, under a starry sky from which the moon had gone down. The girl sat in the back of the car, as before, and no one spoke a word.

When he pulled up before the cottage no one, for nearly half a minute, moved either.

"Will you come in?" Edna Whittington said at last.

"No thank you."

"Then I'll talk to you here." She turned to the girl.

"Go inside, Valerie. Here's the key."

The girl did not move or answer. Harry Barnfield turned, saw her sitting there motionless, mackintoshless, cool in the yellow dress, and said:

"Better go." He took the key of the cottage from Edna Whittington and handed it to the girl. "I think it's better."

"I'm going," she said very quietly. "Good night. See you tomorrow."

Then, and he could only guess what it cost her to do it, the girl leaned over, turned his head with her hand and kissed him on the lips, saying:

"Thank you for everything. Good night."

Before he could move to open the door for her she was out of the car, running. He heard the key scrape in the lock of the cottage door. Then the door opened and shut and he was alone, in silence, with Edna Whittington.

He said at once: "I don't know what you have to say, Edna, but it's very late and I'd like to get home."

"How long has this been going on?" she said.

"About twenty years."

"If you're going to be flippant I shall probably lose my temper and—"

"I'm not going into explanations," he said, "if that's what you want, and the sooner you get it into your head the better."

She gave the distasteful beginning of a laugh.

"All right. I'll just ask you one question. If that isn't too much?"

"Ask."

"I suppose you're going to tell me you love this child?"

"Very much."

"Setting aside the word infatuation," she said, "do you suppose she loves you?"

"I do, and she does," he said.

This time she did laugh. It was husky, unpleasant and briefly sinister.

"I honestly think you're serious about this."

"I'm not only serious," he said. "It's my whole life. And hers."

She started to light a cigarette. He disliked very much the idea of smoking in cars and he was annoyed as she saw the thin masked face, so drawn that it was almost skeletonized, in the light of the match and then in the burning glow of the cigarette held between the drooping magenta lips.

"You know, Henry," she said. She blew smoke with what appeared to be unconstricted ease. "Somebody will have to be told."

He instantly thought of Katey: Katey the shabby lioness, passing through her blonde phases, her gin-mists; Katey yelling at him, calling him a squeak-mouse; messy, lost, groping, scrofulous Katey.

"Oh! Katey will be told," he said. "I'll tell Katey. Tomorrow."

Edna Whittington blew smoke in a thin excruciated line.

"I wasn't thinking of Katey."

He couldn't think who else could possibly be told and for a moment he didn't care.

"I daresay my friends have put two and two together," he said, "if that's what you mean."

"I wasn't thinking of your friends."

"Who then?"

She drew smoke and released it. The smoke had a strange repugnant scent about it. He saw her eyes narrowed in the narrow face, the mouth drawn down, almost cadaverous, and he grasped that this was a smile.

"Valerie," she said. "Valerie will have to be told."

"Told?" he said. The car was half full of smoke, tainted with the scent of it. He felt his annoyance with her rising to temper. "Told what, for God's sake?"

"About us," she said. "You and me."

"Us?" And what about us?"

He suddenly felt uneasy and on edge, nerves probing, the smoke sickening him.

"I think she has to be told,"she said, "that you and I were lovers. Of course it was some time ago. But wouldn't you think that that was only fair?"

He could not speak. He simply made one of his habitual groping gestures with his hands, up towards his face, as if his spectacles had suddenly become completely opaque with the white sickening smoke of her cigarette and he could not see.

"Not once," she said, "but many times. Oh! yes, I think she has to be told. I think so."

She did not know quite what happened after that. He seemed suddenly to lose control of himself and started yelling. She had never known a Harry Barnfield who could yell, show anger, make foul noises or use violence and now he struck her in the face. The blow partially blinded her, knocking the cigarette from her lips, and in the confusion she heard him yelling blackly as he turned the key of the car.

When she recovered herself the car was travelling down the road, very fast. As it turned under dark trees by a bend, she realized that the headlights were not on. He was bent forward over the wheel, glaring wildly through the thickish spectacles into a half-darkness from which trees rushed up like gaunt shadows.

"I'll kill you, I'll kill you," he kept saying. "I'll kill you first."

She started screaming. Out of the darkness sprang a remembered figure of Harry Barnfield in a white straw hat, white flannel trousers and a college blazer, a rather soft Harry Barnfield, simple, easy-going, good-time-loving, defenceless, and laughing; one of the vacuous poor fish of her youth, in the days when she had kept a tabulation of conquests in a little book, heading it *In Memoriam: to those who fell,* her prettiness enamelled and calculated and as smart as the strip-poker or the midnight swimming parties she went to, with other, even younger lovers, at long weekends.

Almost the last thing she remembered was struggling with the door of the car. When at first she could not open it she struck out at Harry Barnfield with her hands. At the second blow she hit him full in the spectacles. She heard them crunch as they broke against the bone of his forehead and then the car door was opening, swinging wide, and she was out of it, half-jumping, half-falling on to the soft frosted grass of the verge.

The car, driven by a blinded Harry Barnfield, swerved on wildly down the hill. She was conscious enough to hear a double scream of brakes as it skimmed the bends and then the crash of glass as it struck, far down, a final telegraph pole.

[12]

On the afternoon of Harry Barnfield's funeral the wind rose greyly, mild in sudden rainless squalls, across a landscape bare of leaves.

The heads of many of the mourners were very bald and as they followed the coffin, in a long slow line, they gave the appearance of so many shaven monks solemnly crossing the churchyard.

At the house, afterwards, there were tea and coffee, with whisky and gin for those who preferred something stronger. The Hunt was well represented. The city gentlemen, J. B. (Punch) Warburton, Freddie Jekyll, and George Reed Thompson, were there. The Sheriff of the County was represented. The Masters of several other Hunts, two from a neighbouring county, together with three local magistrates and two doctors from the local hospital were there. Colonel and Mrs. Charnly-Rose, Justice Smythe and his two daughters, both excellent horsewomen, and several clergymen, farmers, horse dealers, and corn merchants were there. It was impossible to say how many people, from all sections of society, from villagers to men of title had come to pay tribute to Harry Barnfield, who as everyone knew was a good huntsman, a good sort, a great horse-lover, and a man in whom there was no harm at all.

In addition to the tea and coffee, whisky and gin there were also cucumber sandwiches and many people said how excellent they were. Several people, as they ate them, walked out of the crowded house into the garden, for a breath of fresh air. Others strolled as far as the edges of the meadows, where Harry Barnfield's horses were grazing and his run of brushwood jumps stood dark and deserted beneath a squally sky.

As they walked they wondered, as people do at funerals, about the future: what would happen, who would get what and above all what Katey would do. Across the fields and the hillside the wind blew into separated threads the wintry blades of grass, over the parched fox-like ruffles of dead bracken and, rising, rattled the grey bones of leafless boughs. "We'll miss him on the five o'clock," the city gentlemen said and confessed that they had no idea what would happen, who would get what or above all what Katey would do.

Nor could anyone possible hear, in the rising winter wind, in the falling winter darkness, any sound of voices weeping across the hillside in the nighttime.

THE WHITE WIND

The lagoon had the hot brilliance of a stretch of celluloid constantly ignited by sunlight into white running flame. From far beyond it the Pacific galloped ceaselessly, charging, white-maned, against the coral reef. At each point of the gap, where the swell poured in, flew great conical flags of splendid spume.

"Does the boat go fast?"

"Like the wind."

"How fast?"

"Like the wind, boy. I told you. Like the wind."

In the shadowy shed, half tin, half palm frond, the boy fed into a strange rattling wheel-like contraption, not unlike a roundabout at a fair, another soda-water bottle. The machine filled it, sealed it with a sound like that of gnashing iron teeth and bore it away.

"How long to go to Papeete in the boat?"

"No time."

"And Bora-Bora?"

"No time. Just like the wind, I tell you. No time."

On the far side of the machine sat a mass of yellow indolence on a box. It stretched out at mechanical intervals a soporific crab-like hand that grasped the filled soda-water bottles and dropped them in a crate. It had grown over the years so completely into the lethargy of this rhythm that occasionally, when it fell asleep in the heat of oppressive afternoons, the hand kept up its fat, slow clawing, independently.

The boy knew this mass of odiously distended flesh as Fat Uncle. He knew of no other name than Fat Uncle.

"Fat Uncle, is the boat faster than Pierre's?"

"Pierre, Pierre, who's Pierre? Boat?—you call that a boat? That fish barrel?"

The flesh of the face was so solidly inflated, like a hard tire, that the simple eyes appeared in it merely as two long slits nicked there by a knife held in a hand that had grown suddenly unsteady as it traced the left-hand eye.

This eye seemed not only larger than the other. It slanted upwards and backwards, jaggedly. The appearance achieved by it was one of idiotic cunning. It was then repeated, astonishingly, in the centre of the naked, soapy paunch below. There the navel lay like a third snoozing eye, the creased lid of stomach folding across it, heaving deeply up and down.

The boy's own eyes were black and listening. He was slightly over four feet in height, rather squat, with thick yellow skin and a mat of black shining hair that was never combed. There was nothing in these rather inconspicuous features to distinguish him from a score of other boys who ran about the waterfront except the eyes. They were farseeing, arrested, solemn eyes and they were inclined to fix themselves for long periods on distances away at sea, without the trace of a smile.

When he was not working with Fat Uncle at the soda-water machine he spent most of his time working and running errands about the port for an American named Edison. Edison owned, among other things, the soda-water plant. He also owned the tin hut, Fat Uncle, the schooner that Fat Uncle said was as fast as the wind and a hotel on the waterfront.

"Faster than the wind," Fat Uncle sometimes said. "Faster. Like a hurricane."

The hotel was a broken-down weatherboarded building with a balustrated upper veranda and a number of open cubicles for drinkers facing the street below. The outside had not been painted for many years but the cubicles inside were raw with violent scarlet, freshly painted, impressed here and there with what seemed like crude transfers of Polynesian girls, with purple *leis* about their necks and green and yellow bark-shirts, dancing.

Edison was fond of purple. Most days he wore a purple shirt, sometimes with large designs of dragons across it, sometimes with rosettes of vast, purple flowers. This colour threw into sickly relief the thin, balding head, the long neck and the scooped dark cheeks with their two-day beard.

On Saturday nights, when the boy spent most of his time helping a Chinaman to wash glasses in the kitchen at the back of the hotel,

Edison thumped away at an out-of-tune piano, Fat Uncle played a ukelele and the floor between the cubicles thundered with sweating, stampeding dancers. In the wild heat of these Saturdays the boy heard men mouthing across the floor untranslatable violent slogans, sometimes in English, sometimes in French, which he did not understand, and occasionally in his own language, which he merely thought he did. Somehow he knew that these were dirty men.

At night he dropped to sleep in the shed. He did not mind the shed. He was in fact very glad of the shed. The shed had become an almost solitary means of comfort to him. It reminded him always of Fat Uncle and the boat, the schooner that went faster than the wind. Sometimes too there was a bottle of soda water that had not been properly sealed and at night he lay down in the warm darkness and drank it, chewing a little raw fish at the same time, or a little coconut.

Occasionally Edison got hold of a sucking pig, invited people to the hotel and gave a big meal, with dishes of hot rice, fish salad, tuna, breadfruit, shrimps and yams. After it was over the boy could sometimes find among the dishes a few unchewed ribs of pork that he could take away to the shed and gnaw there like a dog.

Over and over again, during the daytime, he found some chance to speak with Fat Uncle about the schooner.

"How long was the schooner yours?"

"Years. Years."

"Why did you sell her to Edison?"

"Bad luck, boy. Bad luck. We all have bad luck sometimes."

The accumulated effect of these conversations on the boy was one of wonder. Even when a sudden elephantine hand struck out at him because the soda-water machine had jammed he was aware of no resentment, no bitterness, against Fat Uncle.

For some reason these blows seemed always to strike him on the right hand side of the face, so that his head appeared to have developed a slight and permanent list to one side. It was this list that gave to his eyes the remarkable impression that he was always listening to half-formed, distant sounds. It deepened his air of being fascinated. It made him seem to regard Fat Uncle as a sort of demi-god, part sinister but full of gripping, fathomless sources of wonder.

"Did you once take her to the Marquesas?"

"Once? Once? About a million times!"

"Samoa? You said you once took her to Samoa."

"Samoa—I took her everywhere. Over the whole Pacific. The whole world, I tell you. The whole word. Everywhere."

"Tell me abut Samoa."

In Samoa, Fat Uncle said, the men were big and vain. The villages were neat and pretty, with big round huts of palm. There was much cocoa, a lot of copra. Lazy and easy, the voyages to Samoa, to pick up cocoa. Good profits. Plenty of dough.

"Where is Noumea? You said you once took her to Noumea."

The yellow crab-like fingers would wave with exhausted disdain in a direction vaguely westerly.

"A million miles that way."

As he spoke of these distances, totally incomprehensible to the boy, who had never even sailed beyond the reef, he would actually open his eyes to their full simple width, as if the very fact of their being open was proof of candour, and then wave his hand again.

"Look at her. You'd think a man would take her out sometimes, wouldn't you? A man who was a man."

A great hand would grab with bloated impatience at a soda-water bottle. A great mouth, with scornful looseness, would spit at the floor.

"Look at her. By God, only look at her."

On the dingy waterfront, from which every turn of wind licked up from the many potholes a darting tongue of dust, the schooner lay squat and desolate, listing to one side. She had all the beauty of a floating henhouse dragged from the sea.

"Goes like the wind, I tell you. Like a bird."

As she stared at the schooner and listened to these things the boy ceased to exist as a mere half-naked figure in the shed. He walked out into a great world of water and islands beyond the reef, beyond the farthest rim of horizon, and found that Fat Uncle was king of it.

The discovery, for all its wonder, was incomplete in itself. He knew it could never be complete until he himself was part of it. And always, at night, in the shed, he would lie for some time awake, however tired he was, openly dreaming, trying to think of devious situations in which Edison, by some miracle, would one day take the schooner out of the harbour and beyond the towering reef, to distant places.

"Couldn't you buy the boat back from Edison?"

"Me? What with? It's his. He owns it. He should take it out."

"It's a pity you sold it."

"A pity—too true it was. Everything was going well. And then there it was. Suddenly. Like I told you. Bad luck. I wanted the money. Every man has bad luck sometimes."

"Perhaps one day Edison will have bad luck."

"You tell me why. Edison's always had the luck. You tell me why."

There were times, in more fabulous moments of memory, when Fat Uncle also spoke of fish.

"Until you get out there—" the disdaining obese fingers waved to the far corners of the world—"you've never seen a fish. They're like ships, the fish there. Like ships. The sharks have mouths like doors."

"And the wind? You said once about the wind."

"The wind will drive you for days. Weeks sometimes. Down to Australia before you can catch a rope or get your breath or turn a hair."

"Do you wish you were out there again? With the big fish? With the big wind?"

"Wish it? By God, wish it!—"

It ended one morning with Fat Uncle kicking over the crate of soda-water bottles, grabbing up a bottle as he passed and then heaving himself in outrage, blowing hoarsely, towards the door, to emerge there like an obese blanched maggot hunching itself from the dark core of a rotting fruit, half-blinded by sunshine.

"I gave her away. That's the truth of it. I should have got three times as much for her. Four times as much. I gave her away. Six times. He got her out of me."

He sucked coarsely at the soda-water bottle like a vast baby tugging at a glassy teat.

"I could prove he got her out of me. Six times as much—that's what I should have got for her."

"You said once the wind blew you for ten days. Were you frightened?"

"Of a thing like that?" He laughed his cackling, simple-minded laugh. "The sea's your friend. I was never frightened. It never does to be frightened."

In the complication of feeling that the schooner was beautiful, that Fat Uncle was never frightened and that Edison was a person of sinister design who had achieved the unforgivable outrage of robbing Fat Uncle of the schooner and laying her up to rot, the boy stood staring at the lagoon with solemn musing eyes.

A girl in a white and crimson *pereu*, hatless, with a single yellow hibiscus darting a pistil tongue from her waistlength blue-black hair, walked a moment later across the waterfront, away from the hotel.

"Ginette, Ginette." The fat lips of Fat Uncle sucked the name in and out, grossly, as they had sucked at the soda-water bottle. "Look at her. Ginette. They all love to call themselves by French names. Where do you suppose she's hurrying off to?"

"To get fish."

"Fish. Fish." The squelching lips made noises of scorn. "Perhaps he's a man with her, eh? Perhaps even half a man—"

The boy, without warning, suddenly lifted his face. The eyes, darting sideways, caught out of the glittering sky, from the south, a half-formed distant sound.

A moment later he was running. His voice leapt out in a sudden little yell of surprise that made the girl in the *pereu*, walking across the dusty potholes of the waterfront, suddenly halt and turn, as if he had yelled for her to wait for him.

"It's the day for the little plane," he was shouting. "The day for the little plane."

The girl had disappeared by the time he reached the end of the waterfront, where a belt of palms, very tall, sprang out of a shore of graphite-coloured sand. Beyond these palms the airstrip opened out, a dusty stretch of uneven grass across which the plane was taxiing, wings dipping up and down, like a bird faking a wound and limping for cover.

The boy looked more than ever inconspicuous under the tall thin palms, the fronds of which began to flap above him like steel feathers as the little plane, taxiing in, stirred up currents of air with its dusty slipstream.

From the plane came two men, the older, taller one spectacled and rubbery, in crumpled grey suit, carrying a brown leather bag, the smaller with a pigskin briefcase under his arm, neat and studious, with immaculate white shirt and shorts and thin white stockings.

The boy ran towards these men with excitement, waving both hands in greeting.

"Dr. Gregory! Monsieu' Longuemart! Dr. Gregory!"

Dr. Gregory, the rubbery, spectacled American, waved a hand in reply. The Frenchman merely smiled at the sight of the boy stumbling down towards the airstrip and it was Gregory who called:

"Hi, Timi! How are you? What goes?"

He held out a cool greyish hand to grip the boy's dusty palm and the boy in turn held out his other hand to grasp the bag.

"I may carry the bag?"

"One of these days the bag will carry you."

"Please?"

"Never mind. Skip it," the doctor said. "Have you been a good boy? That's the thing. Did you take your pills?"

"Yes, doctor."

"All of them? How many left?"

"Four. I'd forgotten it was today you came."

"Good boy."

The boy walked the rest of the way to the waterfront between the Frenchman and the American. The Frenchman was speechless, reserved and smiling. It was always the American who talked.

"Did Ginette take her pills?"

"I think so."

"Anybody else you know take them? What about Fat Uncle?"

"He was going to take them one night and then he went fishing. Another day he was sick."

"Where? How sick?"

"Here."

The boy put his hand on his stomach. The doctor said, "They are always sick, aren't they?" and the Frenchman, to whom the remark was really addressed, smiled, a little more broadly this time.

"Have you been sick?"

"No, doctor."

They were by now on the waterfront, in sight of the short cluster of houses, the schooner and the hotel.

"I see Pierre's boat isn't here," the doctor said. "Where's Pierre?"

"I think he has taken the boat to Apia," the boy said. "He went yesterday."

As they walked the rest of the distance down the waterfront the doctor felt a sudden compulsion to muse aloud to the Frenchman.

"One of these days they'll be in a fine jam here. Pierre will have the boat in Apia or Suva or somewhere and we won't have the plane fixed and something'll break out and there'll be a fine mess. Like the epidemic on Bora-Bora. There'll be hell to pay."

He waved seemingly tired loose-jointed hands at housefences on which trailed creepers of tender golden bells. His grey, rather globular eyes rested on bright barriers of red ginger-lily and hibiscus, the hibiscus full blown, crimson and yellow, but still unshrivelled by glaring sun.

"Beautiful, isn't it?" the doctor said. "Incredibly beautiful. I must get some pictures before I go back. I've got a batch of new slides. Look at the crotons. They always remind me of snakes, those yellow ones. They come out well in colour."

They presently drew level with Edison's schooner, the semi-derelict henhouse rocking gently up and down against the wooden waterfront piles, and the doctor stopped to regard her with a certain ironic sadness.

"All so beautiful, Jean, but no telephone."

Gazing from the schooner, he turned with shrugged shoulders to the Frenchman.

"How do you like your lines of communication?"

The Frenchman, staring at the schooner, smiled too and also ironically.

"She goes like the wind," the boy said.

"Does she now? Who says so?"

"Fat Uncle. Faster than the wind. She goes faster than the wind."

"Does she?" the doctor said.

He strode out, too affected to look at the boy, feeling it time to move on. He rested a hand on the boy's shoulder, as if in comfort or tenderness, or merely confidentially. "So you haven't been sick? Nothing? Not once?"

"No, doctor."

"And you know why you haven't been sick?"

"Yes, doctor."

"Why?"

"Because I take the pills."

"Good boy," the doctor said.

They were already within fifty yards of the hotel. Abruptly the doctor stopped again, eyes protuberant with moderately pained disgust as he stared at Edison's crumbling frontage.

"How do you suppose it holds up?" he said. "The only good thing about it is the soda-water. Every time I come here I expect to see it flat. Which way do you suppose it would fall, Jean? On its face or on its backside?"

The Frenchman spoke with meticulous, pointed effect for the first time.

"On its knees, I hope."

"Yes? I suppose a short prayer would do it no harm," the doctor said.

The first of these ironic flippancies was lost on the boy. He understood the doctor only when he spoke of pills. In a simple illustration, months before, the doctor had made him understand, perfectly and for all time, the meaning of the pills.

"I want you to look at this. The picture of a girl. Do you think she's beautiful?" The doctor, who was fond of photography, had drawn from his case a coloured slide. The boy held the translucent glass to the light and gazed at it. "Yes, she is beautiful. Something like Ginette," he said. The doctor retrieved the slide and held out another. "Now look at this. Would you think, perhaps, she was the same girl?"

"No. Not the same girl."

"Why not?"

"She looks very old and she has the elephant legs."

"She is the same girl," the doctor said. "She has the elephant legs. Only ten months later."

After this the doctor took him by the hands. The doctor's loose large-jointed fingers were surprisingly cool and tender.

"Nothing like that can happen to you if you take the pills," he said. "You understand? Nothing can ever happen to you."

They were by now outside the front of the hotel. The doctor and the

Frenchman went inside and sat at one of the scarlet cubicles, followed by
the boy. "I guess a gin-fizz is called for," the doctor said. "Perhaps two
gin-fizzes." White globes of sweat from the short exertion of the walk
had begun to drip from his face and neck and chest and with a large
white handkerchief he started to mop them away.

"Tell Edison two gin-fizzes," he said to the boy. "Two really nice
long gin-fizzes. Special ones."

"Special ones," the boy said. "Yes, doctor," and moved away
from the cubicle.

It was the girl and not Edison who eventually brought the gin-
fizzes, carrying them in on a round bamboo tray.

"Ginette," the doctor said and both he and the Frenchman
halfrose from their seats in greeting.

"Eddo will be here in a minute. Oh! don't get up." Her mouth,
red and rather full, broke at once and for no reason at all into bright
beating laughter. "He's in a temper at me because I was late getting
the fish."

"Please sit down," the doctor said. "Have a drink with us."

"Oh! no, I'm quite happy."

She laughed again, too readily and too loudly, the doctor
thought, with head thrown back, thick red tongue quivering in the
broad but pretty mouth.

"The boy could get it."

"Oh! no, I'm really quite happy."

She sat down. The doctor could not help admiring, as he always
did, the sumptuous golden arms, the primitively sensational shoulders rising smooth and naked from the cavern of blue-black hair, as
she leaned her elbows on the table and laughed splendidly again, for
the third time. There was always something extraordinarily lovable,
simple and touching, he thought, about that laughter. But today it
struck him as being not only physically rich and splendid but also,
in some way he hadn't yet fathomed, uneasily sad.

"Well, have a drink of mine," he said.

She laughed again.

"Well, all right, doctor, a drink of yours." She picked up the long
glass and half looked at the doctor, then the Frenchman, through
the rim of it. "*Santé!*" She drank gin-fizz, very briefly."How long
do you stay?"

"It depends," the doctor said, "on how good people are. If they take their pills. Did you take your pills?"

"Of course."

"If they were all as good as you," the doctor said, "we'd be away the same afternoon."

"Then I'm glad they're not all as good as me."

This was the signal for new and louder laughter and this time the doctor and the Frenchman joined in.

The laughter had hardly died away before Edison appeared in sloppy purple shirt, skyblue trousers and a growth of beard that was like a pale sandy scrubbing brush.

Slouching, he shook hands loosely with the doctor and the Frenchman, and then sat down, scratching his bare chest.

"Fish salad all right?" he said. "Raw fish? All I can do today. I know you always like it."

"Fine," the doctor said.

"Might get a sucking pig next time you come," Edison said, "and Ginette'll get some shrimps. She'll do that favourite curry of yours."

Suddenly Edison got up, went to the corner bar, beyond the cubicle, and poured himself a neat deep whisky to which he added a gill of soda. Then he came back to the cubicle, bringing the bottle and drinking from the glass as he walked along. It was a favourite habit of his.

"Fit?" the doctor said. "I'll bet you didn't take those pills?"

"No," Edison said, "and you know I never will. Whites don't get elephantiasis. You know that." He held up his glass. "This is my bug-killer. Served me well and faithfully, man and boy, for many years."

The doctor looked away. He was not anxious to pursue any further the discussion of a subject on which he was aware he was liable to grow distastefully fanatical when roused. He stared instead at Edison's schooner, moored across the waterfront.

"I see Pierre's away. What do you do for supplies when Pierre's not here?"

"Oh! people call. Boats. You'd be surprised."

"Something you'd like when we come next time?"

"Don't think so," Edison said. "We always manage. Nothing ever happens here."

"Supplies of bug-killer good?"

"Splendid. Never been exhausted yet."

It pained the doctor to sit through the remainder of the drinks, through lunch and through some minutes of coffee afterwards, during which Edison lowered the level of the whisky bottle by several further inches and Ginette laughed at every other sentence or so. He did not know why he now felt unusually discomforted and pained at the impression of some rift between the drinking Edison and the laughing girl, but his heart felt curiously sore and sick whenever he looked at her.

He found relief in praising the coffee. The only really tolerable thing about Edison, he thought, was the coffee.

It was really quite remarkable coffee that Edison made. Perhaps, in relief, he praised it overgenerously:

"This is not only the best coffee in the islands. It's the best coffee in the world."

"I know it."

"It's nectar. It's perfect. You could never ask for anything better."

"And you tell *me* how to live," Edison said. "On pills."

Only a sense of irony kept anger pinned at the back of the doctor's throat.

"I don't tell you how to live," he said. "I don't tell you how to die either."

He was relieved and glad to escape to the soda-water bottling shed, where he found the boy feeding bottles into the rattling roundabout and the indolent yellow mass of Fat Uncle responding mechanically, three-parts asleep, in the oppressive afternoon.

He shook hands with the massive bloated mountain and, while Longuemart got ready a notebook in which to record figures, if there were any figures to record, introduced the subject of pills.

Pain and nausea, with actual imitations of the process of vomiting, sprang sweatingly from Fat Uncle's face. The slits of eyes actually opened, dark with simple despair.

"Sick," Longuemart said. "He's been very sick, he says. For several days."

Gregory did not bother to use his own bad French, but said simply, in English:

"Give him two pills. Explain to him that the boy takes the pills."

Longuemart, in French, explained this, at the same time holding out the pills. The eyes of Fat Uncle rolled open and then shut themselves tightly. The big soapy hands groped at the air like shaggy spiders crawling up and down invisible webs.

"He says he's sick enough already. The pills made him vomit twice as much. He cannot eat his food."

"Hurt his pride," the American doctor said. "Shame him. Ask him if he wants to be thought less courageous than the boy."

Fat Uncle held out his hands, flatly this time, in an appealing gesture of mute despair and Longuemart took the opportunity of placing the pills in the right hand palm. Fat Uncle recoiled as if cut, speaking quickly.

"He says it is not a question of being as courageous as the boy. He knows the boy is very courageous but he is also younger. He says youth is everything. It never knows what it is to be tormented."

"Tell him—no, don't bother."

In despair, too, mildly tormented himself, the American suddenly gave up.

"We'll talk to him tomorrow before we leave," he said. "Give the boy his quota."

The boy, with one of his rare smiles, held up his hands for the pills. Gregory patted him on the shoulder, smiling and saying:

"See you later, Timi. Ask Ginette to find me a watermelon."

Together the two doctors started walking up the slight incline at the back of the hotel, away from the waterfront. A sun like a burnished wheel flared down nakedly on that part of the road where there was no shade of palms. Its force struck the American with such unexpected brutality after the shade of the hut that he paused suddenly on the hillside to pass his hand across his face. He was a great believer in the virtues of tabulation. He was a firm worshipper of efficiency. As a consequence he had made up his mind to record every house on the island, to give it a number and to make up a case history of every inhabitant, giving them numbers too. It would take many weeks, but he was determined to see it through.

"Where do we start today?" he said.

"House number four. Just along the road. Three Chinese. Numbers thirty-seven, thirty-eight and thirty-nine—S."

The S, the doctor was aware, stood for Suspect. He twisted loose fingers across his chin. He was suddenly oppressed by heat, by the meaningless mass of trivial details which he himself had helped to devise and which now seemed of less consequence, than the occasional snaking curls of dust that a light hot sea-wind blew from the potholes.

He looked back down the hill, towards the scrubby waterfront, the hotel, and the flat dust road running beside the lagoon. He could just make out the shape of the little plane on the edge of the airstrip and it was as if, for a moment, he wanted or had decided to go back to it.

"Something the matter? Did you mean to bring your camera?"

The American shook his head, seeming to sniff something. Cursorily he gave another glance at the hotel, so insubstantial-looking and tinder-like that he would not have been surprised to see it at any moment suddenly crumble or ignite in the torrid air.

"I just thought I smelled corruption," he said. "That's all."

* * *

With increasing despair Gregory followed the Frenchman along the dust track by the lagoon at noon the following day. Both men were riding bicycles, the only form of transport, apart from horses, the island knew. The further bay of the island was too far away for walking and the American already felt exhausted as he tried to plough the bicycle along a track that the past rainy season had left like a scoured riverbed.

All morning his mind had been alight with irritating warning signals about the perils of inefficiency. His entire training and nationality revolted against the mere notion of mess. He disliked the idea of riding a bicycle not so much for its own power to discomfort but because his mind clamoured constantly that there must be some simpler, more efficient, less sweatily wasteful way of achieving the same end.

He got off the bicycle.

"Jean." The Frenchman, riding ahead, turned and got off his bicycle too. "Jean—do you think you could manage here by yourself for a time?"

"I think so."

"Perhaps a week? Maybe ten days?"

"I think so. Why?"

The American raised loose irritated hands and let them fall deprecatingly back on the handlebars of the bicycle.

"Two successes, ten failures, four pill-spitters and one who actually palmed it," he said. "We're great. We move mountains."

"The vale of prejudice."

"We've got to re-attack," the American said. "Re-form, I mean to say. If we're even going to reduce the incidence of this thing, let alone stamp it out, we'll only begin to do it by efficiency. And riding bicycles isn't efficiency."

"Nor is it a cure for filariasis."

The doctor, though fond of the Frenchman's habit of talking sense with light flippancy, did not smile.

"I'm going to take the plane back," he said, "and get scooter engines fitted to the bicycles."

"You think they will prove more effective than pills?"

"I've got another idea in my mind, too," he said, "but first the bicycles."

He actually turned his bicycle round in the track and stood with one foot on the pedal, preparing to get on.

"It'll take a few days to work out," he said. "But if you wouldn't mind staying on here—"

"Of course. Not at all."

"Let's get back then. We'll have lunch and then load the bicycles into the *Rapide* and I'll be away."

Riding back to the hotel the American, less oppressed by the guilt and irritations of inefficiency now that he had expressed his thoughts about it, found himself sometimes glancing from side to side. Beyond the masses of bright yellow and carmine crotons, with their twisted elegance that he was so fond of photographing, and beyond the rampant hedges of hibiscus and ginger-lily and creeper and the trees of *tiare* and jasmine that would smell more and more exquisitely as dusk came on, lay the stilted huts of palm-thatch that he knew so well. Above the huts spread the palms; and below the palms ran the little streams, open sewers, crossed here and there by crumbling bridges, that did not smell so exquisitely in the heat of noon. Under the palms, with their fallen coconuts, ran the rats, eating at the coconuts. Into the half-eaten nuts fell the rain and in the cups of rain bred the mosquitoes. That was his constant, evil cycle. With a revulsion that never lessened with each experience of it he longed to sweep it all away.

From one of the huts a half-Chinese woman, seeing the two doctors bicycling past, rattled with a length of bamboo on the edge of a tin roof, attracting their attention, calling something at the same time.

"What does she say?" the American said.

The Frenchman alighted from the bicycle and stood listening.

"Something about someone being ill there."

"Did we call there already?"

"We called there yesterday. But there was no answer. We thought they were out. Fishing."

It did not seem to the American worth the bother of getting off the bicycle. The pattern was one, he thought, he knew too well.

"Getting sick in readiness for us," he said. "Sickness is better than cure. We know that one."

"Ought I perhaps to go in?"

The woman again shouted something as the American bicycled on.

"Come back after lunch. It's only five minutes," he said. "Tell her you'll be back in an hour. Tell her to stay there."

At lunch the American was pleased to see the melon, a sugary-golden variety, with black frosty seeds, that the boy had told Ginette to get for him. Edison's coffee was again quite beyond praise and the only trace of the doctor's irritations of the morning arose from the fact that the coffee was too hot to drink as quickly as he wanted.

"I'll be back in a few days," he said to Edison. "At the most a week. Was there something you wanted?"

"Hell, no," Edison said. "I keep telling you. We've got everything here."

"Including yaws, T.B., three sorts of—" the doctor started thinking and then checked himself abruptly. There was no time, even for the sake of candour, he told himself, to get himself involved in newer, further irritations. He would even decline, he thought, to take too much notice of how drunk Edison was, much drunker than at noon the previous day; or that on the face of the girl the sense of rift that had troubled him so sorely at yesterday's lunch had grown more pressing and more mystifying, a sharper pain.

"Do you wish me to ride the other bicycle to the plane with you?" Longuemart said, "or could someone else perhaps ride it? I ought to get back to that woman. I think I ought to see what's the trouble there."

"Timi can ride the bicycle," the American said. "The boy can ride it. If that's O.K. with Eddo?"

"Everything's O.K.," Edison said.

"I'll come down to the plane with you," the girl said suddenly, "I'd like to. I'll ride the bicycle."

Riding the bicycle along the waterfront to the airstrip beyond the belt of palms the doctor noticed that the girl hardly spoke at all. He could not help admiring, once again, as he always did, her sumptuous strength as she helped him load the bicycles into the little plane; but he was inexplicably touched too by the brooding rift in her face, by the emotion in the broad, quivering nose, and he said, just before preparing to climb into the cockpit:

"Like to come to Papeete? Room for you if you cared to come."

"No, thank you."

"Would do you good. Nice for you."

"No, thank you."

Before speaking again the doctor performed once again his sudden trick of sniffing at air. He looked instinctively along the waterfront in the direction of the crumbling hotel and thought that, once more, as yesterday, he caught a sudden smell of corruption in the air.

"Is something the matter?" he said.

From the cavernous mass of her dark hair, turning her face away, she looked down at the dust of the airstrip, not answering.

"Is something wrong?" he said. He was moved to put his hand on her shoulder.

"I know something's wrong because you laughed too much yesterday."

"He is taking another vahini," she said. "That's all."

Half an hour later she was still standing on the airstrip, gazing across the empty sky above the lagoon, as if halfhoping that the

Rapide would for some reason appear and come back, when Dr. Longuemart suddenly came running along the waterfront at an agitated trot.

"Has it gone? Has Gregory gone?"

The stupidity of the question, aimed at an airstrip quite empty except for herself, made him stop short, white as his own shirt with exhaustion, panting self-reproaches.

"I might have caught him if I'd had another bicycle," he said. "But I couldn't find Eddo. I might have caught him—"

She stared at him with sudden bitterness.

"I could have told you where Eddo is," she said. "Why do you want the doctor? What's wrong?"

With difficulty the young Frenchman pulled his words together.

"There are three cases of typhoid in that house," he said. "And two in another."

On the floor of the shed, in the stifling heat of the afternoon, Fat Uncle slept like a tired ape. The machine had stopped. The boy was dozing too.

Half dreaming, he could hear nothing but the sound of the Pacific beating against the reef. Of all the sounds in his life it was the one he heard least consciously. It simply beat through the days without rest, so that he heard it only as he might have heard the constant and ceaseless tick of a clock on a wall.

It occurred to him suddenly in this half-dream that the sea had begun to speak to him with several voices. Across the hot air these voices were arguing with complexity about something, uplifted.

He listened for several minutes, slowly waking, and then got up. It was not until he reached the door of the hut that he realised that the sea, or the envelope of hot dead air enclosing the sea, had played on him the oddest of tricks. The voices were real voices. He could in fact already hear Edison's voice among them, louder than the rest, and they came from inside the hotel.

He walked across the yard. Between the yard and the cubicles that faced on to the waterfront was a kitchen where cockroaches as large as mice ran for cover when the evening lamp was lit and where a lean and almost hairless Chinaman prepared fish and vegetables, cooked and washed up dishes. This Chinaman too was asleep, his head resting on the comparatively cool edge of the sink, one yellow hand on a tap, as if in the act of turning it.

The boy remembered then that it was another of his tasks to pump water. If he forgot to work the rotary pump that pushed water up to the tank in the roof then the Chinaman turned his taps in vain and consequently came out into the yard and beat him, as Fat Uncle sometimes did, with a thin, spearlike length of bamboo.

He was only too well aware of the significance of the hand on the tap and he slipped through the kitchen swiftly and soundlessly, bringing himself up sharply beyond the door that led into the front saloon, where the first figure he saw was that of Edison, who was waving a drumstick, and the first voice he heard was that of the young French doctor:

"I simply ask you this—is the schooner seaworthy? That's all. And you answer me neither one way nor the other."

With a gesture of expansive sarcasm Edison waved the drumstick.

"Seaworthy? Seaworthy? Of course she's seaworthy. Take a look at her before she falls in half."

Cane blinds drawn against the heat across the openings beyond the cubicles made the interior of the hotel shadowy and it was some moments before the boy could make out the figures of both Edison and the doctor, sitting in one of the cubicles, and the face of a girl he thought at first was Ginette.

As his eyes became used to the shadows he saw presently that it was not Ginette. The hair of the girl who sat in the cubicle was less dense and was plaited. Her body was feline, compact and rather small and sometimes she sucked at a long glass, through a straw.

"You don't seem to be able to get it into your head that the schooner is the only means of communication we've got," the young doctor said. His voice was restless with urgency. "Can't you see that? Don't you understand?"

"Communication?"

Edison said, "God, there's bags of communication." He waved the drumstick. "Walk along the waterfront. You'll find twenty canoes. They'll take you."

"A hundred and thirty miles?" the doctor said. "It would take a week. I want someone there tonight. Tomorrow morning anyway. That's why it's got to be the schooner."

"Got to be? Got to be? Hark at that," Edison said. "Hark at that."

There was hardly more than a word or two in this conversation that the boy could fully understand. He watched with fascination the sarcastic swings of Edison's drumstick and the upraised restless hands of the doctor, fingers upstretched in protest or appeal.

"Will you take her?" the young doctor said. "That's all I'm asking. Will you take her?"

"Not on your life."

"I'm not asking you on your life," the doctor said. "I'm asking you on the lives of the people on the island. Perhaps all of you. God man, in three days we'll have a ramping, raging epidemic here!"

"Will we?" Edison said. "If I'm going to snuff it I'll snuff it here in the hotel. In comfort. Not in that bloody colander out there."

"I don't believe you even half grasp what the situation is," the doctor said. "Not a quarter—"

"Hell, it's probably only bellyache." Edison, picking up a whisky bottle, poured out half a tumbler and pushed the bottle across the table towards the doctor. "Help yourself. Give 'em all a shot of bug-killer."

Before the doctor could move or speak again the boy saw Ginette, for the first time, as she moved across the cane blind beyond the cubicle. Half encased in her mass of black hair she had been so much part of the shadow that he had never noticed her there.

Now she simply came forward, halted a foot or two from the table and looked at Edison.

"If you won't take her, Fat Uncle will take her."

"Fat Uncle. That fat idiot? My God, Fat Uncle?"

"And if Fat Uncle won't take her I'll take her myself."

"You. Fat Uncle. Fat Uncle. You."

With contempt Edison threw away the drumstick. It landed among the drums and cymbals on the little dais where Edison and Fat Uncle sat on Saturdays to play for dancing. In the silence that followed Edison drank again. The doctor did not speak and the girl sucked at her straw.

In fascination the boy stood watching Ginette. He saw her put her hands, palms outspread, on the flanks of her big hips. He watched her throw back her head, tossing the thick mass of hair from her shoulders. On her face was a look he had never seen there before. It struck him as being a look of calm, proud loathing.

A moment later she started to move towards the door where the boy stood watching. She still did not speak. As she moved away from the cubicle, Edison, in a further gesture of contempt, put one arm round the waist and under the naked arms of the girl beside him and the girl, in the act of sucking at her glass, laughed suddenly so that she seemed to spit down the straw.

"I'm going to ask Fat Uncle. Even Fat Uncle has grown up from being a sucking-pig."

The boy saw Edison seize the bottle as if it were a hammer and a moment later he himself was through the kitchen, running, afraid the crash of the bottle would wake the Chinaman, who in turn would start yelling for water. But the crash, for some reason, never came and he was beyond the kitchen and across the yard and inside the shed, waking Fat Uncle, before he recovered from fear and astonishment.

In the shed he had a further moment of astonishment when the girl arrived. In a few seconds it rose to a strange elation. Suddenly, and for the first time, as the girl began to speak to Fat Uncle, now pulling himself lethargically and still only half awake to sit on a soda-water crate, he began to understand what had been going on between Edison, Ginette and the young French doctor in the front part of the hotel.

He surmised, with exultation, that the schooner might, at last, be going to sea. The boat that went like a bird and in which Fat Uncle had splendidly roved the world, in the fashion of a sea king, was about to sail, miraculously and unbelievably, beyond the reef again.

"There is great danger," the girl said. "I mean not with the boat. From the epidemic. We have to be in Papeete tomorrow morning and pick up things for the doctor and then come back quickly. Does the engine work?"

Ape-like and groping, Fat Uncle sat shaking his head.

"It's not my boat. It's Edison's boat."

"He'll come. He's drunk now. But he'll come."

"Will the doctor come too?"

"No: the doctor won't come. He'll stay here, with the sick ones. But I'll come."

It did not seem to the boy that there was either fear or reluctance on the face of Fat Uncle, scratching his head as he pored, eyes groping, over the soda-bottling machine. It was altogether impossible for Fat Uncle, the man of great voyages, the creator of infinite legends, to show fear or reluctance. Fat Uncle was the man who had never been afraid. He interpreted it merely as the uncertainty of a man suddenly waking from sleep and finding himself momentarily stunned by the shattering import of news he had long wanted to hear.

"Does the engine work, I asked you?"

"I can't do it. I could never do it. It's Edison's boat."

"You've got to do it. The whole island may die if you don't do it. All of us. You too."

The shattered, crumbling figure of Fat Uncle stood up. The boy looked up at him with sensations of rising, exultant pride. He felt too that he suddenly loved the gross, simple, bloated mass of flesh in a way quite unexperienced, quite unknown, before.

"It's Edison's boat. He'll never let me."

"He'll let you. I'll see to it. He'll let you."

"And what if he won't? What then?"

"He'll come," she said. "You didn't see him when I called him sucking-pig."

In another moment a sensation of exorbitant impossible hope ran through the boy. In a dazzling second of revelation he realised that he was within reach of becoming one with Fat Uncle, with the girl and perhaps with Edison, on the schooner. He too might be able to go.

"Fat Uncle, Fat Uncle," he started to say and touched the arm of the quaking mass of flesh still groping about the centre of the hut.

The shock of his touch on the nervous flesh of the man was so great that Fat Uncle swung the elephantine arm that so often hit him when the soda-bottling machine became jammed. But now the arm trembled so much that it did not strike him and a moment later the Chinaman was yelling across the yard:

"No water! No water! I kill you one of these days!"

The voice seemed to give Fat Uncle a remarkable burst of courage. The boy, caught between the stumbling sweating figure and the menace of the Chinaman in the yard, darted to one side, trying to escape, only to be caught this time by a lumbering backhander that knocked him off his feet.

"Get out of my way!" he shouted. "I got things to do—I got things on my mind! Can't you see? Things on my mind!"

For the rest of the afternoon the boy pumped water. Sometimes on days when he forgot to fill the tank he heard a distinct sharp snarl of steam as water hit scalding metal on the exposed rooftop, but today he did not listen for the sound. His ears were on the sea.

From time to time the Chinaman, who did not take his pills either, came out of the kitchen to squeak thin admonitions across the yard:

"I keep you pumping till midnight! See! I teach you to forget to pump! Keep you pumping till midnight!"

When darkness fell with sudden swiftness the boy was still pumping. At intervals he paused to listen, looking across the yard with solemn eyes in the direction of the hotel, but there was never a sound that would tell him what was going on there or if anything was going on at all.

Some time later darkness filled him with a new fear: the fear that Edison, the girl and Fat Uncle might have already manned the schooner, crept beyond the lagoon without his knowing it and disappeared. He could not bear this thought. He instinctively stopped pumping and ran out of the yard and across the waterfront without stopping to think of the Chinaman or what he would do when he found he was no longer pumping.

To his great surprise and delight the schooner was still moored at the jetty. He ran on and stood at the waterside, looking at her. A great change, he thought, had come over her. Someone had left a lighted hurricane lamp hanging on the side of the deckhouse and the light gave to the entire scabby structure of the boat a golden, ethereal glow.

He had never seen her looking like that; it made him catch his breath to see her bathed in light, mysterious and glowing. Across shallow parts of the lagoon beyond her a few men were already fishing, wading waist-deep in water, carrying their flares above their heads, or in canoes that carried flares on poles.

A moment later he actually felt a flame run through his body as he saw Fat Uncle and the girl appear on deck. He wanted to run forward. Fat Uncle had an oil drum in one hand. He swung the drum lightly as he crossed the deck and the boy knew that it was empty.

In his excitement he was ready to run forward to meet them when he heard, from behind him, the sound of other figures crossing the waterfront. He instinctively turned and darted away, as he so often did, from the menace of approaching men, hiding himself behind a palm-roofed structure of three sheets of corrugated iron that formed a stall where, in the day time, a woman sold fruit, green coconuts and slices of watermelon.

From there he saw Edison arrive with the young French doctor. It struck him at once that he was a surprisingly sober Edison. He did not shout or stagger. His voice was hardly upraised at all as he called to Fat Uncle.

"Does she go?"

"No."

"I told you she wouldn't."

"I'll have another go at her when it's daylight."

"She'll never go," Edison said. "I tell you. She never was any damn good anyway."

"She'll go like hell when she gets started," Fat Uncle said.

"When," Edison said. "When."

He approached the gangplank that connected the schooner with the jetty. He spoke now with compressed sarcasm.

"Another thing you forgot," he said. "It costs money to run that thing. Who's paying that?"

The boy saw the girl fling up her head, for the second time that day, with a gesture of proud, sharp loathing.

"So that's what's worrying you," she said.

"Gas costs money," Edison said. "Oil costs money. And it's a damn long way."

"To where?" she said. "Hell?"

The boy heard Edison laughing.

"A damn long way in that thing," he said. "Well, who pays? I don't pay, I tell you that."

The young doctor, approaching the gangplank, spoke for the first time.

"I will pay," he said, "or rather the *Institut* will pay. Dr. Gregory will see to that."

"Suits me."

"Now you have to be shamed into it," the girl said. "Now it's money."

"Don't goad me," Edison said.

"Goad you? Let your heart goad you," she said. "If that's possible."

"Get off the boat!" Edison started shouting. "Go on!—the pair of you. Come off her!" His voice started to raise itself, for the first time in cold fury. "She stays where she is!"

He seemed about to spring forward, as if ready to snatch Fat Uncle and the girl from the deck with his own hands, but the young doctor took several strides forward too.

"It's imperative that she goes," he said. "Edison, I tell you it's absolutely imperative that she goes."

"Goes? I tell you she'll never get beyond the reef—"

"I will buy the boat," the young doctor said. "I will give you a cheque on the *Banque D'Indo-China* as a deposit and we will fix the rest when Dr. Gregory comes back. How is that? Will you sell her?"

"No."

"All right. I will hire the boat. I will give you a cheque for that. I will pay for the oil too." The doctor spoke with succinct, flat contempt, not raising his voice. "I will also pay Uncle to take her. I am even willing to pay you if it will make you happy."

"All right!" Edison started shouting. "All right! So you hired yourself a tea chest! Now what? All you have to do is pull a string and she's off like a bomb."

"She'll start."

"And who's going to start her?" Edison said. He lifted thin, jeering hands in the direction of Fat Uncle. "That baboon? That bladder? He's been trying all night!"

"I am going to start her."

"Confident man. Confident man," Edison said. "All confidence. She's never been started in six months. Nine months. How do you know she'll start?"

"Because," the young doctor said. "I have faith she will start.

And because—" He was already walking towards the plank, rolling up the long white sleeves of his shirt—"I like talking to engines. They'll start if you talk to them the right way."

The doctor walked across the plank to the deck of the schooner. Edison retreated a few paces, preparing, it seemed, to go back to the hotel. And then suddenly, as if actually shamed by something the girl had said or as if the thinnest of the doctor's veiled ironies had at last begun to have their effect, he turned and shouted towards the doctor:

"She kicks like hell. She kicks back at you."

"I'll manage."

"There's a knack in it. You can stop her kicking if you know the knack."

"Thanks. I'll manage."

His voice faded as he disappeared into the well of the boat below the little deckhouse. For a few moments longer the hurricane lamp remained suspended where it was. Then Fat Uncle took it off its hook, ready to follow the doctor below, and Edison called:

"Hey, Fat Uncle!"

"Hullo?"

"I'll be back in ten minutes if you want me."

"Back?"

"We'll need food, won't we, you fat ape?" he called. "We may be days in that thing. We'll need a case of bug-killer."

Edison turned abruptly and walked across the waterfront. For a moment longer the hurricane lamp illuminated the deck. Then Fat Uncle took it away.

The girl did not move from her position in the stern of the schooner. In darkness broken only by the occasional passage of a fishing flare across the lagoon behind her she leaned on the wooden rail of the boat, staring ashore. Something about her seemed to brood profoundly, in some way mutinously, with sadness, in the darkness.

What it was the boy had no means of knowing. He crouched for a long time behind the watermelon stall. He saw Edison reappear from the hotel, carrying crates and a second hurricane lamp, and then some time later appear a second time, carrying drums of oil.

All this time the girl did not move from the stern of the schooner, but some hours later the boy heard on the night air a new, thrilling and altogether miraculous sound. It made him start to his feet so suddenly that he cracked his elbow on the corrugated iron of the little stall. He was afraid for a moment that someone from the schooner would hear the sound and come down and find him hiding there, afterwards surrendering him to the Chinaman and the tortures of the pump again. But the girl lifted her head no higher than she might have done if she had heard the sound of a rat exploring a tin can across the jetty.

He listened to the sound of the schooner engine for a long time. When finally it stopped on the night air and Fat Uncle had taken away the second hurricane lamp and there were no more figures on the schooner he felt he could still hear it, wonderfully beating through the darkness. All his blood was on fire with that sound.

Even when he climbed on board and lay down in the hold, in the bows of the boat, in complete darkness, he still imagined he could hear it, a great pulse marvellously driving his blood, miraculously ready to bear him out to sea.

He dozed off and came to himself some hours later, in the first light of morning, in a world of shaking timbers. The reality of the engine actually running in its confined cradle at the foot of the small companionway no longer struck him as beautiful. He felt his blood begin to blench at the smell of engine oil. His veins felt white and cold. His impression was that they were filled with whiteness.

After he had been sick two or three times, retching as quietly as he could into a sack, he sat up. The boat progressed in a series of deep fat rolls that were so regular that after a time he let his body go with them without any attempt at resistance. Presently, in this way, he beat the last of his sickness.

He was not afraid. He remembered over and over again some words of Fat Uncle's: "The sea is your friend. There is no need to be afraid of the sea." At the same time he experienced occasional short moods of disappointment. The boat seemed to progress neither like the wind nor like a bird. It seemed much more like a thick slow slug crawling its way through waters he could not see.

He longed to go on deck. He began to feel, and then to be sure, that the world on deck would be the world he had imagined: his

promised world, the world in which the boat flew on a strong white
wind, the world of great fish with mouths like doors, the world of
Fat Uncle, the King, and the far, long voyages.

The heat of the day was already rising when he dared at last to
crawl on deck. Sun struck him brassily as he lifted his face above the
companionway. At this moment, he feared Fat Uncle. He was sure
that Fat Uncle would strike him.

Instinctively he searched the deck for Fat Uncle and at first saw
only Edison, standing at the wheel, looking ahead, his back towards
him. Then he saw Fat Uncle lying flat on his belly, face turned
sideways across the deck. It astonished the boy very much to see
that his lips were grey.

With wide eyes Fat Uncle lay and stared at him. His mouth fell
open. A dribble of yellow moisture poured from his lips. He raised
himself on one elbow and with the other hand pawed at his face,
gropily, as if pulling at invisible cobwebs.

Then like an enormous frog he inflated his chest and face and let
out a gigantic croak that brought Edison whipping round from the
wheel. The croak became a thinning whimper. The eyes squeezed
themselves shut. They remained shut for the space of a quarter of a
minute or so. Then suddenly they shot open again and Fat Uncle,
with a yell, told himself of the reality of the boy:

"It is you! It is you! You came up there like a ghost."

"For Christ sake," Edison said.

The boy stood at the head of the small companionway, waiting to
be struck. It surprised him greatly that no one moved to strike him.
It surprised him still more to see that Fat Uncle, the man of the sea,
lifting himself to his knees, face grey and sickened, looked as
frightened as he felt himself.

"How in hell did you get here?" Edison said.

He started trembling and had nothing to answer. His veins ran
white again. The sea ran white about the schooner. He felt sick
again as he stared at its running whiteness and the faces of the men.

In a third great moment of surprise he saw the girl walking up
from the stern of the schooner. He had never remotely expected to
see her there. He had expected the world of men to be completed,
for some reason, by the young French doctor.

Fat Uncle, as the girl appeared, experienced one of his sudden waves of courage and waved an elephantine fist at the boy. He lurched unsteadily as he threw the blow with vague menace, like a drunk, but the blow missed by a yard.

"That's right. Strike him," the girl said. "Be brave. Strike him."

"I ought to throw the little squirt overboard!" Edison said. "Sharkwards."

"That's it. You be brave too," she said.

It was Edison now who started yelling. He yelled for Fat Uncle to take the wheel. Then he grabbed the boy by the shirt and yelled into his face:

"How the hell did you creep in?" With an open hand he cuffed him first on one side of his face, then the other. He bawled incomprehensibly, narrow face raging. Then he turned on Fat Uncle, yelling: "You were supposed to keep him working, you fat baboon, out back there. What in hell were you up to?"

After this, since there was no answer from Fat Uncle, he cuffed the boy about the face again, knocking him from side to side.

"You are very brave, too," the girl said.

"Shut up and lie down somewhere!" Edison yelled.

"You didn't used to talk to me like that," she said.

"I talk how I like."

"Everybody knows."

"And another thing—I'm in charge here," Edison yelled. "I'm skipper. This is my boat."

"Come with me. Come this way," the girl said and held out her hand to the boy.

The boy followed her to the stern end of the deck. She was preparing food there: bread, with a little rice and scrapings of raw fish and a few red peppers. A half stalk of bananas lay on the deck, together with Edison's crate of whisky.

"Why did you come?" she said.

He did not know why he had come. He stared at the sea's running whiteness. A snowy wake between himself and a jagged glitter of horizon held him transfixed. He discovered that he could no longer tell why he had come, why he wanted to come or of the great thoughts that had once pounded through him. Most of all the great thoughts had vanished, meaningless or incomprehensible, and would not come back.

"There's no need to be afraid of anything," she said. "Don't be afraid."

"Why did you come?" he said.

She did not answer. She turned her head away, face half-hidden by the huge black mass of her hair. She sat cross-legged as she busied herself with the fish, her big legs and feet bare, her knees golden and shining, her *pereu* drawn up above them. Her hair, when it fell the full length and she was sitting down, as she was now, was thick and long enough to spread about her like a cloak.

"Why did you come?" he said. "I didn't think you were coming."

"I came like you did," she said. "Hiding."

He sat cross-legged too, staring at her. He remembered how she had leaned against the stern of the schooner, in complete darkness, brooding. Was it possible that she brooded about coming? He watched the whiteness of the sea, the hot, glittering light, running past her dark head. Her splendid, gentle, brooding face was carved against the skyline that ran in the heat of the morning like pure flame.

He started wondering, for some reason, how old she was. She looked, he thought, much older than yesterday: much older than the day he had heard her laughing so loudly in the presence of the two doctors. He could not remember seeing her laugh ever since that time.

He guessed that she would be old. Everybody who was grownup was old. That was natural. It was only people like himself who were not old and he said now, solemnly:

"How old are you? I never knew how old you were."

She actually laughed a little, showing her broad white teeth.

"As old as my tongue and a little older than my teeth," she said. "So am I."

"Sixteen," she said. "That's how old I am."

"Is that old?" he said.

"I sometimes think," she said, "it's as old as I ever want to be."

They went on talking together, sometimes busy with the food, sometimes doing nothing, for most of the morning. The swell across the ocean seemed to lengthen with the heat of the day. The candescent wake of the slugging schooner grew no faster but simply whitened more fiercely, blinding in the perpendicular sun.

Towards twelve o'clock Edison came aft for a few minutes, picked a whisky bottle out of the crate and stood with it in his hand, drinking, staring out to sea. The girl did not speak to him. Edison did not speak to her either. A two-day growth of beard seemed to make the long lean face appear more cadaverous in the fierce upward reflection of sea light. Sweat gave it a thin oily gleam, the naked ball-like head quite shadowless in the ferociously burning glow of noon.

He spoke only once, and then not to the girl. Walking away, pausing half a dozen paces up the deck, he waved the bottle in a starboard direction, out to an ocean apparently empty except for a distant, long-winged sea bird flying low above the water.

"Look, boy. See that?"

The boy looked up in time to see, fifty yards away, the explosion of a single rising shark. It sprang from the water like a suddenly discharged torpedo and then vanished instantly, seeming to leave on the hot air an echo that in reality was Edison's voice, laughing.

"See you behave, boy," Edison said, "or that's where you go."

He swung away towards the wheel, lifting the bottle to his mouth, indulging his favourite habit of drinking as he walked. From the wheel the boy heard him laugh again, as if perhaps he were repeating the joke to Fat Uncle, who in turn laughed too.

After that the boy sat for some long time quite silent. It was beyond him to know if the threat of Edison were real or if the laughter of Edison was only laughter. He was aware, in a strange way, of a growing expansion of the sea about him. Noon now seemed to impose on it a sombre, heartless enormity. The shark that had sprung suddenly out of the heart of it was an evil vision that was also a threatening voice. The recollection of its moment of furious savagery made him shudder.

There was no way he knew of expressing himself about these things and he simply sat staring at the gentle, brooding face of the girl.

"When will we arrive?" he said. "Today?"

"Perhaps tonight. If all goes well."

He wanted very much to arrive. The air was growing thicker and more oppressive every moment and he was glad to see the girl pouring out, into an enamel cup, a drink of water.

Drinking the water, he sat staring, in his long-sighted, solemn fashion, far out to sea. It had occurred to him suddenly that he might see land there. By searching for land he might project himself into a still further world, beyond Edison's sinister jocularities and the voice of the shark, where no one could threaten him any more.

For the space of a few seconds he actually believed he could see land, in a purplish, uncertain mass, looming from the horizon. He watched this mass for some moments longer without certainty. Then it began to seem to him nebulously, ominously, unlike land.

He spoke to the girl, pointing.

"Is that where we're going?" he said. "Is that the land?"

The girl rose on her knees in order to look more easily over the side of the schooner. In this alert, upright posture she let out a sudden gasp of alarm. A moment later she had twisted herself completely to her feet and was running along the deck.

"Look there! Look there!" she was shouting. "That way! Look there!"

The boy stood motionless, watching the horizon with its ominous flower of darkening cloud, and knew suddenly that it was not the land.

He lay below in the hold, side by side with the girl, in complete darkness, when the storm hit them from the south.

All morning he had been aware of a wind of splendid whiteness on the sea. Now he knew that what hit them was a black wind. It was a wind of solid, driving water. He felt it pounding against the wooden bows of the schooner in an unbroken attack that sent him rolling like a light and helpless barrel across the timbers and then pushed him back again. He yelled in pain as his head cracked on the bulwark and for the first time in his life he could hear no responsive sound of his own voice against the roar of wind and rain.

Somewhere in the middle of this maelstrom of driving sound an object crashed with sickening thunder down the steps of the companionway. The boy did not know until afterwards that this was Fat Uncle. With a tremendous clang that seemed for a moment like the side of the ship exploding inwardly, the hatch-cover closed behind him, battening the three of them down.

It was impossible for him to know how long the black wind beat at them. The squat flatness of the boat kept her riding down long troughs that, just as she seemed to be free, curled like vast conical hooks and clawed her back again. At each end of these raging troughs she was so low in the water, leaking at the seams, that he lay half-drowned.

When the wind began to lessen with a sinister abruptness that startled him far more than his first sight of the storm cloud had done, he became gradually aware of an ominous situation. He could not hear the engine beating. All he could hear above the dying wind were the elephantine hands of Fat Uncle, clawing their way, ape-like, up the totally dark steps of the hatchway.

An astonishing shaft of metallic sunlight seemed to dart down through the opening hatch and scooped Fat Uncle up to the deck. The boy heard Edison yelling. In a sudden list of the schooner water from the deck poured down the steps and it was as if Fat Uncle had turned and spewed.

Edison yelled again. In stumbling response Fat Uncle reappeared at the top of the hatchway and a moment later slithered down it. He began to make frantic and misdirected attacks on the engine, banging pointlessly with spanners. Water sloshed about the hold, drenching the boy as it climbed up the bulwarks and bounced back again.

He stared at the fumbling figure of Fat Uncle with a mixture of brooding hope and pity. The huge hands, convulsively picking up tools and groping about the engine cradle, were pathetic in their obstinate impression of doing something useful. Now and then they hovered, jelly-like, above the puzzle of plugs and mechanism, fingering objects with timidity, as if they were monsters that would sting.

Suddenly an enraged, half-drunk Edison threw himself down the hatchway. He yelled incomprehensible threats at Fat Uncle and struck him flat handed about the face. The great yellow ape dived sideways as the boy so often dived in retreat from him and then fell, deflated, into the sloppy water of the hold.

"Get up on deck, you fat bastard!" Edison yelled. "Get hold of the wheel and try to keep her steady when she goes!"

Watching the drenched and yellow figure heaving itself up the hatchway the boy suddenly felt infinitely sorry for Fat Uncle. A moment later he saw Edison pounding the gross flopping back with his knee.

"Get up there! Go on, you bastard! Out of the way—I want to get on deck. Move yourself!—God, you got us into this thing, didn't you, but you've got about as much bloody idea how to get us out as a sea egg."

The two men disappeared on deck. A rush of wind blew away the last of Edison's disturbed threats. A minute later it seemed to blow the man himself back again. He had armed himself with two bottles. He was actually performing, as he came down the hatchway, his trick of drinking as he walked.

He too made attacks on the engine. A thin enraged strength gave the white unmuscular arms a wiry, clockwork activity. It was unbrutal but sinister. At intervals he slapped his mouth against the bottle. With the return of sunlight the air had become cinderous again and presently Edison ripped off his shirt. The prominent white ribs, curiously hairless, were bathed in sweat, and the boy suddenly saw him as a living, clawing, mechanical skeleton.

An hour later the engine was still not working and periodically Edison stormed at it with disjointed shouts. In a lurch of the boat an oil drum freed itself from somewhere and rolled against his shins, setting him yelling in a venomous tirade against Fat Uncle, the French doctor and above all the monstrous stupidity of ever having come on the boat. Fat Uncle was mad. The boat was a deathtrap. Longuemart was mad. Who ever had the damn crazy idea of taking her out in the first place?

"You did, you fat bastard, didn't you? You did!"

Time measured itself in the emptying of a bottle. He uncorked another. As the level of this second one lowered itself the skeleton-like figure of Edison seemed to disappear. A trapped, blasphemous prisoner took its place: a prisoner of an engine that would not work and of a vision so disturbed that he actually started to aim misplaced blows at the bulwarks as if hammering to be free.

In a final abusing storm of threats he lurched wildly up the companionway, swinging the spanner. The boy heard him scream hoarsely on a harsh upward scale of abuse, incoherent to him except in a final repeated phrase:

"I'm coming for you, you fat bastard! I'm coming for you!"

At the moment Edison's disappearance the boy saw the girl emerge from the darkness behind the engine cradle. Her *pereu*, like her arms and legs, was drenched in oil and water.

She picked up a hammer left by Edison on the engine cover. She stood for a moment at the foot of the steps. The boy scrambled across the partly flooded hold, stumbling in water. She seemed to take pity on the anxious brooding eyes and put one hand on his shoulder.

He heard running feet on the deck.

"Stay here," she said. "Don't come up. Keep away."

She started up the steps. A gust of wind shuddering down the companionway blew away the complete coherence of whatever she said next but he thought it sounded like:

"He gets filled with madness. The whisky blinds him. He doesn't see—"

In three or four leaps she was up the steps. Sheer curiosity could not keep him back and less than half a minute later he was crawling after her.

He emerged on to what seemed to him a steaming, deserted deck. Heat was burning up the last of the flood of spray and rain. The deck planks were giving off grey rising vapour.

He found himself suspended in fear and excitement at the head of the companionway. His hands and knees felt locked. When he did move at last it was to retreat a step or two as Edison tore blindly past him, yelling, with Fat Uncle a yard or two ahead.

He heard Fat Uncle fall, screaming, against the wheel. He knelt cold and transfixed as Edison beat at the yellow mass of flesh with the spanner.

The girl came running too. She aimed a single blow at Edison's shoulder with the hammer. A second before the impact Edison turned his head sharply as if to shout to her to keep away and the blow crushed into the smooth white top of the balding skull.

Edison fell sightlessly. A moment of awful surprise seemed to click his mouth open. A gust of sea wind seemed to blow a thin feather of blood from his lips. A second gust of wind caught the entire body as it fell, pitching it suddenly, frail and more than ever skeleton-like, against the wheel, where Fat Uncle lay.

The boy stood for what seemed to him a long time surveying the dead. It would not have surprised him very much if the girl had been dead too. She sat stiffly against the side of the deck, head bowed, face completely hidden in the mass of her hair.

He was disturbed at last by a vague notion that the dead ought to be covered. He walked back towards the stern of the schooner and presently found a tarpaulin in a locker. He dragged it back along the deck, spread it out and threw it at last over the bodies of Edison and Fat Uncle.

Turning away, he felt his veins run white again. The wind was white on the water. The heat of the afternoon was incredibly, cruelly white as it beat up from the drying decks and the sea.

He turned at last to the girl. With relief he saw her lift her face, as if she had actually been watching him from the cavernous shadow of her hair. The most mysterious thing about her face, he thought, was that she seemed now to be in one respect like Edison. She could not see.

He was prepared for her to start screaming. She did not scream. Instead she turned her face slowly in the direction of the wheel and held it there, transfixed by the sight of the tarpaulin.

He also stared at the tarpaulin. The flaring realisation that it covered the body of the man of legends, the great, long voyager, filled him with sudden waves of sorrow for Fat Uncle.

He turned and saw this sorrow of his reflected in her face. Somehow he grasped, incredibly, that it might be sorrow for Edison. He could not understand this. He could remember nothing good of Edison. His abiding impressions of Edison were of a man repellent, sneering, drunken, wasteful, odiously sinister. Edison was of the breed for whom he played on Saturday evenings at the screaming dances: a dirty man.

It even occurred to him, as he stood there for a few moments longer, that sorrow for Edison was a mistaken thing. It even seemed to him possible to be glad that Edison was dead. He even thought the girl might be glad.

When he spoke for the first time it was with an odd detachment, about something he felt to be far removed from these realities.

"That was a great storm," he said. "I've never known a storm like that."

"No," she said. "It was a great storm."

As she spoke she turned to look at him, for the first time directly, with large black eyes. A sudden burst of wind blew her hair free of her face, leaving it fully exposed. Its sightless lack of expression seemed to imprison her in a terrible bond.

In this same imprisoned, expressionless way she spoke monotonously of the engine:

"Does the engine work?" she said. "What about the engine?"

He was glad to follow her down the steps of the companionway. In the hold it was easier, now more secure; the sea was calming down. In the partial gloom he could not see her face so well and he was glad of this. He was glad too to be out of sight of the humped black mound that was Fat Uncle and Edison.

"When did you hide?" she said.

"In the morning. Early. After everyone had gone."

"I think I was asleep when you came," she said. "Do you remember they went back to the hotel and then came back again? That was when I hid. I heard the doctor working on the engine for an hour."

As she spoke she seemed to be searching for something and a second later he knew what it was.

"We must have the spanner," she said.

With nausea and fear he remembered where the spanner was. As she realised it too she stood imprisoned more terribly than ever, unable to move or speak to him.

He went up the companionway. Once more, on deck, his veins ran with whiteness. The sea, running with whiteness too, blazed at his eyeballs.

For a few seconds longer, standing over the tarpaulin, he played a game of hideous guesswork. He guessed that the larger, humpier mound underneath the tarpaulin was the body of Fat Uncle. He guessed that Edison had the spanner.

He snatched at the tarpaulin with sudden desperation and the empty hands of Edison were revealed underneath it. He flung it back again and turned to find himself mocked in the glitter of whiteness prancing up from the sea.

The spanner lay all the time on the deck, six feet away.

"Here it is," he said to her.

It was the instinctive thing to give her the spanner as he reached the foot of the hatchway and she promptly dropped it.

He picked it up. Something about the feel of the spanner made him suddenly recall Fat Uncle. He was abruptly glad of Fat Uncle. Sometimes when the soda-bottling machine jammed it was a favourite theme of Fat Uncle's to bludgeon him into the business of mending it again. His hands, in consequence, had grown quite agile with spanners.

He began to tinker with the engine. The girl brooded beside him, somberly, terribly quiet. By contrast he began to feel less and less of his nausea, his fear and his horror at the bloody secrets of the tarpaulin up on deck. The spanner gave him the means of grasping at tangible things and he began now to try to cheer the girl up with recollections:

"Fat Uncle went on long voyages in this boat," he said. "Once he was blown by a big wind like that."

"Yes?"

"To Australia. All the way to Australia the wind blew him."

"I never heard him talk of that."

"A million miles,"he said.

"There is no such thing as a million miles."

"There must be," he said. "Fat Uncle told me so."

He felt himself become buoyant at these recollections.

"Long, long voyages he went. To Noumea. Across the world. Everywhere."

"Long ago?"

"Oh! long ago."

"I never heard him talk of it."

Two hours later he could no longer see to work on the engine. In his own mind he had long since given up the idea that anything he could do would make it work again. His pretence of solving its mysteries was merely part of his pride.

He followed the girl up the hatchway. With averted eyes the pair of them went aft along the deck.

"There is a little food left," she said, "if you feel like it."

He could only shake his head. A spurt of sickness squeezed itself acidly up his throat. He managed to say:

"Do you feel like it?"

"Some water, perhaps. Could you drink some water?"

He could not speak this time. He simply nodded his head.

"The sun has gone," she said.

Holding the water cask in readiness to fill the mug with water, she paused and stood for some time staring at the horizon. The sun had gone down in a startling agony of carmine, purple-black and flame. A few pinkish clouds, like high birds, were flying far overhead, delicate, broken-feathered. The sea, calm now except for the faintest ripples, collected these colours and cast the mingled glow of them back in her face. The features of the face were set and grim, as if carved, their proudness undissolved.

Ten minutes later it was utterly dark except for a slowly expiring gap of rosy copper low down and far away, against the face of the dead calm sea. Something about this calmness, on which the schooner now rode as if locked to an invisible anchor, filled the air with a sense of foreboding so ominous that when the boy finally lay down on the deck, side by side with the girl, it was with his face downwards but slightly averted, listening.

It struck him suddenly that they were there for ever. The schooner was locked against a sea permanently held in deathly silence. Its searing flare of daylight whiteness had given place to a darkness that imprisoned every scrap of motion. He could not detect the slightest drift of the boat one way or another or the faintest rise of it up and down.

He lay there for a long time in this motionless attitude, completely locked in silence. The girl too was lying face downwards, head buried in her hair. Her hands in turn clutched the side of her hair, as if in a nightmare of remorse and terror she was suspended in the act of tearing it out by the roots.

The horror of what she must be thinking broke on him very gradually. After a long time he turned and lay face upwards, staring at the stars. The sky, like the sea, seemed to be held in a formidable, dark paralysis.

Staring upward, he wondered what he himself could possibly feel like if he had killed a man. Through a horror of his own he passed into a stage of sheer fright at the mere recollection of what lay under the tarpaulin along the deck. When the horror finally lessened and passed it gave way to an enormous sense of wonder: a thankful wonder that he had not, after all, killed a man, and then a terrible wonder that he had actually seen the act, survived it and was alive to remember it all.

He lay for a little longer in a senseless vacuum, no longer even thinking. A dozen times before this he had expected her to cry. The fact that she did not once show the faintest sign of tears had helped to keep him from weeping too. Suddenly he could not bear any longer her tearless agonised attitude of seeming to tear her hair out by the roots as she lay there in the darkness. It filled him with a boyish rush of compassion in which he could no longer refrain from touching her. He moved towards her and put his hands on her shoulders and her hair.

She at once interpreted this groping touch of his as a sign of fear. She turned instinctively and with big naked arms held him against her. She rocked him backwards and forwards, motherwise, murmuring quietly at the same time.

He found something more than comfort in the touch of her body. It did for him what the sky and the sea had failed to do. It drove away the last impression of ominous foreboding, his feeling that the two of them were locked there for ever. It coaxed him out of his senseless vacuum.

The girl too began to come alive. She actually pressed her mouth against the side of his face. Then he heard her voice framing words for the first time since darkness had come down.

"Don't be afraid."

"I'm not afraid." As he said this she enveloped him still more closely with her body. "Are you afraid?"

"It is not a question of being afraid."

He did not understand this remark and for some moments she did not explain it. Instead she held him still more closely to her, arms completely round him now.

"There is something more than being afraid."

For a second time he did not understand her. He was bewildered by a growing sense of mystery about her. Her flesh quivered as she held him. An impression that all the pores of her skin were about to shed their own terrible fears gave him an overwhelming sense of sorrow that he could not bear.

"What is it?" he said. "What is more than being afraid?"

She spoke with distant calmness in answer.

"I have a child inside me."

He did not speak. The gravity of his pride that she had decided to tell him this was so great that he felt suddenly, inside himself, a new stature. He was also old. He also felt he had become, in some strange way, part of her.

"Shall we try to sleep now?" she said.

Her voice had taken on a further spell of calmness. The infinite sense of brooding sorrow was at last dispelled.

"Come closer to me," she said. "Lie close to me."

He had already closed his eyes. He started, a little later, to sleep peacefully in the warmth of her arms. In the uncanny silence of the completely motionless boat she slept too, holding him like a mother.

He awoke, some time after dawn, to strange noises. He thought at first that the sea had risen and was beating against the sides of the vessel. He opened his eyes and stared upward at a repetition of the flocks of clouds travelling, like pink birds, high across the morning sky.

The sounds troubled him. Like part of a half-remembered dream they mocked at his expanding consciousness with strange familiarity.

Finally he got up. He could no longer resist the reality of the sounds. He walked along the deck. Half way to the bows he stopped, horrified by the astounding emptiness of the deck about the wheel, stunned by an incredible illusion that the tarpaulin had been carefully folded up and laid at the head of the hatchway.

In the moment of realising that the bodies of Edison and Fat Uncle no longer lay there he realised also that the engine was running.

He stood staring down the steps of the hatchway for fully a minute before realising that the blood-stained face of the man bending over the engine was the face of Fat Uncle.

A new horror rose up in him. The impression that he was staring down at a figure spirited back from the dead was too much for his calmness. He felt his veins run sick and white again.

Almost at the same moment he heard Fat Uncle begin speaking.

"I remembered we only put half a tank in," he said. The half-idiotic lips gaped upward, brown with blood. "No wonder we stopped."

The boy started to answer with a series of broken phrases that made no sense with the exception of the word "Edison? Edison?" which he blubbered over and over again.

With fat crooked fingers Fat Uncle waved upwards, towards the rising light.

"He's gone where he said he'd send you," he said. "Out there."

For the first time the boy broke into weeping. His choking tears had nothing to do with Edison, nor with the sudden appearance of Fat Uncle, back from the dead. He was weeping at an unknown horror that seemed to be crawling up from the whitening sea, on all sides of him, in a nightmare.

The sound of his weeping brought the girl running along the deck. She too heard the sound of the engine and stopped abruptly.

"Timi! Timi!" she was shouting. "Timi!" The sudden joy on her face woke in him fresh bursts of weeping. "Why do you cry? How did you make it go?"

The head of Fat Uncle rose above the top of the hatchway. And the girl, seeing it, let out her own grievous cry.

A land rose from the sea. A long serrated cockscomb of green and violet seemed to float out of the horizon under a scalding sun.

Like a caricature of a warrior scarred in battle, Fat Uncle stood grasping the wheel with enormous, aggressive hands, staring straight ahead. His face, with muscles set, no longer seemed flabby. It seemed to be contained in a metallic, greasy mask. Dark crusts of blood had congealed and dried across the forehead, heightening the yellow of the skin and giving the impression of a man wrapped in a brooding, savage frown.

The girl once dipped a bucket into the sea. She was moved to bathe the bloodstained face and started to tear a strip of cloth from her *pereu;* but Fat Uncle bashed into the silence of the deck with a slam of a vast hand against the wheel and a bruising cry across the white calm sea.

"Let them stop there! Let the world see them! Let them see how he tried to kill me!"

After that the girl crouched against the side of the boat, head enclosed in the falling mass of her hair, hands flat on the rail. She stared for some hours in speechless concentration at the land enlarging with incredible slowness on the horizon while the boy, ordered by Fat Uncle, washed blood from the deck.

Now and then Fat Uncle broke into long, senseless abuse of Edison. He shouted with lunatic contempt at the evil of fate, spitting at the sea. At the end of these outbursts he struck at the wheel again with a strange mixture of pride and childishness, laughing, giggling fatly.

"Now she's mine! Now I've got her back!" His idiot pride in the material possession of the boat made him seem more than ever swollen. "She was always mine! She always belonged to me."

The boy was struck by these outbursts into a watchful awe. He tried for a long time to work out a reason for Fat Uncle's pride in his scars. He understood the pride in the schooner, but that of the scars eluded him completely until Fat Uncle yelled:

"You saw the fight. How did I kill him? Tell me that."

It did not occur to the boy that this was evidence of cowardice in Fat Uncle. He heard the words with amazed bewilderment. He heard Fat Uncle give a laugh of triumph, as if actually glad that he had killed a man.

He was about to shatter this illusion by telling Fat Uncle the truth when he saw the girl, moving for the first time for some hours, slowly turn her face, pushing back her hair with both hands. The face, paralysed with fright, looked unbelievably cold in the heat of the day, frozen against the background of an ocean across which, at last, a wind was rising, cutting brief slits of foam from the crests of the long smooth swells.

"Tell me how I killed him! I don't remember." Fat Uncle struck attitudes of boldness, flinging out oil-stained contemptuous arms. "I remember he came up behind me—like that"—he crouched with grotesque ape-like fury in imitation of Edison—"Like that he came up, didn't he? I remember that." He spat again with galling, contemptuous laughter. "From behind! Like a rat—from behind!"

For a long time the boy nursed his dilemma, watching first the girl, then the land becoming more and more clearly defined every moment across the white-fringed sea. He could actually make out now the collar of the island's enclosing reef and soon he could see the colour of the mountains beyond, yellow-brown at the foot, sharp emerald high up the slopes, with dark palm tufts on the shore and in between.

Once or twice he opened his mouth to speak, but the words never framed themselves. Hearing Fat Uncle laugh again, he pondered gravely, with eyes that seemed as always to be listening to half-formed sounds, on the astonishing fact that a man might be glad to kill a man. Held in a horror between truth and silence, he was troubled by a growing recollection, more bewildering to him now than when it had happened, of the girl telling him of the child inside herself and of her mystifying words:

"There is something more than being afraid."

These were all strange mysteries, not of his making. He could not interpret them. He could only interpret the embalming warmth of the girl's arms in the depth of nighttime, quieting him to sleep, holding him so closely that he was almost one with the other body inside her own.

That was a still stranger mystery: the child inside herself. He brooded on that until compassion and wonder held him in a trance, sightlessly.

He was woken out of it by a yell from Fat Uncle:

"I see the gap!" With the quaking, triumphant fingers of a man who might have made, single-handed, an uncharted voyage across cruel waters, he pointed ahead. "We're nearly there! Boy, take the wheel a moment while I get below!"

The boy grasped the wheel. In the few seconds while Fat Uncle was below the girl came and stood beside him. He turned, not speaking, and looked at her sad, gentle, brooding face, wrapped in dignity. He searched it for a sign of fear and at the same moment searched his own mind for something to say to her.

A second later the engine slowed to half-speed. She smiled gravely. Without a word she put her hand on his shoulder and a moment later Fat Uncle came up on deck.

"I'll take her now." He brandished, in his ape-like, childish fashion, a pair of arms that seemed as if they were about to embrace himself. "I'll take her in."

As he moved to grasp the wheel the girl spoke quietly.

"Let the boy take her a little farther," she said. "He deserves that. It would make him very proud to take her a little farther."

There were still a few hundred yards to go.

"Take her!" Fat Uncle again waved generous, expansive arms, laughing. "How does she feel? How do you like her?"

As the boy, grasping the wheel, stared into hot sunlight with solemn far-seeing eyes, a strange illusion affected him. It was that the boat, though down to half-speed, was travelling faster than ever, running with flying swiftness across white-flecked water towards the steaming gap and the mountains beyond.

"How does she feel?" Fat Uncle shouted. "How does she go?"

The veins of the boy ran with pride. The entire sea about him ran with wonderful whiteness. He turned swiftly to show his pride to the girl and saw that there were tears in her eyes. These tears, unfallen, imprisoned her brooding eyes with a troubled, crystalline brightness. She too was proud.

Exultantly he half threw up his hands. A boy might travel a million miles and never see what he had seen. He might live through a million nights and never hear what he had heard. Solemnly he was glad he had been afraid with her and because of it he felt he understood, at last, her tears, her pride and above all her brooding darkness.

"She goes like the wind!" he shouted. "Like the wind!"

ABOUT H. E. BATES

H. E. Bates was born in 1905 at Rushden in Northamptonshire and was educated at Kettering Grammar School. He worked as a journalist and clerk on a local newspaper before publishing his first book, *The Two Sisters*, when he was twenty. In the next fifteen years he acquired a distinguished reputation for his stories about English country life. During the Second World War, he was a Squadron Leader in the R.A.F. and some of his stories of service life, *The Greatest People in the World* (1942), *How Sleep the Brave* (1943) and *The Face of England* (1953) were written under the pseudonym of 'Flying Officer X'. His subsequent novels of Burma, *The Purple Plain* and *The Jacaranda Tree*, and of India, *The Scarlet Sword*, stemmed directly or indirectly from his war experience in the Eastern theatre of war.

In 1958 his writing took a new direction with the appearance of *The Darling Buds of May*, the first of the popular Larkin family novels, which was followed by *A Breath of French Air, When the Green Woods Laugh, Oh! To Be in England* (1963) and *A Little of What You Fancy*. His autobiography appeared in three volumes, *The Vanished World* (1969), *The Blossoming World* (1971) and *The World in Ripeness* (1972). His last works included the novel, *The Triple Echo* (1971) and a collection of short stories, *The Song of the Wren* (1972). Perhaps one of the most famous works of fiction is the best-selling novel *Fair Stood the Wind for France* (1944). H. E. Bates also wrote miscellaneous works on country life, several plays including *The Day of Glory* (1945), *The Modern Short Story* (1941) and a story for children, *The White Admiral* (1968). His works have been translated into sixteen languages and a posthumous collection of his stories, *The Yellow Meads of Asphodel*, appeared in 1976.

H. E. Bates was awarded the C.B.E. in 1973 and died in January 1974. He was married in 1931 and had four children.

THE REVIVED MODERN CLASSICS

H. E. Bates
A Month by the Lake & Other Stories. Introduction by Anthony Burgess. Seventeen "nearly perfect stories" *(Publishers Weekly)* by the English master (1905-1974)—"...without an equal in England in the kind of story he made his own."—*London Times.* Cloth & NDPaperbook 645.   (In preparation: *A Party for the Girls: Six Stories*)

Kay Boyle
Life Being the Best and Other Stories. Edited with an introduction by Sandra Whipple Spanier. Thirteen stories from the period when Kay Boyle lived as an American expatriate in France. "Boyle's writing captures the moment of visionary realism when sensation heightens and time for an instant fixes and stops."—Margaret Atwood.   In preparation: Cloth & NDP654

Mikhail Bulgakov
The Life of Monsieur de Molière. Trans. by Mirra Ginsburg. A vivid portrait of the great French 17th-century satirist by one of the great Russian satirists of our own century. Cloth & NDP 601

Joyce Cary
"Second Trilogy": *Prisoner of Grace. Except the Lord. Not Honour More.* "Even better than Cary's 'First Trilogy,' this is one of the great political novels of this century."—*San Francisco Examiner.* NDP606, 607, & 608. *A House of Children.* Reprint of the delightful autobiographical novel. NDP631

Maurice Collis
The Land of the Great Image. "...a vivid and illuminating study written with the care and penetration that an artist as well as a historian must exercise to make the exotic past live and breathe for us." —Eudora Welty. NDP612

Ronald Firbank
Three More Novels. "...these novels are an inexhaustible source of pleasure." —*The Village Voice Literary Supplement.* NDP614

Romain Gary
The Life Before Us (Madame Rosa). Written under the pseudonym of Émile Ajar. Trans. by Ralph Manheim. "You won't forget Momo and Madame Rosa when you close the book. 'The Life Before Us' is a moving reading experience, if you don't mind a good cry." —*St. Louis Post-Dispatch.* NDP604. *Promise at Dawn.* A memoir "bursting with life...Gary's art has been to combine the comic and the tragic." —*The New Yorker.* NDP635

Henry Green
Back. "...a rich, touching story, flecked all over by Mr. Green's intuition of the concealed originality of ordinary human beings." —V. S. Pritchett. NDP517

Siegfried Lenz
The German Lesson. Trans. by Ernst Kaiser and Eithne Wilkins. "A book of rare depth and brilliance..." —*The New York Times.* NDP618

Henri Michaux
A Barbarian in Asia. Trans. by Sylvia Beach. "It is superb in its swift illuminations and its wit..." —Alfred Kazin, *The New Yorker.* NDP622

Kenneth Rexroth
Classics Revisited. Sixty brief, radiant essays on the books Rexroth called the "basic documents in the history of the imagination." NDP621

Raymond Queneau
The Blue Flowers. Trans. by Barbara Wright. "...an exuberant meditation on the novel, narrative conventions, and readers." —*The Washington Post.* NDP595

Robert Penn Warren
At Heaven's Gate. A novel of power and corruption in the deep South of the 1920s. NDP588